Fair game

The Chalcot estate, a piece of leafy, traditional England hidden away behind high creeper-covered walls, was caught in a time warp.

Once again, as every year in late autumn, the killing season was about to begin. The predestined victims, hundreds of purpose-bred pheasants, their copper and red and bronze and green plumage echoing the colours of the landscape, wandered and pecked without heed while the shooting party assembled.

The landowner, Lewis Glaven, had arranged the shoot to introduce his son Will's shy fiancée to country house living. Hope Meynell was lovely, but most unsuitable for Chalcot, and Lewis was not the only one who disapproved of the engagement.

On that crisp November day, as the shoot reached Belmont wood, tensions began to rise. The shooting party – local gentry, including a discarded girlfriend of Will's, and an upwardly mobile CID officer, Martin Tait – waited eagerly for the beaters to drive the pheasants out of the trees and over their shotguns. Spectators, including Hope, waited with revulsion for the slaughter to begin. And then, as trespassing Animal Rights protesters tried to put a stop to the killing, an event occurred that would change forever the lives of those for whom the estate was home.

Martin Tait reported it as a tragic shooting accident. But when DCI Douglas Quantrill, head of Breckham Market divisional CID, took charge of the investigation, it became apparent that a murder had taken place.

Sheila Radley, a celebrated author of eight previous crime novels, brilliantly reveals the still potent attractions of country life in all its socially divisive rituals.

Also by Sheila Radley

Death and the maiden (1978)
The Chief Inspector's daughter (1981)
A talent for destruction (1982)
Blood on the happy highway (1983)
Fate worse than death (1985)
Who saw him die? (1987)
This way out (1989)
Cross my heart and hope to die (1992)

FAIR GAME

Sheila Radley

Constable · London

First published in Great Britain 1994
by Constable and Company Limited
3 The Lanchesters
162 Fulham Palace Road
London W6 9ER
Copyright © 1994 Sheila Radley
The right of Sheila Radley to be
identified as the author of this work
has been asserted by her in accordance
with the Copyright, Designs and Patents Act 1988
ISBN 0 09 473750 9
Set in Linotron Palatino by
CentraCet Limited, Cambridge
Printed and bound in Great Britain by
Hartnolls Limited, Bodmin, Cornwall

A CIP catalogue record for this book
is available from the British Library

For Sue, Rachael and Jessica

A Father's Advice to his Son

If a sportsman true you'd be,
Listen carefully to me.

Never, never let your gun
Pointed be at anyone;
That it may unloaded be
Matters not the least to me.

If 'twixt you and neighbouring gun
Birds may fly or beasts may run,
Let this maxim e'er be thine:
Follow not across the line.

'Stops' and beaters oft unseen
Lurk behind some leafy screen;
Calm and steady always be:
Never shoot where you can't see.

You may kill or you may miss,
But at all times think of this:
All the pheasants ever bred
Won't repay for one man dead.

abridged from verses written in 1909 by
Commander Mark Beaufoy MP for his son
Henry on reaching the age of thirteen.

1

Laura woke with a start, and a sense of foreboding. For a few moments she lay tense, wondering what was wrong, her head turned to the window where the dark oblong of curtain was outlined by the morning's grey light. All was quiet as usual, in the house and outside. And then, close by, she heard the raucous *kurrr-kuk* and the wing-flap of a crowing cock pheasant, and she knew at once why she was uneasy.

Today was the first of November. The killing season was about to begin.

She jumped out of bed and pulled on her old tracksuit trousers and the first sweatshirt that came to hand. Its message was SAVE THE WHALES, but her immediate concern was not for marine life or even for wildlife in general. Living as she did in the heart of the Suffolk countryside, on a landowner's shooting estate, what she was intent on saving from slaughter were the local gamebirds. It horrified her to think that the hundreds of pheasants that strutted so handsomely through the fields and woods, filling the air in spring with their calling, were soon going to be flushed out, panicked into clumsy flight, and driven over a line of guns to be shot in the name of sport.

Pausing only to splash the sleep from her eyes and sweep a brush through her long pale hair, she ran downstairs and along the back corridor. The door to the kitchen was open but her mother was refuelling the Aga and didn't notice her. In the lobby, where the outdoor clothes were left, she hurriedly pulled on her wellies and her padded jacket. Then she seized the bag of pheasant food and let herself out through the back door into the cold misty air.

Once outside, in what was still called the stable yard although it was where the cars were garaged, she slowed down.

'Chuck-chuck-chuck,' she called, crossing the gravelled yard as quietly as possible and walking on over the wide back lawn towards the shrubbery. The cobweb-spangled grass had been drenched by overnight fog and the trees were limply hung about with dripping yellow leaves. As she neared the shrubbery, she tossed out handfuls of grain and peanut kernels. The wary cock pheasants had run for cover as soon as they heard her open the door, but the more trusting hens were peeping eagerly from beneath the evergreens, waiting for her.

'Chuck-chuck-chuck,' Laura reassured them, and the drab birds, smaller and with much shorter tails than the cocks, came scurrying out like domestic fowls to feed at her feet.

Her mother was always snapping at her for wasting her pocket money on feeding wild pheasants, but at the moment they mattered more to Laura than anything else. Twice a day throughout the hard weather of the previous winter she had fed a cock and three hens; and in May, at least one of the hens had repaid her by nesting under the bushes and producing a family of chicks.

Soon after they were hatched, Laura had been lucky enough to glimpse them. She was crossing the back lawn when she had heard a hidden bird give an anxious cluck. Stopping abruptly, she had seen a patch of shade-dappled grass at the edge of the trees come magically alive as ten or a dozen little balls of fluff, yellow with dark brown bars, scurried to their mother for protection. And on the following day she had seen the hen pheasant ushering her brood down towards the insect-rich meadows, encouraging them with throaty murmurs as they scrambled and tumbled through the grass, and crouching to shelter them under her wings when they were caught by a heavy shower of rain.

All the pheasants left the shrubbery during the summer in search of good pickings in the fields. They were difficult to see, then, when the hedges were in leaf and the grasses were high; but there were occasional distant calls to be heard, and sometimes a cock's long neck would rise up out of growing barley like a multicoloured periscope.

8

Laura had worried about the chicks, though. She knew how vulnerable they were to cold, rain and predators, and she had wondered whether any of them would survive and return to the shrubbery for the winter. To her joy, as the evenings drew in, three cocks – one of them last year's original – and at least half a dozen hens had begun to make their way back each night to roost. If only, she thought, she could persuade them to remain in or near the shrubbery in the daytime instead of roaming away in their restless search for food, she could save those few, at least, from fear and violent death.

Like most country children, just-fifteen-year-old Laura had grown up taking the wildlife about her for granted. It was there; always had been, always would be. What she had been most concerned for when she was young were the spectacular endangered animals, the whales and tigers and elephants. Then as she grew older and began to understand the importance of the environment, she had been indignant about the destruction of the tropical rain forests. It was only in the past year that she had really appreciated that the English countryside and its wildlife were endangered too.

It seemed that things were not in fact the same as they always had been. There were fewer meadowlands, wildflowers and butterflies; fewer wet places, frogs and newts; fewer old barns and barn owls, hedgerows and birds, woods and wild animals. And unless something was done to save them, there would be fewer still by the time Laura had children of her own.

Living on the Chalcot estate, which had seemed such a paradise when her mother took the job as housekeeper to Mr Glaven four years ago, now burdened Laura's conscience. She didn't see how she could stay in a place where wild creatures were killed for people's pleasure. Not for the first time in her life – her parents had divorced when she was eight and she had been desperately unhappy for years afterwards; still was, whenever she thought of her father – she had contemplated running away from home.

But that would mean abandoning her special pheasants, Fitzroy and Francis and Fred and their plain little wives. She couldn't just leave them to their fate, not after encouraging them to rely on her for food and safety. Besides, here was a wonderful opportunity to put her beliefs about conservation into practice.

She knew that Mr Glaven was not a wicked or a cruel man. He had always been kind to her, and he seemed very fond of dogs and horses. She couldn't believe that he would continue to shoot pheasants once he realised how wrong it was. Conceiving it her duty to tell him, she had made the mistake of saying so to her mother one Friday evening when they were preparing supper for his homecoming.

Her mother, nearing fifty, a thin cross woman with gypsy ear-rings, her black-dyed hair cut sharp and short, had been furious.

'Don't you *dare* do any such thing. Don't be so stupid, girl! Mr Glaven's a good employer. We're lucky to live here, and if you go offending him with your righteous notions we shall be jobless and homeless as well. If you don't like what goes on, just keep your eyes and ears shut. *And* your mouth.'

But Laura cared about the pheasants more than anything else. As soon as she could find an opportunity to speak to Mr Glaven, she had no intention of keeping her mouth shut.

Chalcot House was a gentleman's residence of comparatively modest size. It had been built in the classic style, of local grey brick, in the late eighteenth century. There were six principal bedrooms, and three more in the Victorian kitchen wing where the housekeeper, Ann Harbord, lived with her daughter. The wing had been built at a right angle to the back of the main house, at the same time as the stable block that formed the third side of the yard.

The Glaven family had owned the 440-acre Chalcot estate for over a hundred years. William Glaven, a prosperous Yarchester grain merchant, had bought the estate in 1885 as a wedding present for his son Lewis.

Keen sportsmen, the Glavens had remodelled the woodland in defined belts and clumps so that driven shoots could be organised. Good hosts, they had provided winter weekend guests with at least a thousand pheasants to shoot in the intervals between lavish meals. The gun room at the back of the house was lined with photographs of those old shooting parties, the men in tweeds and stiff white collars, the women in vast skirts and amazing hats.

The days of such extravagance were long gone, of course. The Glavens had continued to prosper, and to shoot, but they now entertained on a much smaller scale. The present head of the family, Lewis – the names William and Lewis were passed alternately from father to eldest son – had been a widower for four years. He was chairman of a major insurance group, and lived during the week in a penthouse flat over the headquarters building in the City of London. He came home every Friday to Monday, sometimes with guests, sometimes alone.

Lewis Glaven had two married daughters and five grand-children, but he rarely saw them. Both families lived near Perth, one in Scotland, the other in Australia. His son and heir, Will, was unmarried; he was in the army, a squadron commander in an armoured regiment, with a social life that kept him away from Chalcot most of the time. When he did come home, often bringing a girl but never the same one twice, he preferred riding to shooting.

Will was thirty-four, and in his father's opinion it was high time he settled down and set about producing a son and heir of his own. Lewis had always intended to hand over the manage-ment of the estate to Will when he left the army, and the ending of the Cold War had brought that event nearer than they'd anticipated.

Lewis looked forward to it. He wanted Chalcot to be properly lived in again. He and his wife had always hoped that Will would marry a childhood friend, the horsy daughter of a neighbouring farming family; but though the girl seemed keen enough, Will was reluctant to come under starter's orders. Most of his girlfriends seemed to be fashionable and city-smart, and where would be the sense in bringing a wife like that to Chalcot? He needed to marry a practical girl with an unsqueamish country background, someone who would be perfectly happy to muck out her own horse, pluck a brace of well-hung pheas-ants before cooking them for a dinner party, and of course breed and bring up the next generation of Glavens.

None of the girls Will had brought home came into that

11

category. Not one of them, in Lewis's opinion, was appropriate as the future mistress of Chalcot, and some were definitely less appropriate than others. On his son's most recent visit, Lewis had tired of dropping hints.

'If you can't find a more suitable wife than that,' he had said exasperatedly of Will's latest girlfriend, 'you'd better not marry at all.'

He should have kept his opinion to himself, of course. Will hadn't been home since, and Lewis could only hope that he wouldn't go and marry the girl out of sheer perversity.

Lewis himself, still attractive to women in his vigorous late fifties, had no intention of making a second marriage. He had married early, and though he'd never regretted his choice of wife and had mourned her sincerely, he was frankly enjoying his freedom. He had a number of good-looking women friends – as fashionable and city-smart as Will's, though rather more mature – but he made a point of keeping them well away from Chalcot. He was essentially an outdoor man, a country sports-man, and his Suffolk estate was his refuge.

Lewis Glaven loved Chalcot. When he was in London he always looked forward to walking his fields in the company of the farm manager, and checking the progress of his prized herd of pedigree beef cattle. Most of all, he enjoyed discussing plans for the shooting season with his gamekeeper.

Shooting had always been Lewis's favourite sport. It was a disappointment to him that his son was neither a keen shot nor a particularly good one, but he was confident that Will would improve as soon as he returned to Chalcot and applied himself to country living.

The history of the estate was of never-ending interest to Lewis. He particularly enjoyed reading the old game books begun by his great-grandfather in 1885, although he deplored the wholesale slaughter that was recorded in them. The object of those old shooting parties had been to kill as much as possible; anything that flew or ran was, it seemed, fair game.

Lewis's own principle was quality, not quantity. What he enjoyed about shooting was the skill and excitement involved, the challenge of birds that flew high and fast overhead. That was why, although the pheasant-shooting season begins on the first of October, the season at Chalcot always began at least a month later. Lewis raised fewer than a thousand pheasants a year, and disdained to shoot until the young cock birds were strong enough to go up like rockets, tails streaming.

It was his custom to hold driven shoots five times a year, the first in mid-November. He would sometimes invite business acquaintances to take part, but only if he knew them to be experienced guns. What he liked best was to invite six or seven local friends – neighbouring landowners or farmers who could offer him a day's sport on their own land in return.

He was becoming increasingly disenchanted, though, with the quality of the sport provided by driven shoots. The keepering involved in rearing the birds, even when they were bought from game farms at six weeks old, was unjustifiably expensive. The birds themselves, hand-fed and half-tame, were sometimes sluggish and reluctant to fly.

Wild birds were leaner, fitter and wilier, and in Lewis's opinion they provided much more testing sport. He anticipated killing no more than fifty per cent of the birds he raised each year; the remainder lived wild, often in the hedgerows, and when he wasn't holding a driven shoot he liked to go out with his gun and his well-trained dogs to walk them up. One good wild pheasant, cleanly shot, gave him far more satisfaction than several half-tame birds.

The keeper had told him, a few weeks ago, that some wild pheasants had taken to roosting in the shrubbery just behind the house. Wily old devils, thinking they could winter safely on his back doorstep! Lewis was looking forward, when he went home for the first weekend in November, to putting 'em up high and taking aim.

'Chuck-chuck-chuck.'

The hen pheasants were feeding happily, and now one of the cocks found the courage to approach. This was Fred, one of the young birds, his plumage an unusually dark reddish-copper colour, barred with black. He turned his wattled head a little anxiously from side to side as he stepped out of cover, his long tail trailing, but he broke into a scurry as he neared the food that Laura had scattered. He was followed almost immediately by the other young cock, Francis, a handsome fellow with his tail held high, his bronze plumage separated by a narrow white half-ring from the shining bottle green of his neck.

It was only right that Fitzroy, the most splendid and lordly of birds, should make his appearance last of all. Laura thought he was by far the most magnificent cock pheasant on the entire Chalcot estate. Like the others he had scarlet wattles, scarlet rings round his eyes, two eared horns of green feathers on his head, and sharply pointed spurs on his legs. But his head and neck were a deep iridescent blue, like a peacock's, and at the base of his neck was a perfect ring of white feathers; his body plumage was the colour of burnished copper, each delicately patterned feather laid on like chain mail; and his gracefully narrow tail, as long as his body, was cross-barred with blue and black.

Laura stood absolutely still as Fitzroy came stalking out of cover. Although he was an older bird, one she had fed last year – or perhaps *because* he was an older bird, and knew the blood-red reason for being wary of human beings – he would run at the slightest disturbance. Keeping his distance, he looked down at the scattered food with what seemed like disdain, turning the grains over with a languid scrape of his claw; but then he found a peanut kernel, his favourite snack, and another, and soon he was feeding eagerly.

Laura stood watching, a pleased smile on her face. And then the quiet was shattered by a rough, mocking voice coming from the far edge of the lawn.

'*Chucky-chucky-chucky!*'

Alarmed, the pheasants instantly scuttled for cover. Laura whirled round on a tall sixteen-year-old with cropped hair, dressed in dark green waterproofs and carrying a broken shotgun under his arm. She'd never seem him with a gun before. If he was trying the impress her, he hadn't succeeded.

'You creep, Darren Jermyn! Why did you have to frighten them?'

'They're gamebirds, that's why. They belong out on the estate, you've no business feeding 'em near the house. You want

14

to feed birds, you get yourself some fowls. *Chucky-chucky-chucky . . .'*

Laura often wondered how she could ever have loved him. He'd been different when he was at school, of course, They'd been a couple, an item, for the whole of his last term. Darren liked wildlife and was every bit as keen on conservation as she was, so they'd had a lot in common.

He was her first serious boyfriend. She'd loved the way his eyes crinkled up when he laughed, and the way his hair grew in loose dark curls round his ears, and their hugs and kisses, and the way he'd told her that he loved her more than he'd ever loved anyone else in his whole life.

They'd both been desolate as the time approached for him to leave Breckham Market High School. Darren lived miles away, out in the country on the far side of town, and they didn't know how they were going to be able to go on seeing each other. He was hoping for some kind of outdoor job, preferably with animals; but jobs of any kind were hard to find.

Then, just before the end of term, he had come away from a visit to the careers office buzzing with excitement. He'd been told there was a Youth Training Scheme place available on – wait for it – *the Chalcot estate!*

They couldn't believe their luck. Laura had been every bit as excited as Darren, until she'd discovered that the job he was applying for was that of trainee gamekeeper.

They'd had a fierce row about it. Laura was disgusted that he could even think of taking a job that involved killing. For his part, Darren couldn't believe that their love, and the opportunity to see each other every day, wasn't more important to her than a few dead birds.

He was so sure she would come round that he'd applied for the job anyway, and had started at the end of July, just when the pheasant poults were bought in and penned in the woods. His job was to feed and protect the growing birds, and control vermin. The hours were long, the outdoor life he'd looked forward to meant walking miles carrying heavy loads of feedstuff, and he hated being constantly bawled out by the keeper, Len Alger, a sour old slave-driver. And although he was well

15

fed by the granny he lodged with in the village, Mrs Alger's sister-in-law, she niggled away at him worse than his mother did at home.

None of that would have mattered to Darren if only Laura still loved him. It had taken him a long time to realise that she didn't. He just couldn't accept that he'd been dumped.

How could she reject his love, when he'd done everything he could to please her? Losing her meant having a constant pain gnawing away inside him. He was lonely and depressed, and it tormented him to know that Laura was living so near. If he behaved badly when he saw her, it was only because he loved her so much.

Laura had turned her back and begun walking away. Darren was determined not to be ignored; that was why he'd brought the gun with him. Mr Glaven, the Guv'nor, had given him some shooting lessons one weekend, lending him the 20-bore shotgun to use against crows, magpies and other predators.

He cocked the gun and raised it to his shoulder. 'There's the ol' pheasant!' he shouted, aiming towards the shrubbery but watching Laura. She whirled round, wide-eyed, her hair flying like a waterfall, twisting his guts with longing.

'Don't you dare!' she shrieked at him. 'Don't you *dare* – '

'Don't be stupid,' he said, jeering to hide his pain. He broke the gun and showed her that it was unloaded. 'Anyway, I'm here to protect the birds, not shoot 'em. You know that.'

'You're here to help other people shoot them, though! I don't know how you can bear to rear them just to be killed. It's *wicked*.'

'Rubbish! Pheasants are a crop,' Darren said, repeating something he'd heard from the keeper, 'same as everything else on the estate. The Guv'nor grows barley so's he can harvest it, and rears pheasants so's he can shoot 'em. Same as he breeds the cattle, so's he can send 'em to be slaughtered for nice juicy beef.'

Laura turned away again. She couldn't bear the thought of eating something that had once had a face, and feelings. 'You're *disgusting*,' she said.

'Still a vegetarian, are you?' he mocked. Then he remembered that he'd offered to come up to the house on the pretext of saving the keeper's wife the bother of telephoning Laura's mother.

'Listen, I've got a message. The Guv'nor rang Len Alger late last night. Seems he wants a driven shoot set up for this Saturday. And he said to tell your Mum there'll be eight people for the shoot lunch.'

'A driven shoot? As soon as this?' Laura was appalled; frightened, too. She hadn't expected Mr Glaven to hold his first big shoot for several weeks. With just two days to go, she'd have no chance at all to convert him before the slaughter started. 'Oh no, he can't . . .'

''Course he can,' said Darren impatiently. 'He's the boss, and if he wants to hold a shoot we've got to get on with it. He said he was sorry for not giving us more notice – it's a special occasion or something. Soon as I've finished the morning feed, I've got to go down to the village and ask who'll do the beating for us. Want to come on Saturday and help?'

He was mocking her again. Laura was so high on fear and anger that she answered him off the top of her head.

'Oh, I'll be there!' she said. 'Don't worry about that. But I shan't be helping the shooters – I shall be there to stop them.'

2

A much-too-familiar vehicle drew up just before Laura reached the yard, adding annoyance to her anxiety. The Daihatsu turbo diesel Fourtrak, in metallic black and silver, was ornamented with an inconceivably needful bull bar and every possible extra in the way of wheel trims, roof rack, tow bar, fog lamps and spotlights. Laura thought it ridiculously over the top for an ancient driver who never chugged further than Breckham Market, and anyway she detested Reg Brunt. The fact that he was a butcher (now in prosperous semi-retirement) would have turned her against him even if he were a nice man, but he wasn't.

He rolled down from the driving seat, a squat person with a

17

bald head, round baggy eyes, a wide slit of mouth and a shapeless body inside a bulky sludge-green winter jacket. It was said in the village that he could turn nasty if he was crossed, but Laura had only ever seen the smarmy, boastful side of him. She always thought of him as Mr Toad.

'Hallo, girlie!' he wheezed, smiling his large ingratiating smile. He produced a package wrapped in thick white paper. 'Brought some lovely sausages for your brekkie – made 'em meself this morning – own secret recipe, finest in the county.'

'I don't *eat* sausages,' said Laura through her teeth. He knew perfectly well she was a vegetarian; even her mother, who was always impatient with what she called Laura's 'fads and notions', had tried to get it into his head. But he didn't seem capable of understanding.

'Oh-ho, you'll love these when your Mum's cooked 'em! Best sausages you'll find anywhere, fried to perfection if I know your mother. Fine cook – fine woman.'

Laura didn't invite him in but he followed close on her heels, convinced of his welcome. "Morning, 'morning,' he cried, bustling into the kitchen. Laura's mother gave him an unenthusiastic nod of greeting, and put a large frying pan on the Aga.

'One egg or two?' she asked in a resigned voice.

Laura kicked off her wellies and ran upstairs to change into her school clothes. The relationship between her mother and Mr Toad was something she preferred not to speculate on. He was said to be a widower, and he lived alone in a bungalow next to his shop. He paid a woman to look after him, but that didn't stop him from turning up at the back door of Chalcot House several times a week, when the Glavens were not in residence, offering meat in return for a meal.

As far as Laura could tell, her mother didn't like him. (How could she? How *could* she, after having been married to a wonderful man like Laura's father?) But she didn't discourage him, either. Laura made up for that by being deliberately rude to him, but his skin was as thick as a toad's warty back.

She usually made herself a piece of toast for breakfast and ate it on the way to school, but when he was in the kitchen she preferred just to snatch up her gear and go. This morning, though, her mind was on Saturday's shooting party; she was determined to stop it somehow, but she supposed she had better deliver Mr Glaven's message to her mother. No sense in getting herself into trouble in advance.

The smell of frying sausages and bacon turned her stomach even before she entered the kitchen. Mr Toad, slurping a mug of tea as he goggled at her mother, already had his jacket off, his feet well under the table, knife and fork to hand and a napkin tucked under his chins.

'Ah, girlie!' He always addressed her as if she were four years old. 'Coming to join me for brekkie?'

'I'd sooner starve,' snapped Laura, hunting for her school-books.

'Oh, you mustn't think of starving yourself! No need for you to be dieting at all – taking after your mother, I can see that – fine slim figure of a woman.'

Clearly unflattered, Laura's mother slapped a laden, sizzling plate in front of him. 'Do you want toast with it?'

'Bread'll do nicely, thanks.' He blew on a forkful of fry, and filled his mouth. 'Soon as I've eaten,' he mumbled, spitting fragments, 'I'll drive this young lady to school.'

'I'd rather walk,' said Laura. 'All the way to Breckham Market,' she emphasised.

'Keen on exercise, eh? Same for me when I was your age – won medals for athletics – running, jumping, best young athlete in the county.' He shovelled in another greasy forkful.

Her mother poured her a mug of tea. It would be nice, Laura thought, if they could exchange a private snigger over Mr Toad's ridiculous claim. But they didn't have that kind of relationship.

'Darren Jermyn came over with a message while I was outside,' she reported distantly. 'Mr Glaven rang the keeper late last night, to say he wants a shooting party set up for Saturday. He said to tell you he wants a shoot lunch for eight.'

'This Saturday? The day after tomorrow?' Her mother was offended. 'He might have given me more notice – it's not just the shoot lunch, I shall have to feed all the beaters as well.'

'Cert'nly should've given you more notice,' Mr Toad blustered, indignant on her behalf. He mopped up his fried eggs with a hunk of bread. 'Taking advantage – diabolical liberty!'

'I wouldn't mind,' Laura's mother went on crossly, ignoring him, 'if only Mr Glaven had rung to tell me himself. It's not like him to be so inconsiderate . . . Why's he in such a hurry to hold a shoot, anyway?'

'I don't know, do I?' said Laura, exasperated. She took a banana and an apple from the fruit bowl and stowed them in her school-bag. 'Darren said something about a special occasion.'

'Private shoots – ha!' Mr Toad passed his mug for a refill, just as there was a ring from the telephone on the wall beside the door. Laura's mother went 'to answer it, and Laura had no intention of serving him, so he had to wait.

'Gentry only!' he wheezed on. 'No chance of being invited to shoot if you're in trade. I could show 'em how to do it – still a crack shot – finest in the county when I was younger.'

It wasn't worth a comment. Laura gave him a contemptuous look, sloshed the remains of her tea down the sink, and stalked past her mother who was talking too eagerly to notice her.

'Not at all, it's perfectly all right, Mr Glaven! . . . No trouble, I'll have everything done in time. . . . Oh, it'll be so nice to see Major Will again! And one guest? No trouble at all, Mr Glaven . . .'

Laura forgot her anxieties over the shoot. What she had just overheard made her so happy that she didn't even feel irritated with her mother, who always behaved stupidly when she spoke to Mr Glaven. It was ridiculous for her to be like that at her age, all pink-cheeked and eager and over the top. Normally, Laura was desperately embarrassed by it.

But today it didn't matter, because the great news was that Will was coming! Darling, darling Will, who'd been so brilliant to her soon after she and her mother moved to Chalcot.

She was only eight when her parents divorced, and she hadn't known how to handle what was happening. She was sure she was the cause of all the rows, and when her lovely Daddy left home she knew it was her fault. What with the guilt, and missing him, her life had at first been a misery.

But her father had written to her regularly to tell her how much he loved and missed her, and gradually she began to believe him. His letters from Saudi Arabia were decorated with

20

fun sketches of palm trees and camels, and they always finished, 'All my love, Daddy XXXXXX'. Laura had depended on the letters, and clung to the hope that one day he would send for her to live with him.

Then, at Chalcot, a letter had come to tell her about a special friend he'd made. It finished, 'All our love, Dad and Judy XX'.

She'd blundered out of the house, flung herself face down on the back lawn, clutching the letter, and cried her eyes out. That was where Major Will had found her, on his way from the stables. Her mother wouldn't have understood or cared how she felt, but Will did. He had sat on the grass beside her, listened, read the letter, and put comforting arms around her. Enveloped in his heady smell of good soap, sweat, horses and leather, Laura had fallen headlong into love.

Ever since then, Will had given her a hug whenever they met and parted. He called her his girlfriend, and sometimes sent her picture postcards – 'with lots of love' – from foreign countries. Laura didn't much like it when he brought one of his glamorous women home, but he always gave her a conspiratorial wink and whispered that she was still his favourite. And because he never brought the same woman twice, Laura felt secure in his affection.

It was a long time since she'd seen him, but she never wavered in her love. Even though she'd had that silly relationship with Darren Jermyn, Will had always been the one she thought of last thing at night and first thing in the morning. He was so good-looking that just to day-dream of him made her feel shivery.

And now she would soon be seeing him again! Elated, Laura wound her long scarf round her neck and ran out of the house, past the shrubbery, along the field path under the dripping November trees, and out into the village street just in time to catch the school bus.

'Leave the pattern, for goodness' sake!'

Ann Harbord snatched the empty plate out of her guest's way while he was still trying to mop up the last globule of grease. She deplored Reg Brunt's liking (so different from Lewis

Glaven's) for enormous fried breakfasts, but if he were determined to give himself a heart attack she saw no reason why she should try to prevent it.

'First class . . .' he sighed, sitting back satisfied. He pulled his napkin away from his chins, and belched politely into its folds. 'You're a fine cook, Ann.'

'That's what Mr Glaven pays me for,' she said tartly. 'Don't hang about, Reg. He'll be home this evening to arrange his shoot, and I've got more than enough to do. Here's the list of the meat I shall want tomorrow. Now be off with you.'

'You're a fine woman, Ann. The offer's always open, you know that.'

She pointed to the door and he shambled off, looking pleased with himself as usual. She had lost count of the number of times she'd rejected his repulsive offer of marriage, but it seemed to make no difference to him, he still came back for more. And Ann was glad of that, on the quiet, because when Lewis Glaven was away she was as lonely as Reg was. Repulsive he might be, but at least he enjoyed her cooking and her company. Which was more than she could say of her own daughter.

Laura was impossible – faddy, moody, untidy, rude, no company at all. They had never been close. Laura had always made it clear that she loved her father best, despite the fact that Terry Harbord was totally unreliable. Even so, Ann had felt slapped in the face when the child had said she wanted to live with him after the divorce.

Though Ann had won custody, she could never forgive Laura for that rejection. A thin-skinned woman, quick to feel slighted, she had spent her life in a semi-permanent state of resentment and anger. Laura had given her yet another grievance to feed on, and she had made a long meal of it.

But at Chalcot House, Ann was as nearly happy as it was possible for her to be. For the first time in her life she felt that she was properly appreciated. Lewis Glaven never failed to tell her how well she took care of the house while he was away, and how excellently she cooked for him and his guests.

Ann's only regret was that he wasn't there more often. She longed for the time when he would retire and come back to

Chalcot for good, so that she could get rid of old Reg Brunt and devote the rest of her life to looking after Lewis.

She knew her place, of course. Even though he always came down to the kitchen to thank her on a Sunday evening after his guests had gone, and often lingered to chat about the family history, she knew better than to indulge in foolish day-dreams. She had no doubt about the nature of their relationship; it was and always would be 'Mr Glaven' and 'Mrs Harbord'. But that in a way was a comfort, because Ann had been hurt often enough to know that intimate relationships always turn sour.

Yes, she ached for him sometimes. He was a very fit, distinguished-looking man, and she was only human after all. But as long as she could stay there to take care of him, receiving courtesy and consideration in return, she would be satisfied.

That was why she'd been so furious when Laura had had the nerve to say she was going to tell Lewis that shooting was wrong. Ann knew he was easily angered – she'd heard him having more than one shouting match with his son – and he couldn't be expected to take kindly to being lectured about animal rights by his housekeeper's daughter.

Naturally, Ann loved Laura. That went without saying. But she was deeply in love with Lewis Glaven. Having at last found some happiness of her own, she was determined not to let her selfish daughter ruin it.

The school day seemed longer than usual. Laura was one of the leading Greens at Breckham Market High, and she knew she could count on her friends to support her in stopping the pheasant shoot. But she didn't want to tell them about it until she had planned what to do. And that was very difficult to decide, particularly with Will coming for the weekend.

Sitting unusually quietly in the classroom, Laura nibbled a strand of hair and debated with herself. She would have to start her campaign by trying to convert Mr Glaven. That would be worth more than any amount of confrontation. But would Will support her? He rarely joined a shoot, but she didn't know whether that was because he was a conservationist at heart, or simply because he preferred riding.

23

And supposing Will wouldn't support her. Supposing his father refused to be converted, and the shoot went ahead? Worst of all, supposing Will decided to join it? That would be a real test of her commitment.

Will was the one person who cared about her, and the one she loved best in the world. Yes, of course the pheasants mattered to her desperately; but without Will to dream of and depend on, she would have nobody.

How would she feel, though, if she saw him shooting at her specials birds? How if he were to blast her glorious Fitzroy out of the air and drop him tumbled and bloody at her feet?

Fear for the pheasants rose thickly in her throat. She swallowed hard. Will couldn't be so callous, surely? He'd understood how she felt about her father, and so he'd understand how she felt about the birds. If he was as fond of her as he said, he would be able to convince Mr Glaven that she was right.

She didn't want to think too much about the alternative. As far as she could see, the only way for her to stop the shoot once it started would be to run out of hiding and make a stand in front of the guns.

3

As she waited for Lewis to arrive, Ann spent a happy evening cooking and freezing in preparation for the weekend. He had told her he would be later than usual, and that he wouldn't want a meal that evening. But he always came to greet her before he changed out of his city clothes, and she planned to suggest a light, late supper of scrambled egg and smoked salmon.

Lewis always travelled to London by train. The gamekeeper, Len Alger, who looked after the dogs while Lewis was away, ferried him to and from Breckham Market station in the Range Rover. Eager as any loving wife – and looking her best, she hoped, with discreetly applied eyeshadow, lipstick and blusher – Ann listened for its return and fretted when it wasn't on time.

Infuriatingly, Laura chose to make her nightly appearance in the kitchen just at the moment when the vehicle came crunching back into the gravelled yard. As usual the girl was wearing a glazed look and her Walkman, so as to avoid conversation. Ann regarded that as a deliberate snub. When Laura wasn't out with friends (or, thinking her mother wasn't aware of what she was doing, chattering to them on the telephone extension in the gun room) she shut herself away in her bedroom every evening. She said she had homework to do, but from what Ann could hear she spent most of her time watching the portable TV that Major Will had lent her.

Ann deplored the fact that her daughter got away with calling him 'Will'. She resented the brotherly attention he paid to the girl. It wasn't right, when she herself took such care to remain properly deferential towards the Glavens. It wasn't fair. And it was particularly unfair that Mr Glaven should hold her responsible (though he was too gentlemanly ever to mention it) for the size of his telephone bill, when she herself never used it socially because she had no one to ring.

'Hurry up!' Ann mouthed at Laura. 'Mr Glaven's coming!'

She washed her hands at the sink, pulled off the cooking apron she was wearing over one of her nicest dresses, and ran to her bedroom to check her hair and ear-rings and face. When she returned to the kitchen Laura was still mooching about, making a major performance out of topping a slice of wholemeal bread with curd cheese and beansprouts.

Ann was annoyed. Quite apart from wanting Lewis to herself when he arrived, she felt embarrassed by her daughter's sloppy appearance. It might be the height of fashion, according to TV, but Ann considered it downright ugly. With her long thin legs in dark leggings, her microscopic skirt, her baggy black sweatshirt, and her big eyes staring from an unusually pale set face, the girl looked as though she ought to be on stage doing a mime. Exasperated, Ann snatched off Laura's headphones.

'Take your supper and go! Mr Glaven will be here any minute.'

Laura snatched the headphones back, though she didn't put them on again. 'I know that,' she snapped. 'Why else d'you think I'm waiting?'

It was then, just as she heard Lewis's footsteps coming down the corridor, that Ann realised why her daughter was so pale. Laura was trembling with nervous tension. Despite Ann's previous warnings, the wretched girl was obviously determined to upset him. Her sweatshirt bore a hand-made legend: SHOOTING PHEASANTS IS WRONG.

Lewis was in the open doorway before Ann could say another word. As always the sight of him – so upright and distinguished, with his high cheekbones, his trim moustache, and his greying hair winged back above his ears; so immaculately dressed in a double-breasted city suit and a handsome silk tie – reduced her to a breathless, adoring silence.

There was, though, something different about him this evening. His blue eyes were distinctly bloodshot. His complexion, which was normally as pink as if he'd just come in out of a sharp wind, was definitely red. Ann knew that he would sometimes drink the best part of a bottle of claret when he dined alone, and that he liked a night-cap of malt whisky, but she had never before seen him come home so well-oiled. Or carrying a bottle of champagne.

'Good evening to you, Mrs Harbord! And to you, Laura!' His voice, usually abrupt, was positively jovial. 'This weekend's going to be a family celebration, and I'd like you both to share it.' Not noticing – or ignoring – the message on Laura's sweatshirt, he began to tear the gold foil from the neck of the bottle. 'Three glasses, Mrs Harbord, please.'

Ann was both flattered and flustered: 'Oh thank you, Mr Glaven! But Laura's only fifteen – '

'Just the right age for her first glass of champagne! Eh, Laura?'

Obedient to his wishes, Ann put three flutes on the table. Laura, keyed up to make an impassioned speech and now obviously thrown, looked paler than ever. 'I don't *want* any of your champagne,' she said through her teeth.

'Oh, come now,' Lewis said amiably, twisting the wire and loosening the cork. 'Just a little to humour me, eh?' He gave the girl a charming smile, one that Ann would have preferred for herself. 'No reason why vegetarians shouldn't drink wine, y'know.'

Ann gave her daughter a 'don't-you-dare-refuse' look. 'What are we celebrating, Mr Glaven?' she asked.

'Some excellent news. Something we've all been hoping for.' He paused, and drew breath: 'The official announcement isn't being made until next week. But I'm happy to tell you that my son is engaged to marry Miss Hope Meynell.'

The cork popped. Lewis filled the glasses with an unsteady hand, foaming them over. 'Do please join me in a toast,' he said: 'Will and Hope!'

Laura made a small noise, something between a gasp of protest and a moan. Her mother gave her a warning glance and a heavy nudge. 'To Major Will and Miss Meynell!' Ann said loudly, raising her glass.

The next sound was an unmistakable sob. With the back of her hand pressed against her mouth, Laura fled.

Ann was mortified. Far from being concerned about her daughter, she was annoyed that Laura might have offended Lewis. 'I do apologise for her, Mr Glaven! I'm afraid she's been a bit, well, silly over Major Will – '

'Silly?'

'Over-fond of him, I'm afraid. Not that Major Will encouraged her, of course, but she's at an awkward age.'

Lewis stared after the girl as though he had become aware of her for the first time. 'Ah, I see . . . Well, she'll soon get over it.' He drained his glass, and then – unusually – sat down at the kitchen table and unbuttoned his jacket. His joviality had evaporated with the foam from the champagne. He was tired, Ann could see that. She longed to put out a hand to him, but made do instead with more apologies.

'Not your fault, Mrs Harbord,' he interrupted her, refilling both their glasses. 'Difficult time, adolescence. A lot to be said for being our age and on an even keel, eh?'

'Oh yes – yes indeed . . .' Ann took a wry gulp of champagne and pulled herself together. 'I really am so pleased for you about the engagement, Mr Glaven. It will be lovely to have a little Lewis to hope for, to carry on the family tradition. Miss

Meynell is the rather shy, beautiful young lady who came last Easter, isn't she?'

'Yes. Quite different from most of Will's other girlfriends. Seems to have bowled him over.' Frowning, Lewis knuckled his moustache. 'Pity of it is, she's not a country girl. Lives in suburban Hertfordshire. Works in a London bank, plays tennis and badminton, sings in a choir – that kind of thing. Perfectly good upbringing, but not right for Chalcot. Doesn't ride. Half-scared of the dogs. Wouldn't know a pheasant from a partridge.'

He drained his glass and became more positive. 'Still, she's young. She'll learn. That's why I've arranged a shoot for this weekend. Give her a good introduction to country life.'

Ann had been brought up in Breckham Market, where her father had owned a hardware shop. She'd lived in a village for most of her married life, but she wasn't at all keen on what Lewis thought of as country living. Not that she had her daughter's emotional objection to shooting, but she couldn't imagine what pleasure there could be in spending a cold November weekend standing about on the edge of a wood watching birds being killed. She certainly didn't envy Hope Meynell the introduction she was going to be given.

'Have you met her family, Mr Glaven?' she asked.

'I called on them recently. Met her father and brother – her mother's dead.' Lewis reached absently for the champagne he had poured for Laura, and downed it. 'Father's a dentist. 'Strordinary profession, dentistry. Who'd want to spend a lifetime peering into people's mouths?'

'And what about the wedding?' Ann asked eagerly. 'Has a date been fixed?'

'No, no, plenty of time for that.' Evidently disinclined to discuss the subject, he topped up the glasses with what remained in the bottle.

'They'll be living in army quarters when they're married, I suppose?'

'What?' Lewis seemed to have something else on his mind. 'Oh no, I shouldn't think so. No, Will's army career's just about finished. He's going to come back to Chalcot next year and run the estate for me.'

Ann was as physically shocked as if a bee had plunged its sting into a sensitive spot. She felt the blood drain from her face. She shuddered, and heard herself utter just the kind of whimpering noise that Laura had made when she heard that Will was getting married.

'But – but if they come and live here,' she protested through numbed lips, 'you won't want a housekeeper any more!'

He seemed not to hear. Preoccupied, he pushed back his chair and rose to go.

Ann had always prided herself on keeping her distance from Lewis: on being unobtrusively helpful, on making no personal requests, on never revealing her emotions. Now, utterly shaken, she heard a cry of desolation emerge of its own accord.

'What about *me*, Mr Glaven?' She ran to him and seized his sleeve. 'What about me!'

It was clear that Lewis had never given the matter a thought. He looked down in astonishment at her detaining hand. 'What?' he said.

'This job – it's my whole life! When the Major brings a wife here, you won't want me.'

'Oh for God's sake, Mrs Harbord!' He pulled away from her hand on the pretext of buttoning his jacket, but there was no mistaking his irritation. 'We can discuss all that when the time comes. They're not even officially engaged yet. Anything could happen before they're married. Just let's concentrate on this weekend's shooting party, eh?'

He walked to the door without giving her another glance.

Laura, lurking in the passage, had heard and understood. She had no sympathy for her mother, though. She had no sympathy now for anything but the pheasants.

She'd done with crying, at least for the moment. The news of Will's engagement had hurt her deeply; she felt deserted, betrayed, completely alone in the world.

But now she'd got over the first shock, she was angry. When she had agonised over whether or not to try to stop the shoot, she'd been afraid of losing Will's approval. Now that she knew he no longer cared about her, the problem was solved. She was determined to go ahead with her protest, just to show him that she didn't care about him either. If she ruined the weekend for him and his stupid girlfriend, good. Saving the pheasants was going to be the most important, worthwhile thing she had ever done.

The best way to save them was still going to be by convincing Mr Glaven, though. This was the opportunity she'd hoped for, but it took some courage to block his way as he emerged from the kitchen. He wasn't as tall as his son but he seemed to tower over her, red-faced, radiating suppressed displeasure.

'Mr Glaven,' she began, resolute but nervously breathless: 'I'm asking you please to cancel the shoot. I don't think you realise just how cruel it is to – '

Eyebrows and moustache bristling, he gave her a thunderous look. 'Young woman,' he interrupted, pointing a stern finger at her, 'I've seen the message you're wearing. I know exactly what you're going to say because I've heard it all before. You people don't begin to understand the values and traditions we live by in the country. You don't know what you're talking about. Now please let me pass, and let's hear no more of this nonsense.'

'It's not nonsense!' cried Laura passionately. 'You're the one who doesn't understand! Pheasants have the right to live too. They have feelings, they love and protect their chicks, and they're terrified when you shoot at them. It's wicked, wicked to kill them for your selfish amusement. If you won't cancel the shoot I'll – '

Mr Glaven wasn't listening. He'd already turned angrily to her mother.

'Mrs Harbord, will you please control your daughter? You've both been given every consideration and courtesy while you've been living here. But this is a shooting estate, and I won't tolerate any interference with our way of life. The shoot goes ahead. If there's any attempt at disruption by your daughter, I shall hold you personally responsible. Goodnight to you.'

He brushed past Laura and stalked down the passage to the main house, slamming the dividing door. She stared furiously after him, not knowing which she most hated him for, being patronising or being bloodthirsty. And then she heard a strange hissing noise behind her.

Her mother was advancing on her in a rage, her face a sizzling red, her ear-rings jangling, her mouth ugly, her hands stretched forward as though to grab Laura by the shoulders and shake her.

'You bitch! You little *bitch*. Now you've ruined everything – I've lost his respect and it's all your fault!'

Laura backed, astonished. They quarrelled often enough, but her mother had always specialised in being cold and sarcastic. Laura had never before seen her so nearly beside herself with fury.

'It's nothing to do with me!' she retorted, one foot on the bottom stair ready to make a dash for her room. Her mother hadn't laid a hand on her in years, but Laura was taking no chances. 'If you've lost his respect it's your own stupid fault, drooling over him the way you do. It's *gross*. I heard you making a fool of yourself just now – "Yes Mr Glaven, no Mr Glaven, what about me Mr Glaven?" Can't you see that you're *nothing* to him? He'd never look at you, not in a million years. You'd better settle for Reg Brunt, before you get too old even for him.'

She hadn't reckoned on the length of her mother's reach. The stinging slap on her cheek came as a shock, but the indignity of it hurt more than the pain.

'Right!' she shouted, nursing her face. 'Right, that's it then. I've had enough. By this time on Saturday I'll have gone for good!'

She'd often threatened to leave home, but now she really meant it. There was no point in staying where she wasn't loved or wanted. All she cared about now were the pheasants, and she was determined to save them before she left.

It wouldn't be easy. Running out to stand in front of the guns just as the pheasants came over would be terrifying. And she would have to do it alone, because it didn't seem right to involve any of her friends.

If she were brave enough, though, it would not only stop the shoot but also shame Will and his father. And make her mother sorry she'd slapped her, into the bargain.

31

4

Shooting was on Detective Chief Inspector Quantrill's mind that day too, though in relation to people rather than pheasants.

Douglas Quantrill, head of Breckham Market divisional CID, detested shotguns. Although he was Suffolk born and bred, his agricultural forebears were labourers, not landowners. He didn't doubt that they would have poached rabbits for the pot, but they'd have done it with snares or ferrets, not guns. He himself had never fired a shotgun, and didn't intend to. He'd been obliged to do rifle and bayonet training during his two years' National Service, and that had put him off weapons for life.

What he disliked most about shotguns was the terrible damage they inflict at close quarters. A 12-bore, fired from a distance of ten feet, will cut a fence post in half. Fired from that distance at a human being – deliberately or by accident, the result is equally horrendous – it will blow a hole in the victim about eight inches across.

As he drove home through the rainwashed dark, Quantrill brooded over the alarming availability of shotguns in rural Suffolk. According to statistics, they average out at about one for every third household. And that's just the legally owned ones.

Despite a continuing police campaign to persuade owners to keep all guns in locked steel cabinets, he knew there were still far too many rural houses where shotguns were left hanging on beams or propped in corners. Anyone who had a mind to embark on armed crime would find it easy enough to get hold of a gun.

Worse, their availability meant that shotguns were used in many of the domestic murders in the county. That was what was on Quantrill's mind that evening, because he'd just visited the scene of the second such shooting in the division in recent months. Shotgun murders are, literally, bloody awful. He was longing for a shower and a change of clothes, and a large drink to take away the taste of violent death.

One of the tragedies of domestic murder is that so many of them have similar ingredients. It was all too common, in his job, to attend an incident where the relationship had obviously been in such a state of stress that a violent ending had become almost inevitable. Family, and friends and neighbours, must have seen it coming.

When the man was jealously possessive, the woman was seeking company or affection elsewhere, and threats were known to have been issued, there was bound to be an ugly conclusion. And if the man owned a shotgun, it was odds-on that he would either attempt or commit murder.

(That was how it had been with today's incident. Afterwards, the husband had mumbled that he kept the gun in the house because he liked to go out after the odd rabbit. He hadn't intended to kill his wife, of course not. He *loved* her. He loved her so much that he just couldn't take any more. If he couldn't have her, no one else was going to; and so on. Another characteristic of domestic murder, in Quantrill's experience, was that most men who commit it say much the same thing by way of explanation.)

Quantrill was not himself a possessive husband, and he found it impossible to imagine what the condition must be like. According to his sergeant, Hilary Lloyd, who was in charge of the current investigation, it probably resulted from emotional insecurity.

If she was right – and he had such high regard for her judgement that he had no reason to doubt it – then it explained why such men were drawn to shotguns: not to have a go at rabbits or whatever, that was just an excuse, but to bolster their own egos. And an emotionally insecure man was the last person who ought to be in charge of such a dangerous weapon as a shotgun.

Mulling it over, as he peered ahead through the clacking windscreen wipers, Quantrill realised why he'd been having a niggling personal worry all afternoon.

He dearly loved his younger daughter Alison, and couldn't bear to think of her being involved with a man who was

33

emotionally insecure. But how do you tell? If insecure men are drawn to shotguns, does it follow that men who like shooting make risky partners?

He wasn't querying the stability of real countrymen, of course. For farmers and gamekeepers and landowners, shooting is a way of life. But he couldn't feel the same about gun-happy policemen. Surely no sane detective, who had seen for himself what shotguns do to people, would ever want to handle such a gun for pleasure?

Incredible as it was, though, he knew one of them who did. Alison knew him too, and much too well for her father's peace of mind. It was bad enough to be aware that she was living with the undeserving prat, without the worry of knowing that he'd just taken up shooting as a hobby.

But the thought of Alison always had the power to give Quantrill's spirits an instant lift. As he turned off Mount Street, swished over the mess of fallen leaves that carpeted Bramley Road and eased his large Rover through his gateway, he was heartened to think that he would soon be seeing her. She was coming home – alone, thank God – for supper, and staying the weekend, and he was looking forward to it more than he would admit. It seemed an age since they'd been able to spend any time together, and there was so much he wanted to talk to her about.

To begin with, there was the news that had left him speechless when he was told it this morning. Promotion to Detective Superintendent . . . He could hardly take it in.

Alison would be delighted, of course. So would her mother, there was no doubt about that. But for himself, Quantrill knew that it wasn't going to be easy, after all these years, to come to terms with the new situation.

'Promoted!' Molly's voice rose in a squeak of joy. 'Oh, how marvellous! Does that mean a new job?'

'Deputy head of the county CID.'

'Oh, Douggie – isn't that wonderful?'

'Terrific,' said her husband, a fraction sour. He hated being called Douggie. But excitement suited Molly, pinking her full cheeks (the 'just-one-bite-can't-hurt' phase of her dieting cycle had come round again) and making her look plumply pretty. He wished, though, that she'd left her hair a softly fading brown, rather than experimenting with that unlikely chestnut colour.

'Detective Superintendent . . .' she breathed, bright-eyed. 'Oh, I'm so pleased! And you are too, aren't you, Douggie? Do say you're pleased – '

'Of course I am.'

He had already put the murder out of his mind, and now he tried to do the same with promotion. Sitting in front of the log fire in the comfortable living-room of their bungalow, with a reviving mug of beer in his hand, he was waiting for Alison's arrival. And for his supper. He sniffed the air hopefully, but could smell nothing cooking.

Douglas Quantrill was a typical husband of his background and generation, perfectly capable in his own opinion of fending for himself, but too good a tactician to let on to his wife. He quite liked having an occasional forage in the kitchen, but only when she wasn't there to interfere. Once, when Molly had gone out for the evening, he had offered to initiate his son Peter into the art of cooking a man-sized mixed grill, or at least a bacon butty; but all the idle youth had ever wanted to learn was how to microwave a frozen pizza to eat on the hoof.

Thankfully, Molly had never been an adventurous cook. Douglas was a plain meat-and-two-veg man, and conscious of his good fortune in having a wife who didn't want to contaminate honest English food with olive oil and garlic. But now that she was working full-time as a receptionist at Breckham Market health centre, Molly often came home via the new Sainsbury's superstore bringing something quick and easy for supper, and Quantrill had learned to be suspicious of these ready-prepared meals. Even when they sounded English, they'd invariably been mucked about.

Tonight, he had hoped that Molly would produce something home-made in Alison's honour. In the absence of any cooking smell, though, it seemed more likely that his wife had brought what she called a 'special' into the house. Sighing, he braced himself for some kind of herby foreign pap that would probably leave him burping for the rest of the evening. Sainsbury's, he thought darkly, had a lot to answer for.

But he wasn't going to make a fuss about it. A couple of years ago – before his son had nearly been killed in a motor-bike accident – he would have objected strongly to being given foreign grub; but now he'd mellowed a bit. Much as he liked the steak and kidney pie that Molly used to make, he knew better than to hanker after it. What he'd learned from the family's near-tragedy was that hankering after anything – or anyone – unattainable was a waste of time and spirit.

One thing he could honestly say he'd never hankered after, though, was promotion to superintendent. He hadn't expected or applied for it. It had taken him twenty years' hard slog to reach his present rank, and that suited him well enough.

He liked being in charge of his own divisional CID. His patch was big enough to give him plenty of elbow room, but not so large that he didn't have a fair idea of what was going on in every far-flung village. He liked living at the centre of things in Breckham Market, and he particularly liked his roomy bungalow with its big garden. In fact – apart from his worries about Alison's relationship – he was very nearly happy.

Certainly he was as happy here as he was ever likely to be, and the thought of advancement had never entered his head. Which was just as well, considering that he wasn't the one who was being promoted. The man who was going to become a superintendent, and deputy head of the county CID, was his colleague from the neighbouring division, Detective Chief Inspector Martin Tait.

'Oh, won't Alison be thrilled?' said Molly eagerly as she bustled about setting the table.

She didn't expect or want any domestic help from her husband. Douglas's idea of help was always more trouble than it was worth, and though she sometimes suspected that his ham-fistedness was deliberate, she much preferred him to keep out of her way. Besides, now that a Sainsbury's was sited in Breckham Market, catering for her family had become so much simpler.

She had bought cannelloni for supper, and for Alison's

36

benefit she was going to serve it with a green salad and a bottled vinaigrette dressing, deceitfully decanted into a jug. Douglas wouldn't like any of it, but at least he wouldn't make a fuss in front of their daughter. He could always fill up with biscuits and cheese.

'I do wish Martin could have come with her this evening,' she went on as she dusted two wineglasses. It was no use expecting her husband to drink anything with a meal except beer. 'Then we could have had a family celebration.'

'*Family*?' said Quantrill irritably. 'I'm damned if I'll include Martin Tait in the family when all he's doing is taking advantage of Alison.'

'Oh, don't be stubborn and out of date! Anyway, I'm sure they'll be getting married before very long.'

Molly didn't feel quite as confident as she sounded. Martin was undoubtedly a good catch, charming, well-mannered and with brilliant prospects. It had disappointed her that Alison sometimes seemed very cool towards him, but Molly had kept on hoping for a conventional engagement and a full-scale wedding.

(She could see it all: Alison, dark-haired and green-eyed like her father, in ivory silk; herself in dusky pink with a wide-brimmed navy hat; Peter, her favourite, so unprecedentedly co-operative that he was actually wearing a suit and a tie; and Douglas – tall and still very handsome, she thought, despite some extra weight and the thick salting of grey in his hair – resplendent in hired morning suit and grey top hat.)

It had really hurt Molly when Alison had mentioned during a telephone conversation that she and Martin were already living together. It seemed, somehow, so shabby; not at all what Molly had been brought up to consider right and proper. Unlike her husband, though, she had become reconciled to it. So many of her friends' children also lived or had lived with partners that it was almost customary.

What did it matter, she told herself, as long as Alison and Martin eventually had a wedding of some kind? But they'd been together for almost a year now, and there was still no hint of it.

'When Alison comes to her senses I doubt she'll be marrying

him at all,' pronounced Quantrill, though he wasn't as confident as he sounded, either. 'With any luck she's coming to tell us she's left him.'

Molly was exasperated. 'Why do you always have such a down on Martin?'

'Because he's not good enough for her, that's why.'

'How can you say that, when he's done so well in his career!' She looked scornfully at her husband. 'Ah, that's what's the trouble, isn't it? When Martin first came to Breckham Market he was only your sergeant. Now he's being promoted to superintendent, he'll out-rank you. You're jealous of him, Douglas Quantrill!'

'I'm nothing of the sort.' Smarting, he marched out to the kitchen, poured himself a beer and contemplated the indignity of the situation.

He'd never liked Martin Tait anyway. The man was arrogant, calculating, brashly self-confident. Tait had joined the police on what Quantrill considered a misguided training scheme that guaranteed accelerated promotion to university graduates. When he first came to Breckham Market as Quantrill's sergeant he hadn't known enough about rural policing to keep his feet dry, but he'd made no secret of his ambition to reach the rank of chief constable in record time.

Whereas Quantrill, with no educational qualifications, had come up the hard way, it had taken Tait only six years to reach the same rank. Quantrill had always been prepared to acknowledge that Tait was a good detective, but he found it hard to accept that the man was now mature enough to become deputy head of the county CID; even harder to think of him as his future boss.

And then there was this unsuitable relationship between Tait and his daughter. It had been on-off for years, and Quantrill had kept hoping that it would stay off. Quite apart from his professional resentment of Tait, he didn't consider him personally reliable. More than once, during the years they'd worked together, he'd put a mental question mark against the man on account of his attitude or behaviour.

It was absolutely typical of Tait to expect to live with Alison without marrying her. ('Having his cake *and* eating it,' Quantrill had thought; resentful again, because that was something he hadn't been allowed to get away with when he was young.) But it was on his daughter's behalf that he objected to it, even though Alison had laughed affectionately and assured him that she wasn't being 'taken advantage of'. It was Martin who'd wanted to marry, she said, and she was the one who preferred to keep her independence.

But Quantrill wasn't reassured. Did that mean, he wondered, that Tait was possessive? And was that brash over-confidence merely a smokescreen to conceal some deep emotional insecurity?

'It's not his professional ability I'm talking about,' he told his wife crossly, 'it's his character. His background's unsatisfactory, for a start.'

'For goodness' sake – his grandfather was a solicitor in Woodbridge, and Martin went to Framlingham College and Sussex University. What more do you want?'

'A more stable family history, that's what. I learned about it when we were working on the Fodderstone case. Do you know that his grandmother spent her last years in a private mental hospital? And that his aunt killed herself? And that his father was an irresponsible charmer who gambled away everything he could lay his hands on, and died leaving his widow and young son penniless? If that's the kind of family you want our daughter to marry into, I certainly don't.'

Molly sat down, shaken. 'I didn't know about his father,' she said slowly. 'Nor about his aunt – though Alison did tell me how fond of her he was, and how her death upset him.'

Her frown cleared: 'But I do know about his poor old grandmother, Martin told me that himself. She was ninety when she died, and she'd been suffering from senile dementia. That's a very distressing way to go – I've seen some of our health centre patients in the early stages of the disease, and it's dreadful for them and their families. But it's not *hereditary*. There's absolutely no reason why it should stop Alison from marrying Martin.'

Unwilling to burden his wife with his real worries, Quantrill

39

took refuge in pig-headedness. 'Well, I hope to God she doesn't, that's all.'

'. . . and so we've decided that we'll celebrate Martin's promotion by getting married. We're going to buy a house in Yarchester, settle down and think about starting a family. There, Mum! That's what you've always wanted, isn't it?'

'Oh, Alison . . . I'm so pleased, dear . . .'

Molly was shedding tears, presumably of joy. They were not a demonstrative family and Quantrill sat watching, heavy-hearted, as mother and daughter exchanged unaccustomed kisses. But Molly quickly extricated herself: 'And your father's pleased too,' she said pointedly as she wiped her shining eyes. 'Aren't you, Douggie?'

At least it gave him an excuse to abandon the mush on his plate. ''Course I am,' he said, falsely hearty. He got up to kiss Alison sedately on the cheek, but she met him with such a loving hug that for a moment he felt quite choked.

'Don't be such an old worrier, Dad,' she whispered. 'Everything will be fine, really.'

'Take no notice of your father,' said Molly as he sat down again, embarrassed. 'He's jealous of Martin's promotion, that's all.'

'That's not true, Mum, and you know it! Anyway, Martin has a tremendous respect for Dad – and quite right too. He's sorry about this evening, but may he come to supper on Saturday? He wants to do things properly and ask Dad's permission to marry me.'

Quantrill snorted. 'He's left it a bit late, hasn't he?' he said sourly, reaching for the cheese.

'Do give him a bit of credit for trying,' coaxed Alison. 'I know things were different in your day. But can't you see that it's better to know each other thoroughly first, instead of going into marriage all starry-eyed and innocent?'

Quantrill avoided Molly's reproachful glance. There had been neither starry eyes nor innocence at their hurried wedding, arranged on short acquaintance and at her parents' insistence because he had been careless enough to make her pregnant. It had been what used to be called a shotgun wedding . . . And that reminded him.

'I hear Martin's found himself a new hobby. What was the matter with flying?'

'Nothing, apart from the expense. He intends to keep up his pilot's licence, but now we're getting married he says he can't justify the cost of flying regularly. So he's joined a gun club instead. He's a very good shot, you know.'

'So I've heard. He should be, he's police-trained. But that was using a hand gun, and in controlled conditions on a proper shooting range. At this club of his they use shotguns, don't they?'

'Yes, to shoot clay pigeons. I went to watch him last weekend. He hasn't had much experience with shotguns yet, but he ran up the second highest score. He says it's very exciting and skilful. He's really hooked on the sport – in fact he's just bought his own gun.'

Quantrill's insides took a dip. 'He's bought a shotgun?'

'Oh dear,' said Molly, catching but not understanding her husband's concern. 'That doesn't sound very safe.'

'Of course it's safe, Mum! Martin's terribly conscientious about security, he'll always keep the gun locked away when he's not using it.'

'That's not the point,' said Quantrill. He made an effort to keep the anxiety out of his voice. 'Shotguns aren't just sports equipment, they're lethal weapons. Quite frankly I'm horrified that Martin's bought one. I'd be a lot happier if you could persuade him – '

'Oh for heaven's sake, Dad!' Annoyed, Alison was on her feet collecting dirty dishes with a clatter. 'Honestly, I came here this evening thinking how pleased you'd both be . . .'

'And we are, dear,' said Molly. She took charge of the table-clearing, giving her husband a glare in passing. 'We'll be delighted to see Martin on Saturday evening. Couldn't he come earlier, though – what about lunch?'

'Sorry, but we'll both be out for lunch. Martin's been invited to a day's pheasant shooting – his first ever – at Chalcot House. How about that! Do you know the Glavens, Dad?'

'Not socially, no,' said Quantrill stiffly. Molly was ooh-ing

41

and aah-ing, but he had always scorned Tait's attempts to ingratiate himself with the local gentry. 'How did he wangle that?'

'He didn't *wangle* it!' Alison protested. 'He'd once advised Mr Glaven over some cattle-rustling problem. Then we went to the County Show this year, and Martin congratulated him on his prize-winning herd. Mind you – ' She laughed. Despite her protest on his behalf, she evidently had the measure of her partner. ' – he did make a point of saying he was interested in shooting. But Mr Glaven rang so unexpectedly to invite him, and only last night, that even Martin has to admit that he must be just a stop-gap. He's pleased, of course, because if he shoots well at Chalcot it'll mean other invitations. And I've been invited too, just to watch.'

Quantrill's concern about Martin Tait's possession of a shot-gun receded. Now he had a more immediate worry. He was sure that a private shoot at a place like Chalcot would be well organised, but that didn't exclude the possibility of an accident.

'You're not going, are you?'

'Of course I am! Not that I want to watch birds being shot at, but I'm longing to see what goes on at Chalcot behind those high park walls.'

'Well, if you must go, stay right out of the shooting area,' Quantrill urged. 'I know you think I'm making a fuss – but with shotguns going off all over the place, anything can happen.'

5

In Keeper's Cottage, at the edge of a spinney just beyond the gardens of Chalcot House, Len Alger was spending one of his wakeful nights. The day's rain had given way to a thick mist that should have enabled the gamekeeper to sleep peacefully for once, in the knowledge that no bastard poachers would be about; but he was a lean, angry man with a lurking stomach ulcer, and he couldn't rest.

'Go to sleep . . .' his wife begged wearily, trying to hang on to her share of the bedclothes as he twisted and turned. But Len, with his long bony limbs and long, bony, weather-worn face, was too tense for sleep. There were no end of preparations to be made for the coming shoot, and he resented having to do everything at short notice just for the benefit of Mr Glaven's useless son, who didn't give a damn about shooting anyway.

At the same time, a long-held suspicion was gnawing away at Len's guts that he was likely to lose his job at the end of the season.

'How can I bloody sleep, with you nagging at me?' he raged. Unwilling ever to admit any fault in himself, he always tried to put someone else in the wrong; usually his wife.

Imagining that a hot toddy might appease his ulcer, he jacked himself out of bed, pulled his trousers over his pyjamas for warmth – there was a central heating system in the house, but he refused to pay for its use – and rammed his horny toes into much-mended socks. At sixty-two years old, he knew that his hearing was less sharp than it used to be, and so was his eyesight. Apart from that he considered himself one hundred per cent fit, and he reckoned to pass easily for the fifty-eight which was all he admitted to his employer.

When Mr Glaven was about, Len Alger shaved closely to hide the tell-tale whiteness of his stubble. He'd never been one for conversation, so his defective hearing hadn't been noticed yet. And he knew the Breckham Market road so well that it was no problem to drive the Guv'nor to and from the station, even if he couldn't read the number plate of the car in front.

But good hearing and eyesight are essential to a gamekeeper, and now the season was about to start he couldn't hope to go on fooling Mr Glaven. Only this afternoon, doing his round of the traps and snares in Oak Wood, he'd failed to spot the winged flash of blue that gave away a flying jay. Maddeningly, that bloody boy Jermyn was with him at the time and had brought the bird down with his little 20-bore. It was a fluke, of course, but Len couldn't get over the shame of it.

'You young idiot!' he'd fumed. 'Why d'you think *I* didn't shoot it? I expected you to *observe* it and learn its habits. You'll never make a keeper, you haven't got the patience. Or the sense.' But though his outburst had temporarily salved his pride, Len knew that he'd soon have to submit to eyesight and hearing tests. And whoever heard of a gamekeeper with glasses and a hearing aid?

He thumped down the narrow stairs, careless of the noise he was making, stirred up the ashes of the living-room fire and threw on some kindling. His wife's little brown mongrel bitch, instantly awake and fearful of doing wrong, stood up in its box and waited, quivering, for a command. In Len Alger's opinion it ought to live out in the kennels with the other dogs; if it weren't a useful ratter he wouldn't give it house room.

'Lie down!' he snarled, and it subsided immediately, nose on tense paws, ears pricked, its anxious eyes watching his every move.

He put the old tin kettle on the fire. Mr Glaven had modernised the house by having a small extension built at the back to accommodate a bathroom and an all-electric kitchen, but Len's rule was that the electricity must be used as little as possible. While he waited for the water to heat he put his old jacket round his shoulders, unbolted the outside door, and took a look and a sniff at the weather.

It was nearly 3 a.m. The light from the doorway shone on a mist so thick and wet that he could hardly see the wall of the brick-built kennels by the garden gate, let alone the trees of the spinney. The gun dogs – his own two retriever crosses, and two labradors and a springer spaniel belonging to the Guv'nor – started to bark as soon as they heard the door open, but he stopped them short with a roar of 'Lie down!'

As he closed and bolted the door he hoped to God the weather would clear before Saturday. Mr Glaven had said that he wanted this unexpectedly early shoot because his son was making a special weekend visit; but pheasants never fly well in rain, and in mist they just sit about and mope. Len wasn't going to take any blame for bad weather, but all the same he knew he would feel responsible if the shoot turned out to be a poor one.

He poured himself a whisky, mixed it with hot water, switched off the electric light and sat brooding by the fire. Even if everything went well on Saturday and the Guv'nor was pleased with him, Len had little confidence that he'd still be in work – with or without artificial aids – this time next year. He knew what was in the wind. Mr Glaven was so taken up with his blasted pedigree cattle that he'd lost his old enthusiasm for driven shoots, and that was exactly where skilled keepering was needed.

Ignorant people thought that all a gamekeeper did was stroll about the woods with a gun under his arm, killing vermin and frightening off the odd poacher. They'd no idea what hard, knowledgeable work was involved in rearing and protecting gamebirds, and then driving them up over the guns.

True, the work was easier now than it had been when Len first started, as one of the underkeepers on a big estate where the shooting was let to a syndicate of businessmen. The syndicate demanded quantities of birds and didn't care how low they shot them, so every spring the keepers had to use incubators to hatch pheasant eggs by the thousand.

The chicks were very delicate and it was always the devil's own job to rear them, though that didn't stop them from driving you mad with their everlasting chirping. They were such stupid little buggers that even though you kept gas heaters going in their rearing huts in bad weather, they'd find somewhere cold or wet to lie down and die in just to spite you. Or they'd pile up in a corner and suffocate, or peck each other to death, or die of the gapes. What with watering and feeding 'em, and clipping their beaks, and dosing 'em, and fighting off vermin, the whole summer had been a seven-days-a-week slog for all the keepers from dawn to dusk.

At Chalcot, thankfully, it was a bit easier. As a single-handed keeper on a small estate, Len was allowed to buy in young pheasants from a game farm as six-week-old poults. They were healthy stock, but even so the blasted birds would still die if they were given half a chance. Once they'd arrived he had to spend every waking hour cosseting and worrying about them, until they grew strong enough to serve their purpose in life by getting shot.

As always, he had spent the early part of the summer building large pens of wire netting for them, one in each of the woods on the estate. These kept the poults from straying until they were almost fully grown. The pens were sited in wide grassy rides, and each contained a shed where the young birds could

45

shelter from killers like rain and cold. The other killers, the vermin that were determined to burrow or gnaw their way in, had to be kept out by guns and traps and snares.

Len Alger was proud of his record in keeping down premature deaths, but that was only part of his skill as a gamekeeper. Everything he did was directed towards providing good sport for the guns at the five driven shoots that were the highlights of the Chalcot year. One wood, and its immediate surrounds, would be shot on each occasion. The Guv'nor would plan the shoots in the expectation that each of the woods would yield a bag of 100-120 pheasants, and Len's skill lay not only in knowing how many poults to put in each wood, but in persuading them to stay thereabouts after they were strong enough to be released from the pens.

The secret of holding the birds where he wanted them was in the feeding and watering. At each pen there were water tanks and metal storage bins, which he kept filled with supplies that he took in by Landrover. He fed near the pens, and also, as the birds began to roam, in outlying areas round each wood. And as the birds grew, he knew just what proportion of barley and oats and protein pellets to add to the wheat, and more importantly, how much of it to give them.

The birds had to be kept hungry enough to come back to feed twice a day, but not so hungry that they'd go searching for food elsewhere. You could never be absolutely sure that you'd got it right until the shoot was in progress, but in the whole of his career he'd rarely failed to feel satisfied when he counted up the dead birds at the end of the day.

If driven shoots were abandoned, though, none of that skill and experience would be needed any more. Mr Glaven would never give up shooting, Len was sure of that; but with his son's lack of interest, and a keeper who was showing his age, he might well announce that from next season he would shoot only wild pheasants. The days of proper keepering at Chalcot would be over, and Len would be on the scrapheap, without a job, without any transport of his own, and without a home.

He'd seen it coming, ever since that bloody Jermyn boy had been taken on.

'Seems there's some sort of training scheme available for

school-leavers,' Mr Glaven had said last July. 'Good idea, eh? Keeps 'em off the streets and gives 'em some useful experience at the same time. Thought we might take a youngster on, if we can find someone suitable. Just temporarily, of course. You could use a good strong lad to help with the poults, couldn't you?'

Just temporarily. Hah!

The fact was that as long as there was any shooting on the estate, there'd have to be some sort of keepering. Vermin would have to be controlled, signs of poaching would have to be watched for, and food would have to be put out for the wild pheasants in a bad winter. But it didn't need a skilled game-keeper to do any of that. After a season's experience, even a blasted boy could do it.

Sore in mind as well as stomach, his hands shaking with suppressed anger, Len Alger poured himself another toddy. He had hated Darren Jermyn even before he met him. He was damned if he was going to train the boy to do him out of his own job – but maddeningly, Darren had turned out to be a good observer and a quick learner. And Mr Glaven had taken an interest in him, even teaching him to handle a gun.

Not that Len blamed the Guv'nor. He had too much respect for him for that, and he liked to think the respect was returned. No, he put the blame on Mr Glaven's son, the blasted Major. Some soldier! Will Glaven was a rotten shot, he missed more birds than he hit and he was too vain ever to practise.

And that was where the trouble was. Chalcot was a shooting estate, and Len was sure the Guv'nor would have kept up the tradition in order to hand it on to his son, if only Will had been interested. As it was, you couldn't blame Mr Glaven for losing heart.

What drove Len mad, though, was the Major's lordly attitude towards him. Instead of admitting that he wasn't a shooting man, he made it clear that he thought driven shoots and proper keepering a waste of money.

'Know how much these damn birds cost to rear?' the Major had drawled at the end of the shoot last Boxing Day, when Len had handed him a brace of pheasants he didn't deserve. 'Fifteen quid a beak – and for that I've had to stand about all day in freezing mud! It'd make more sense to have 'em delivered from Harrods.'

He was laughing, but Len knew he meant it. Bloody playboy, wanting to do nothing but ponce about on horseback all day. Never a word of thanks or appreciation for the keeper's skill and hard work . . . Len Alger hated him, almost as much as he hated Darren Jermyn.

Resentment, seething in his stomach, rose thickly in his gullet. He cleared his throat explosively and spat on to the dying embers of the fire, making them sizzle.

To hell with the satisfaction he liked to get from a good shoot. It would give him a lot more satisfaction, this Saturday, if something were to happen to spoil the Major's homecoming.

After all, if anything did go wrong, he could always put the blame on that blasted Jermyn boy.

6

In his lodgings in Chalcot village, Darren had had a restless night too. He couldn't stop thinking about the jay he had shot in Oak Wood.

Len Alger had said it was just a fluke. He *would* say that, the miserable old devil. Jays are wary and like to stay hidden in woodland, so they're difficult to get a shot at. Darren reckoned, from the way the keeper screwed up his eyes when he wanted to focus on anything, that he probably hadn't even seen the bird.

No – there might have been a bit of luck involved in shooting his first jay (he was actually after a rook when he found the bright blue wing in his sights and squeezed the trigger) but Darren preferred to call it quick reaction. Mr Glaven had told him he was a promising shot, and here was the proof. It was a cold wet afternoon and his hands and feet were miserably chilled, but as the bird tumbled through the branches he'd felt elated.

Remembering first to break his gun and take out the remaining cartridge, as Mr Glaven had taught him, he had run squelching into the wood to pick up the bird. Jays are predators, like all their cousins in the crow family, a menace to other birds because they devour eggs and young. But while most predators are black and ugly (or villainously black-and-white if they're magpies) jays are almost exotic, with pinky-brown plumage, black tails, white rumps, black and white bars on their wings and brilliant blue wing-coverts. Darren wanted two of the blue feathers, one to wear boastfully in the band of his jungle hat, the other to offer to Laura (whose eyes it matched) with love and longing.

But when the jay was in his big red hands, he changed his mind.

Darren Jermyn was a country boy, entirely practical about animal life and death. His grandfather, who kept fowls, had taught him the knack of wringing their necks and so he was unfazed when he found the jay still alive. With one wing almost shot away, its eyes staring, its strong beak opening and closing in silent gasps, it was flapping in agony among the fallen leaves. Darren had scooped it up immediately, put two fingers round its throat and ended its struggles with a sharp tug and a twist.

Its nervous system gave its last twitches, and then the bird slumped, neck hanging, eyes closed. Blood, oozing from its shattered wing and matting the creamy-pink down on its wounded breast, mingled with the rain on his hands. And as the diluted blood trickled through his fingers, Darren had felt a sense of unease.

He hadn't hesitated to shoot the bird. It was his job to kill all predators and pests on the estate, and so far he'd thoroughly enjoyed doing it.

He'd lost count of the rats, stoats, weasels and other vermin he'd trapped, and the rabbits he'd snared. But he kept his gun score on the back of the Game Laws leaflet that Mr Glaven had given him to study, and it was beginning to mount: rabbits 12, woodpigeon 17, grey squirrels 4, carrion crows 2, rooks 5, jackdaws 1. No magpies, but that was because Len Alger had already shot them off the estate.

The jay was different, though. It made him stop and think. He knew it was stupidly sentimental to mind about killing a predator just because it happened to be uncommon and attractive, but he couldn't feel easy about what he'd done.

Laura had once said it was wrong to kill any living thing, but that was just idiotic. He'd pointed out to her that if rapid breeders like rabbits and rats weren't kept down, the whole country would be overrun – no food crops would survive, and rats would spread disease throughout the land. She'd gone a bit quiet after that!

But he couldn't use the same argument against jays. There was no way they were ever going to take over from the songbirds. Their numbers were so small, in comparison with even the wild pheasants on the estate, that it wouldn't make any difference to the game population if he never shot another jay as long as he worked there.

After all, the only reason he'd taken the job was to be near Laura, and she'd already given him enough grief. She would be furious with him for killing anything as beautiful as the jay. It would probably ruin his chances of getting back with her.

As he thought it through, he had spread out the dead bird's undamaged wing. The blue wing-coverts he'd wanted were there for the taking. But across them was a trail of blood, each drop a separate bead of crimson against the glossy blue, and he knew he didn't want the feathers any more.

Now, unable to sleep, he relived those few moments when he'd held that shattered little corpse, and felt again the sense of shame that had made him hurl it as far as he could into the undergrowth, before wiping his hands on the wet grass and getting on with his work.

On the day before the shoot he was up in what seemed like the middle of the night – not because that old misery Len Alger had threatened to have his guts for garters if he were late, but because he knew how much work there was to get through, and he didn't see how else he'd have time to do it.

He scrambled into his clothes, breakfasted one-handed on a cheese sandwich as he powered his mountain bike through the misty dark, and arrived at Keeper's Cottage at daybreak. But that still didn't stop Len Alger from bawling him out.

'What sort of time d'you call this, you lazy young devil? You'll never make a keeper, you're too idle!'

Rotten old bastard . . .

Darren had developed a real hatred for Len Alger. He despised him, too, because of the man's attitude to wildlife.

Mr Glaven had emphasised to Darren how important it was to obey the Game Laws. 'It's a great responsibility, being a gamekeeper,' the Guv'nor had said sternly. 'This leaflet tells you what you're legally entitled to kill on the estate at any time of the year. You're allowed to do it because you're my employee, and we preserve game here. But it's illegal to shoot anything that isn't listed, and I won't turn a blind eye if you do. I won't have anything killed here at Chalcot unless it's been reared for the purpose, or is acknowledged to be a menace. Understand?'

Darren understood, and privately agreed. He had no intention of killing anything that was harmless. But Len Alger classed everything on the estate (always excepting Mr Glaven's pedigree cattle) as either game or vermin. As long as the Guv'nor wasn't about, Len shot at anything that moved regardless of the law.

And he was cruel with it. It had horrified Darren to see him shoot at a ginger cat that was mouse-watching at the bottom of a hedge. It was a long shot and the animal streaked off towards the village, apparently unhurt but quite possibly wounded. When Darren had protested that it was somebody's pet, though, the keeper had laughed.

'You bloody great softy,' he'd jeered. 'Anything that's capable of killing young pheasants is fair game as far as I'm concerned. If you haven't got the guts to do a thorough job, you'd better pack it in. Go on, tell the Guv'nor you're leaving.'

But that was Darren's problem. If he went of his own accord, or swore back at the keeper and got the sack, it was Laura he would be leaving. And he loved her far too much to do that.

Easier to put up with a pig like Len Alger. But one day – one day before very long – he intended to get even with him.

*

The overnight mist had thinned, leaving everywhere soaking wet under a low grey ceiling of cloud. Glad of the waterproofs the Guv'nor had given him, Darren hurried off to begin the morning feed round.

It was his regular job, twice a day, seven days a week, to feed Oak Wood and Belmont Plantation. That had been the first dirty trick Len Alger had played on him, sending him out to the woods that were farthest away and then grumbling because the job took him a long time.

After he'd fed the birds at each pen, he had to fill a sling bag from the storage bins and carry it to the outlying feeding places. It was hard work, sweating along under the weight of the bag across ditches and fences, and pushing through bracken and brambles. His boots were soon clogged with mud, and he slipped about on slimy heaps of dead leaves. At one point he got bogged in a ditch, and struggled out with a bootful of cold muddy water.

But he always enjoyed the actual feeding. Len Alger seemed to hate the pheasants, but Darren liked them. As he reached Belmont they were just beginning to wake up, on their roosts on the almost-leafless branches of the beech trees. Once awake, they launched off and came drifting down like free-fall parachutists to land lightly in the straw-strewn ride beside their old pen.

For a few moments they just stood about, looking as dopey as he usually felt when he first woke up. But as soon as he whistled they seemed to gather their wits. The cocks stretched and flapped their wings, stirring the damp air with their cries of *kurrr-kuk*. Still whistling, Darren hurried down the ride throwing out handfuls of grain, and soon the birds came running eagerly to feed.

They were even tamer then Laura's pheasants because they belonged to the first batch of poults, bought in at the same time as he began work on the estate. They had always looked to him for food, even though they liked to eat insects in summer and wild fruits and beechmast in the autumn. Many of them were naturally wary and would scatter if they heard a blackbird's warning cry, but they all knew they had nothing to fear from

52

Darren. The boldest would happily feed at his feet, and he wished he had time to stand still and watch them.

After he'd fed in and around Belmont, and checked his traps and snares, he hurried on to do the same at Oak Wood. When he got back to the keeper's house he had the kennels to sweep and swill, and then the Landrover to hose down and clean out. Everywhere was wet and mucky. His hands felt raw, and a leak from the hose sprayed back on him and ran down his neck, soaking his T-shirt.

The pleasure he'd felt in feeding the pheasants had evaporated. He was very glad of the mug of hot sweet coffee that Mrs Alger sneaked out to him while her husband was somewhere with Mr Glaven, but even that didn't lift his spirits for long.

He began to feel really depressed. It wasn't only Laura's rejection that weighed on him, or the dreary weather, or the discomforts of his job, or even Len Alger's behaviour. He felt uneasy and anxious, and he didn't know why.

He slogged on with his work, clearing up the big shed where the beaters were going to have their midday break tomorrow and heaving in bales of straw for them to sit on. He was just about to sit down himself for ten minutes, and eat his sandwich lunch, when Len Alger came hurtling out of the house wiping his mouth with the back of his hand.

'Come on, come on, you lazy young devil,' the keeper bellowed, onion gravy on his breath. 'Get that Landrover loaded up! Mr Glaven's going to meet us at Belmont to set things out for tomorrow.'

Swearing to himself, Darren stuffed the sandwiches back in his pocket and loaded the various bundles of gear he'd helped prepare during the previous weeks. Len Alger had ordered him to do this and that, without telling him what anything was for, but by now he had a fairly good idea. As they bumped along in the Landrover he looked out at the pheasants that were wandering, unworried, in the open fields, and his stomach began to tighten. He told himself it was hunger, but he didn't feel like eating any more.

Mr Glaven's Range Rover was already parked beside Belmont Plantation. He came to meet them with two black labradors pacing sedately at his heels, a pink-cheeked country gentleman with a greying moustache, dressed in a well-worn Barbour and a flat cap and carrying a thumbstick. He gave Darren his usual affable greeting and added in his posh voice, 'No doubt the keeper's explained what we've planned for tomorrow. You know what to do, eh?'

Darren was going to tell the truth, but Len Alger had been listening intently and now he shoved in first:

'Certainly I've explained, Mr Glaven! But I very much doubt he's taken it in. I'm afraid he'll never make a keeper, he's too unreliable.'

Darren felt the blood in his face rush up to boiling point. He made a great effort to keep his mouth shut, but the Guv'nor couldn't fail to notice the indignation steaming out of his ears.

'Can't expect too much too soon,' said Mr Glaven, giving the keeper a shrewd look. 'The lad's only been with us three months. From what I've seen he's a hard worker. Now, set the pegs out, will you, Len? And you come along with me, young feller. I'll tell you what's what.'

He strode off with his dogs along the stubble field that skirted the wood. 'Now then,' he said, 'you know we're shooting here in Belmont tomorrow?'

Darren hadn't known, and the news came like the twist of a stick in his guts. He ought to have realised what was going to happen, because he knew the Belmont pheasants were the oldest they'd reared and therefore the strongest fliers. But somehow, when he fed them this morning, he'd managed not to think consciously about their fate.

No wonder he'd been feeling depressed, though.

They reached the highest part of the estate, a rise on which the wood had been planted a hundred years before. Mr Glaven pointed out with his stick where the planned drives were to take place, three in the morning, coming towards Belmont across the outlying fields and copses where Darren had been feeding the birds, and two in the afternoon up here in the wood itself. He also pointed out where the shooting party – he called them the Guns – would stand for each drive.

'You'll be walking with the beaters,' the Guv'nor said. 'The keeper will be in charge, but they're all regulars so you'll soon see what to do. The Guns will be spread out in a row at the end of each drive, and you beaters will work your way in line towards them. The idea is to drive the pheasants ahead of you so that they'll fly up over the Guns.'

'Supposing they won't fly?' said Darren, clutching at a twig of hope.

'That's what you beaters are for, to flush 'em out. They won't want to fly, of course. They're heavy birds and flying soon exhausts 'em. They've had no cause to be frightened of human beings, and they'll try to tuck up in the undergrowth. So you'll have to poke 'em out with your stick and keep them running ahead. Don't panic them, just keep 'em going. They'll take off when they run out of cover and see the Guns. Never fails.'

The grey air was still, disturbed only by near and far pheasant-calls. A small group of them, led by a fine russet cock with a parson's collar round his neck, had come wandering out of the shrivelled bracken that edged the wood and were pecking unconcernedly on the corn stubble, no more than a dog's rush away.

But the Guv'nor's labradors were professionals, and knew better than to make the pheasants fidgety. They stayed sitting at their master's feet, watching the birds with nothing more than mild interest. Darren would have thought it an amazingly friendly scene, if he hadn't known that the pheasants had been set up to be shot out of the sky tomorrow, and that the dogs would be there to retrieve them when they fell.

He felt sick. 'I've brought these birds up from poults,' he protested. 'I can't force them out to risk their lives, not when they trust me.'

'Hah! Can't carry your job to its logical conclusion, eh?' Mr Glaven looked fierce, but his voice wasn't unsympathetic. 'Young keepers often feel like that at their first shoot, but they get over it.'

He turned and began to walk briskly back towards the Range Rover, his boots crunching the brittle grey stubble. 'Think of it this way, lad,' he advised as Darren caught up with him. 'These pheasants are hatched to order. If we didn't shoot game on this estate, not one of the birds you've reared would ever have lived. Besides, they've got a fifty per cent chance of surviving – and that's more than you can say of my beef cattle, eh?'

"Spose so,' said Darren reluctantly.

'Well then.' Mr Glaven sounded impatient, disinclined to waste any more of the short November afternoon. 'You must make up your mind. In my opinion you're doing well here, and there may be a permanent job for you if you want it. If you can't face tomorrow, though, you'd better say so before night-fall. Now, have you pulled up your snares in this wood, and put the safety catches on the traps?'

'No – I didn't know I was supposed to.'

The Guv'nor was not pleased. 'Well then, do it right away. We can't risk any of the beaters or dogs being hurt tomorrow. After that, give your birds their second feed. If you decide to leave the job, come up to the house afterwards and I'll pay you off.'

Dusk came very early under the beeches. By the time Darren went to feed the Belmont pen, the wood was rustling with pheasants making their usual lengthy going-to-bed prep-arations, peering up into the trees as if to select a desirable lodging for the night.

At least, Darren thought, they don't know what's going to happen tomorrow. For himself, he felt like an assistant executioner – his stomach was tight, his mouth was dry, and when he pursed his lips he couldn't whistle. But the pheasants came to him anyway, trusting him so completely as he threw out the grain for their last supper that their colours seemed to blur before his eyes.

He hurried away, to do as much as he could of the rest of the feeding before the birds flew up to roost. When he passed Belmont on the way back, the dark wood was noisy with his pheasants' goodnight chatter; but now he had stopped feeling sorry for them. He knew that he would be there at the shoot tomorrow, even though driving the birds over the guns would be a final betrayal of their trust.

It was Laura he had to be there for. She mattered to him far more than a whole woodful of pheasants. If sacrificing the lot of them would win her back, he'd do it gladly.

He had been so busy agonising over their relationship, and over the pheasants' fate, that he hadn't given much thought to what Laura had said at the end of their last meeting. At the time, he'd been so longing to touch her that he hadn't taken in her meaning.

He remembered asking her – mockingly, so as to show how cool he was – if she wanted to come and help him with the beating. And she'd snapped back something about being there anyway, not to help the shooters but to stop them.

He hadn't taken it seriously. He'd thought it was just an off-the-top-of-her-head retort, because it was ridiculous of her to think that she could put a stop to the shoot. But Laura usually said what she meant, and when something was important to her, she'd go for it.

He knew now why he'd felt so uneasy. Everything that had been happening at Chalcot was leading up to tomorrow, the killing day. And if Laura tried to interfere when shooting was taking place, it wouldn't only be the pheasants that were in danger.

That was why he was going to be there at the shoot. He was sick with love and fear for her. Laura was his, whether she recognised it or not, and he would do whatever it took to prove it.

7

As he drove his BMW through the open gates that led to Chalcot House, with his new gun bag stowed in the boot and his new tweed cap tipped over his eyes, Martin Tait was in his element. Or at least in the element he considered rightfully his, though it had been extraordinarily difficult to establish that fact in the minds of those who mattered.

If the classless society evolves anywhere, it won't be in rural

Suffolk. This may not be apparent to incomers who have flocked to live in those grossly expanded villages where the old pattern of country life has been destroyed. But in small villages like Chalcot, on the edge of a country estate that is in private ownership, most of the inhabitants recognise that a social structure still exists. Willingly or unwillingly, they know their own place in it.

The standard is set by 'the County': established upper-middle-class families like the Glavens, who are instantly recognisable by the understated quality of their clothes and their self-assured voices. Many of them own land and provide employment, but not necessarily a lot of either.

Membership of the county set has little to do with wealth and nothing at all to do with conspicuous consumption. It is based on 'old money' and cannot be bought, as some of the newly rich discovered during the booming Eighties, when they acquired country houses in the expectation of instant social success and found that they were ignored. They didn't have the right background, or values, or voices or clothes. They didn't *belong*, and being pushy got them nowhere.

Though the upper classes are thin on the ground, their influence is considerable. By tradition, they devote much of their time to serving the community. Lewis Glaven's grandfather and father had both served as chairmen of the local magistrates, and he hoped to be appointed to the bench as soon as his business commitments allowed. His late wife had been county president of the Women's Institute and an indefatigable fund-raiser for charity. Lewis was a regional committee member of the Country Landowners' Association, and a churchwarden at the parish church where he read the second lesson every Sunday.

Despite their good works, the members of the county set are not always admired by the rest of the community. Their confident enunciation, and their habitual air of quizzical amusement, can get right up the noses of the self-made and the stroppy. People like Reg Brunt, the prosperous Chalcot butcher, are quick to sense that they are being put down, and to become angrily resentful.

On the other hand there are those like Ann Harbord, Lewis

Glaven's housekeeper, who are so charmed by the upper classes that they are only too glad to be of service to them. And then there are those like Martin Tait, who persist in regarding the county set as an exclusive club which they are fully qualified to join, if only they can persuade a member to support their application.

Tait had been trying to join for years. He certainly had the right voice, and the right air of effortless superiority. He wore the right clothes, too, after a youthful flirtation with trend and colour. He had a professional, property-owning middle-class background, at least in his grandparents' generation, and he had been to the right kind of school.

Unfortunately, his school and university were both in minor leagues and he had never been able to build up the right network of friends and contacts. Until now, there had been no one to give him the elusive introductions that are the key to membership of the county set. But today was going to change all that. Today, as he drove between the double row of autumnal lime trees that formed the approach to Chalcot House, Martin was a happy man.

It was just after nine o'clock. Rain was forecast before the end of the afternoon but the morning was just right for shooting, dry and with a strong enough breeze to make the pheasants fly well.

The air and the grass had both been crisped by a touch of overnight frost. Visibility was good under a high pale sky, hazy with cloud, and the brilliant bronze of the beeches and the yellow of the maples made the countryside glow. Martin's spirits were so high that when he glimpsed a cock pheasant pacing out from behind a tree, he couldn't resist doing what he would have done at the age of nine: 'Pchyeeow!' he exploded, taking a pot-shot at the bird with his index finger.

Then Chalcot House came into sight, grey and classically handsome beyond an expanse of lawn, and he grew up again.

The long drive divided and made a sweeping circle round the leaf-littered grass, passing a shrubbery on the left before going on towards the front of the house. On the right, where the drive went past the back of the house, vehicles were parked and there was a lot of activity. Martin turned right and slowed, just for a moment feeling uncharacteristically anxious.

It was going to be so important to make a good first impression. That was why he was glad that Alison wasn't with him. Not, of course, that he was doubtful of her acceptability. But Lewis Glaven had suggested, when he telephoned the invitation, that she might like to join them later, for lunch and the afternoon shoot, and that suited Martin very well. It would be easier to exaggerate his claim to county status if Alison weren't listening.

He parked next to a scruffy Range Rover, unsure whether it was a good or a bad thing that his pride-and-joy BMW 318iS Coupé was by far the newest and cleanest vehicle there. The others were a classic sports car, an MGB GT, two other Range Rovers, a Landrover and a big old Volvo estate that evidently served as a mobile dog kennel.

There seemed to be a lot of people among the vehicles, although in fact there were no more than five men and two women, indistinguishably greeny-brown in comfortable old shooting tweeds. They were exchanging hearty banter as they unloaded guns and cartridge bags and wellington boots and Barbours and shooting sticks. Gun dogs stalked about the yard, their growls as they sized each other up, and their yelps as their owners hauled them off, adding to the noise.

Martin, a fair-haired, spare, sharp man, got out of his car and stood tall. The upper classes always seem to have a height advantage, and at only five foot eight – shorter than everyone there including the women – he hoped that his credibility wasn't going to be damaged.

He looked about him for his host's pink cheeks and moustache. It was six months since he'd last met Lewis Glaven, at the County Show, and what with the uniform appearance of the shooting party, and their uniform height, he needed the moustache to identify him.

'Ah, good morning to you!'

Lewis Glaven saw him first and came over with an outstretched hand. He was wearing a tweed cap and a many-pocketed shooting coat, and shooting breeches with stockings and leather ankle boots. 'Glad you could join us at such short notice. And that charming girl who was with you at the Show – will she be coming later?'

'Yes indeed. Thank you for asking me to the shoot, and Alison to lunch. We're both delighted to be included.'

'Excellent. As I told you, it's my son's girlfriend's first shoot too. Can't expect young women to enjoy the sport if they have to spend the whole of their first day out in the cold, eh? We'll all lunch together and then they can come and stand with the Guns for the last two drives.'

Martin had felt he'd made a good start. Now, though, he had been put on a spot. He knew it had been traditional for an Edwardian lady to stand admiringly beside her man at a driven shoot, but he hadn't realised that the Glavens still kept the custom.

Alison wasn't a country girl, she was a presenter with BBC local radio. She was coming to Chalcot without realising that she would be expected to watch the shoot at close quarters, and he felt sure that if she were beside him when he began bringing down birds, she would be horrified.

'One small problem there, I'm afraid,' he began carefully. The last thing he wanted was to offend his host, but he had to speak out. It wasn't just that he knew better than to commit Alison to doing something she would hate. He was also afraid that she might make a public protest, and disgrace him. 'I don't think Alison's ever likely to be a shooting enthusiast,' he explained to his host. 'What she really likes is photography. If you have no objection, I think she'll be happier taking photographs rather than getting too close to the guns.'

His host gave him a bristly look, all moustache and eyebrows. '*Photographs*? Of what?'

'Well . . . er . . .' Martin wished he'd had the sense to say that Alison would prefer just to go for a walk. The photography had been his idea, not hers. He'd wanted some photographs of himself at the shoot, and he'd instructed her in the use of his Canon EOS for the purpose. 'Mainly of the house and the estate – with just a few action pictures of the Guns at the start of one of the drives. General views, of course,' he added apologetically. 'She wouldn't get in the way.'

Lewis Glaven's pink cheeks darkened to red. His pale blue eyes, their blood-flecked whites a tired grey, seemed to bulge.

'*No* photography – absolutely not! Good God, we can't have novices wandering about with cameras during a shoot! Accidents can happen easily enough, without *inviting* 'em. Never forgive myself . . . No no, she must stand in the safest place, just behind you. Got that?'

Tait drew himself up, sincerely contrite. It wasn't easy to know how to address his host without sounding either obsequious or familiar, so he used the standard police courtesy: 'Yes of course, sir.'

'Right, then.' Simmering down, Mr Glaven gave him a forgiving clap on the shoulder. 'Your own first shoot, so you weren't to know how hectic it can get out there when the birds start coming over. You'll have enough to do and think about, without worrying where your girlfriend is. By the way – have you brought any ear-protectors? If not, I can lend you some.'

'I always wear them when I'm shooting clays,' Tait said, reminding his host that even if he'd never shot pheasants before, he was an expert with a gun. 'Ear muffs are compulsory on the police firing range, so it's become a habit with me.'

'Very wise. We all wear muffs or plugs here at Chalcot, except for my old friend and neighbour Barclay Dodd. He's been shooting without protection all his life, and now the poor chap's deaf as a post. Ah, here's our excellent Mrs Harbord with the coffee. Take a mug, and come with me to meet everyone.'

A thin dark woman with gypsy ear-rings and an anxious frown, her inappropriately smart red coat providing the only splash of colour among the tweeds, was carrying round a tray of steaming mugs. When her employer thanked her, her face brightened and lifted towards him with disproportionate gratitude, as though she felt she had in some way been forgiven.

She was followed – with a reluctance more intense than any teenage sulk – by her daughter, who carried a second tray. The girl's black sweater, with its Wildwatch owl motif, emphasised the whiteness of her face. She kept her eyes well down behind the pale curtain of her hair, and deliberately avoided Lewis Glaven.

For his part, he appeared not to notice her. Producing a

battered silver flask from one of his pockets, he went among his guests offering to lace their coffee with whisky. Tait followed, holding his mug high to keep it from being knocked by the dogs. He preferred animals in a one-to-one relationship, and was unused to being knee-deep in waving tails and over-inquisitive noses.

To his disappointment – he had expected a mention of his rank – his host introduced him with a 'Do you know Martin Tait from Saintsbury?' formula. He learned that his fellow members of the shooting party were from three well-known families of gentlemen-farmers: the Glavens themselves, the Dodds from Ashthorpe and the Treadgolds from Nether Wickford.

Senior in age was Barclay Dodd, perched bulkily on a shooting stick in the middle of the yard. He wore a Barbour and shooting breeches, with an old tweed deerstalker crammed down on his white hair. His complexion was a weatherbeaten red darkening to purple about the nose, and he was beaming; the prospect of the day's sport, unhampered by his deafness, obviously filled him with good humour.

He rumbled a cheerful greeting at Tait, and accepted his hosts's offer of a second slug of whisky in his coffee. When one of the labradors, strutting stiff-legged about the yard intent on marking its territory, cocked its leg against his shooting stick, Barclay Dodd was the first to enjoy the joke.

His daughter Joanna, tall in lean trousers and high hunter boots, with a man's flat cap worn forward on her tied-back chestnut hair, was not in a good humour. She was about Martin's age, a big-boned woman with a long face, handsome but undeniably horsy. Having declined coffee, she was standing by one of the Range Rovers opening boxes of cartridges and loading them into her cartridge belt.

Martin lifted his cap to her when he was introduced. She had such a height advantage that replacing it would mean that he had to peer up at her from under its peak, so he decided to carry it instead. He did his best to charm her, but after one quick comprehensive look and a brusque 'How d'y'do,' she turned dismissively away.

'Joanna is a damn fine shot,' Lewis Glaven told him, clearly

63

trying to coax her into a better humour. 'Very few women shoot, but those who do are good. Joanna must be the best in the county.' But she shrugged off the compliment. As the men left her, she was cramming handfuls of extra cartridges into the pockets of her Barbour.

Tait already knew of the Treadgold family, who owned several thousand acres of Suffolk. They were two bachelor brothers in their mid-fifties, and an older widowed sister, Dorothy Wilson-Brown. She had a formidable reputation, having served for many years on the County Council, most recently as deputy chairman; she was currently a council member of the County Agricultural Association, and also chairman of the governors of Breckham Market High School.

On this occasion she seemed to be in charge of the mobile kennel and most of the dogs. A grey-haired woman, with shrewd brown eyes in a face as wrinkled as an over-wintered russet apple, she wore a rakish old sporting hat, layers of sensible clothes, stout wellies, and a careless fistful of jewelled rings on her gardener's hands.

Mrs Wilson-Brown appeared to be a favourite with Lewis Glaven, who called her Doffy and introduced her proudly as 'Our chief picker-up'. She was a couple of inches taller than Martin, and she looked him over with some suspicion.

'Haven't brought your dorgs, have you?' she demanded.

He gave her his best smile. 'Certainly not, without a specific invitation,' he assured her. He hadn't owned a dog since he was a boy, but he knew better than to let on; dog-owning is taken for granted by the county set. Besides, he wasn't going to turn down the chance of winning a point for good manners.

'Glad to hear it.' She awarded him the point with an approving nod. 'Some new Guns bring 'em regardless, and I can't abide badly trained dorgs at a shoot – can you?' She gave him a smile, then turned to talk to Lewis Glaven, leaving Tait with her brothers.

The two Treadgolds, George and Jim, both had high-complexioned Roman-nosed faces under their flat caps. They were much of a height, with long thin legs and corpulent middles that strained the buttons of their shooting coats. Their public activities extended no further than their own parish, and they were clearly more ill-at-ease with a stranger than their sister was. They stood stirring their coffee and looking down at Tait with a courteous but puzzled air, as though they had no idea what to talk to him about.

'Do much shootin'?' said one of them, in a tone that presupposed he didn't.

'Not as much as I'd like,' said Tait, hoping for a future invitation to shoot at Nether Wickford Hall. 'We don't get much time for it in the CID.'

'Ah,' they said, even more at a loss.

'Detective Superintendent,' explained Tait modestly. Strictly speaking, he was still a chief inspector until he took up his new duties on the first of December, but it seemed a pity not to fix his new rank in their minds.

'Ahh.' They both nodded sagely, clearly no more impressed than if he'd said 'Sergeant', and gulped coffee. Tait began to feel vexed. Then one of them, emerging from his mug inspired, offered a humorous, deadpan contribution to the conversation: 'Police, eh? Better get out and buy our dorg-licences, then . . .'

The brothers grinned at Tait, inviting him to enjoy the pleasantry, and he dredged up a weary smile. Policemen become inured to such juvenile jests. Frankly, though, he was disappointed to hear it from the Treadgolds, particularly on a social occasion like this. He turned away, wondering whether they were really going to be worth cultivating.

And then he caught a glimpse of an extraordinarily lovely girl. She had come round from the front of the house and was standing shyly at the corner of the yard, small and slim, and dressed in soft clear colours that were beautifully out of place in that earthy company. She seemed to Martin as delicate and huge-eyed as a fawn. Her cheekbones were high, and her fine gold hair, gently stirred by the wind, floated in tendrils about her face. He gaped at her, open-mouthed with admiration.

With her was a man of his own age – only taller, dammit, and undeniably good-looking in his shooting clothes; Lewis's son Will, presumably, the only member of the party Tait hadn't yet met.

Will Glaven seemed to be trying to coax the girl to come and meet everyone. It was clear that she was reluctant – even more

65

so when two of the dogs bounded across the yard and leaped up at her. Flinching from them, she took fright and disappeared round the corner. Will called the dogs off and went after her but returned almost immediately, shrugging off the incident, to join the rest of the company.

Martin, who prided himself on missing nothing, was incensed on the girl's behalf.

'What an oaf Will Glaven must be!' he thought fiercely. 'How could he try to drag a girl like that into a crowd like this? She doesn't fit in here and she never will. She's going to hate this kind of country life, absolutely hate it. And if he's too stupid to see that, he doesn't deserve her.'

Disenchanted with some of his new companions, fed up with so many nosy dogs, bowled over by the girl and quite forgetting that he was already spoken for, Martin appointed himself her rescuer.

The housekeeper's daughter had removed the mugs and the shooting party was almost ready to leave. While Tait had been putting on his work-worn wellingtons and Barbour, they were joined by an angular man in weatherproofs, carrying a thumb-stick and with a whistle hanging round his neck. He seemed to know everyone else, and was now respectfully touching his cap and shaking hands all round.

Lewis Glaven brought him over to Tait and introduced him as Alger the gamekeeper. 'How do you do, sir?' the man said, a thin smile cracking his bony face, and Tait realised that he was older than he had at first appeared; probably due for retirement. 'I'm very pleased to meet you, Mr Tait. I hope you'll enjoy the shoot.'

His voice was polite, even smarmy, but there was a sardonic look in his faded eye. Tait felt that he'd been summed up as a novice, and it annoyed him. The keeper's handshake lingered a little, possibly as a reminder that it was traditional at the end of a shoot for each Gun to press some banknotes into his hand by way of a tip. Tait had been thinking in terms of a couple of fivers, but now he decided that one would be quite enough.

'Full complement of beaters today, Len?' asked Lewis Glaven.

'Yes sir, they're now on their way to the first drive.'

'Is the Jermyn boy with them? I wasn't sure, yesterday, whether he'd come.'

'He's there, sir. For all the good he'll do . . .' The keeper's weather-worn face became a deeper red. 'I hope you realise, Mr Glaven,' he burst out, 'that I can't take responsibility for the number of pheasants we'll find in Belmont. I've done my best to teach him, but he's got no aptitude for keepering. He's too idle.'

Lewis Glaven controlled his obvious irritation and made no comment. He gave the keeper some final instructions, and the man sloped off. The members of the shooting party called their dogs to heel, and awaited their host's briefing.

'Well now – ' he began in his clear, assured voice. 'Delighted to see you all here at Chalcot for the start of the season. Couldn't raise the usual eight guns at such short notice, I'm afraid, but we're grateful to Martin Tait for making us up to seven. Let's hope we'll see some good sport.'

Ambivalent as he had begun to feel about the company, Martin was delighted to be singled out for a mention – particularly without any hint that he wasn't as experienced as everyone else. He glowed with a sense of belonging.

'As usual,' Lewis Glaven went on, 'to give everyone a fair chance, we'll draw for our first pegs and then move up two at the start of each drive. And as usual, if you'll bear with me, I'll just go over the Chalcot ground rules before we start.'

Tait had read enough about driven shoots to know the code of good practice already, but he realised that the others weren't to know that he knew. Lewis Glaven was tactfully making sure of it for everybody's benefit, and Tait prepared to listen intently. But at that moment an extravagantly fitted Daihatsu Fourtrak drove into the yard, and a squat man rolled down from the driving seat.

He was half a head shorter than Martin, and dressed up in a shooting suit of best-quality tweed with every possible sartorial extra. He took off his deerstalker, revealing an almost hairless head, and came among them with a swagger and a wide ingratiating smile.

'Good morning all!'

The man advanced on Lewis Glaven and tilted back his head – with some difficulty in the absence of any recognisable neck – in order to address him.

'Ah, Mr Glaven, good morning to you! Won't keep you a moment – my junior assistant is just delivering Mrs Harbord's order for the weekend.'

The junior assistant, an undersized lad almost swamped by a butcher's white trilby hat and long white overall, brought a covered tray out of the vehicle and carried it to the back door of the house.

'Fillet steak for your dinner tonight, I believe,' went on the man, 'and crown of lamb for your Sunday roast. My manager does all the cutting now, of course – first class butcher, trained him myself. Best quality meat, needless to say – finest in the county!'

Lewis Glaven, waiting to resume his briefing, murmured courteous Thank yous and Yes indeeds. The junior assistant took the tray into the house. The seated dogs yawned impatiently. The members of the shooting party, discreetly amused, studied the sky.

'Ideal morning for shooting!' the butcher continued. 'Shooting man myself, of course – crack shot when I was younger, finest in the county. Still first class! Belong to a syndicate over at Horkey. Should have been there this morning – shoot called off at the last minute. All ready for it, as you see – gun and cartridge bag in the Fourtrak. Disappointed, of course . . .'

He stood waiting, a wistful look on his toadlike face, absurdly hopeful of being given an invitation to join them. The junior assistant had returned and was standing by the vehicle, presumably waiting to know whether or not he would have to walk back to the village.

Lewis Glaven merely nodded his understanding, and offered the butcher nothing more than a sympathetic 'Bad luck.'

Undeterred, the man persisted: 'Pay my way, of course! Just as I do at Horkey. Money no object – name your price.'

The other members of the shooting party had turned away and were talking loudly among themselves, all except Joanna Dodd who seemed indifferent to the incident and almost savagely impatient to be off. Lewis Glaven phrased his reply courteously, but his tone and his look put the interloper firmly in his place.

'No one pays to shoot at Chalcot, Mr Brunt. This is a *private* party, d'you see? Now if you'll excuse me . . .' He moved away and joined his friends.

For a moment the butcher stood crestfallen. The voices of the shooting party rose, and peaked in laughter; they were not of course laughing at him, because they had forgotten him already, but it was evident that he thought they were and felt doubly humiliated.

Then he reinflated himself. Beef-red, grotesquely proud, he swaggered back to the Fourtrak; and only Tait, it seemed, noticed the malevolence of his expression as he drove away.

As soon as the briefing had finished, and pegs had been drawn for, the party and their dogs were distributed among the off-road vehicles for the cross-country drive up to Belmont.

Martin found himself sitting in the back of a Landrover opposite the Treadgold brothers, competing for space with their knees, the gun bags, a retriever and two spaniels. The dogs were intrigued by his dogless smell, and did their best to rectify it with licks and snuffles. Absently fondling a spaniel's ears, he thought of Will Glaven's girlfriend and wondered how best to rescue her, without asking himself exactly who or what he intended to rescue her for.

The brothers, meanwhile, still regarded him as a puzzle. They looked at him with frank curiosity, as though he was the first man they'd met socially who hadn't been born with a sporting gun in his hand. Tait decided not to bother to learn which of them was which. It was easier to think of them as Tweedledum and Tweedledee.

'First time you've tried shootin' game, eh?'

There was no point in denying it. Anyway, they could see that his gun bag and his cartridge bag were both brand new.

'I've always shot clays,' he said. 'Excellent sport, and it fits in with my CID work.'

The Treadgolds refused to be impressed by his job. They conceded, though, that clay pigeon shooting was probably

69

better than nothing. 'Keeps your eye in, off-season,' said Tweedledum. He paused, then said to his brother, 'Wonder if Calamity Jane practises with clays, on the quiet?'

'Hasn't done the trick, though, has it?' They gave each other a meaningful smirk.

Tait guessed they were talking about Joanna Dodd. 'Why Calamity?' he asked, insatiably curious. 'I heard she's a good shot.'

'With a gun, yes. Can't get her man, though . . .'

Tweedledee turned to his brother. 'What about that stunnin' new girl of his? No wonder Joanna's in a foul mood this morning.'

'No wonder at all. If Will's serious about the girl, he's going to be in real trouble with Calamity Jane. How does that quotation go? "Hell has no fury like . . ."?'

Tait would have capped it correctly, but the Treadgolds were simply setting up one of their prep-school jokes.

'. . . like a woman's corns?' suggested Tweedledee.

'That's it! Remarkable chap, Shakespeare – or was it Oscar Wilde? Knows what it is that makes people tick, anyway.'

They grinned at each other, and then sobered. 'All the same,' said Tweedledum, 'if I were in young Will's boots, I'm damned if I'd go out in the same shootin' party as Joanna. Wouldn't want to meet with a nasty accident.'

8

The beaters were travelling up to Belmont in style, sitting on straw bales in a covered trailer towed by one of the farm tractors. Another tractor followed, towing the empty game cart. The cart was fitted with wooden racks on which the dead pheasants would be strung up at the end of each drive.

There were nine regular beaters, an assortment of local men who looked forward to a day outdoors in good company, with cash in hand at the end of it. They had come prepared to push through thick undergrowth and were wearing their oldest, toughest clothes. They were armed with heavy sticks, makeshift flags, and thermos flasks containing who-knew-what, and with them were two eager dogs and a despondent Darren Jermyn.

Being left alone to brood about Laura would have made Darren wretched enough. As a novice, though, he had to serve as the butt of the other beaters' dry humour.

'Seems there'll be a new Gun out today,' said leathery old Arthur, the owner of the dogs. 'A townie from Saintsbury. Hope you've put a tin plate down the front of them there waterproof trousers, boy? He's bound to shoot low, and a few stray pellets could ruin your love life . . .'

Darren reddened. He shifted uncomfortably on the straw, endured the laughter, and submerged himself again in angry, anguished thoughts.

He had biked straight up to Chalcot House that morning, arriving at first light just as Laura was coming out to the shrubbery to feed her special pheasants. She'd looked beautifully sleepy, as though she hadn't properly woken up, and he'd longed to hold her in his arms and nuzzle her warm cheek.

But Laura was still hostile. Brushing her fall of hair away from her eyes, she'd said crossly, 'What do you want?'

He tried a subtle approach. 'It's more what I don't want. I've gone off gamekeeping. I don't want anything to do with killing the pheasants. So I'll pack in the job – if you'll promise to stay away from the shoot.'

She'd looked at him as though she despised him. 'I'm not promising you anything! If you've finally realised that it's wrong to be a keeper, good. Just say so to Mr Glaven and walk out.'

'That's not the point – '

She gave him a scornful smile; there was nothing sleepy about her now. 'Too scared to tell him?'

"Course I'm not scared! I was going to tell him anyway. But I don't want you to get involved with the shoot. You could be hurt.'

'The pheasants are going to be *killed* if I don't help them. Stop interfering, Darren. I've made my plans.'

His insides tightened with anxiety. 'This morning?'

'No – I've got to stay and help my mother with today's lunch, worse luck. That's the only way I'll get my week's money out of her. But then I'm going to Belmont to stop the rest of the shoot, whether you like it or not.'

Sick with longing, Darren had tried another approach. 'All right – if you must do it, I'll join you. How about that?'

He had moved towards her. Her nearness made him shake, and snatched at his breath. Unable to keep his hands off her, he reached out and touched her hair. 'We'll find some way of stopping the shoot together . . .'

He slid his hands under her hair and cupped them round her neck. All he wanted was to show her his love, to draw her towards him and feel the softness of her body, to be an item again as they were last summer. But Laura resisted.

'Together?' she'd said scornfully, and the sweet remembered warmth of her breath made him tighten his hold. 'We're not together – we're finished, can't you understand? Get off me, Darren Jermyn!'

She struggled, pushing his arms and trying to break his grip. He pulled her to him, so desperate to prove his love that he hardly knew what he was doing. 'I love you, Laura,' he heard himself croak, 'I *love* you – '

A sudden sharp pain crippled him as she kicked him on the shin. Taken by surprise he had yelped, hopped, sworn and let her go. And now he sat in the beaters' trailer, so deep in misery that he couldn't raise the energy to feel sorry for the pheasants he was about to betray.

At least he knew now that Laura wouldn't be trying to stop this morning's shoot. She was safe for a few hours. But this afternoon . . .

Whatever she tried to do this afternoon, he would be there to stop her. And next time he held her, she wouldn't get away from him so easily.

The keeper's Landrover had overtaken the tractor and trailer. By the time the beaters arrived at the far side of the estate, half a mile beyond Belmont wood, Len Alger was waiting for them.

He was irritable, impatient to start, but the men thought him such an old misery that they refused to be rushed. They knew that experienced beaters are hard to come by, and that he needed them more than they needed him. One of their pleasures was to see him spluttering with rage, and they contrived to wind him up by taking their time over unloading themselves and their equipment from the trailer.

Darren had jumped down first, glad to get away from the lot of them. The vehicles were parked at the end of the track under a tall old hedge, coloured with autumn leaves and hawthorn berries, that formed the western boundary of the Glavens' land. Looking back, across the intervening arable fields and hedges and copses, he could see Belmont wood standing thick and dark against the eastern sky. The sight of it, and the thought of what could happen there during the afternoon drives, made him feel sick with anxiety.

Before they reached the wood, though, there were going to be three drives across the nearer land where he had been feeding the wandering pheasants. He could see some of them now, pecking about in wheat stubble, the cocks occasionally raising their handsome, stupid heads to peer at the group of beaters.

Yesterday he had thought of them as victims, but today he hadn't any sympathy to spare. At least they didn't know what was coming to them. Mr Glaven had said that half of them would survive, and Darren was beyond worrying over the fate of the others. All he could think of was Laura.

'Come on, come on, you lazy young devil! Stop day-dreaming and get to the far side of that kale – *move* yourself. And when I blow my whistle to start the drive, for God's sake keep in line!'

Len Alger, his gun under his arm and his two brown retriever crosses keeping prudently to heel, was now so wound up that his long bony face was visibly twitching. The other beaters, grinning, plodded over the stubble and spaced themselves out in a long line, facing east across a swath of kale towards a narrow plantation known as Long Spinney.

Darren had the farthest to go, naturally. He picked up his ash stick and made for his place. He chose to run, not because he cared what Len Alger shouted at him but just to show the rotten old bastard how young and fit he was.

The kale in front of them was a game crop, planted for the benefit of the pheasants. The birds he'd seen pecking in the

73

stubble had already taken fright and run to it for cover. It was nearly waist high and so top-heavy with coarse green leaves that Darren had no idea how many birds were likely to be in it, but Mr Glaven had told him that it should produce enough for a good first drive.

Darren could see the shooting party taking up their positions at the lower end of the stubble field, in a dip between the strip of kale and Long Spinney. The Guv'nor had explained that the crop had been deliberately planted along the crest of a slight rise. The plan was that when the pheasants were driven out of the kale and flew for the shelter of the trees they would see the guns just below them, put on speed and climb high, so presenting a challenging target.

Darren glanced along the line. The other men stood with their sticks, or flags made of strips cut from plastic sacks and nailed to poles, waiting for the signal to start beating through the kale. The dogs, Arthur's and the keeper's, professionals from nose to tail, stood quivering with eagerness to begin. Their job was to work with the beaters, scouring silently along the line to stop any of the birds from running back, and pointing them out if they tried to lie low.

'Some o' them crafty pheasants'll crouch down and freeze,' Arthur had told Darren. 'When y'see a dog pointing, go you and poke the bird out. Keep 'em all moving forward.'

Len Alger had positioned himself in the centre of the line but about twenty yards back. According to Arthur, this was so that he could bawl at any beaters who didn't keep in line, and also take a shot at any wily pheasant that flew back behind the beaters instead of forward over the guns.

As well as his shotgun the keeper had a walkie-talkie. The Guv'nor would use it to let him know when to start each drive. There seemed to be some delay at the other end, but Darren was hardly aware of what was or wasn't happening around him. He stood with his head down, using his stick as a prop; aching as he thought of Laura, wondering what she was doing and what she planned.

'You, boy!' The keeper's sudden bellow made him start. 'Wake up there, for God's sake! You'll never be any good at this job, you're useless . . .'

74

Kurr-kuk kurr-kuk.

Somewhere down by Long Spinney a cock pheasant crowed; and then another and another. Numbed by his own wretchedness, Darren waited for the keeper's whistle to blow, and the slaughter to start.

Martin Tait was standing beside his peg, a slotted stick which held a numbered card. As he waited in the crisp pheasant-echoing air to take aim at his first live target, he was tense with anticipation. He hardly noticed his host's approach, until Lewis Glaven spoke to him.

'Ah, you've found your peg. Excellent. Mind if I stand here for this first drive? Just to see how well the birds are flying . . .'

Tait could hardly object, but he wasn't too pleased. He was confident that he would impress his host over the course of the day, but he would have liked to get his eye in before being watched.

He understood Lewis Glaven's motive, of course. Safety had been the main theme of the briefing, and no doubt Lewis wanted to assure himself that his new guest was a safe shot. But he need have no fear about that.

Tait had come to Chalcot having already learned the safety rules that apply to driven shoots. As a senior police officer – and therefore well aware of the lethal potential of shotguns – he knew better than his host how important such rules are. He was miffed to think that Lewis Glaven hadn't taken his safety-consciousness on trust; but at least he now had an opportunity to demonstrate that he was not only a safe shot but an excellent one as well.

The other members of the shooting party – his fellow Guns – were positioning themselves on their pegs, which had been pushed into the stubble more or less in a straight line and about thirty yards apart. They stood with their backs to Long Spinney, well out from the trees. Ahead of them, on the crest of gently rising ground a hundred yards away, was the swath of kale.

Behind the Guns, on the edge of the spinney, were the pickers-up. Doffy Wilson-Brown, planted squarely on a shooting stick, was in charge of a small team of local helpers –

superannuated beaters, by the look of them. With them was a posse of gun dogs, patient and observant, waiting until the end of the drive when they would be sent out to retrieve the fallen birds.

Lewis Glaven, his own dogs at heel and a radio in his hand, was looking up and down the line to check that all the Guns were in place. As he did so he offered Tait a quiet word of advice.

'Technique's much the same with pheasants as with clays. Difference is that clays slow down as they come over, birds accelerate. Takes a bit of getting used to. No shame in missing. Always go for the challenge of a high bird, never for an easy target. I'd rather you missed than made an unsporting kill. All right?'

'Right,' agreed Tait, hoping that rising tension hadn't made his voice breathy. He would hate to sound like a beginner. He decided against putting on his ear muffs immediately, in case his host had anything more to say. Impatient to begin, he longed to load his gun, but it was against the safety rules to do so before the drive started.

Then everything began to happen. Lewis Glaven radioed 'Ready? Start!' to the keeper. Almost immediately they heard the blast of a whistle, coming from out of sight on the far side of the kale.

Tait snatched a couple of cartridges from his belt. Over-eagerness and cold fingers made him fumble. He heard a few distant shouts and then a steady outcry as the beaters began to move forward. Almost dropping the second cartridge in his haste, he swore under his breath.

'Don't rush it,' murmured his host. 'Plenty of time.'

Tait slid the cartridge home and cocked his gun. He looked towards the kale and saw two birds rising from it, encouraged by the beaters' flags. The pheasants were slower starters than clays because of their weight, but the wind under their wide-spread tails was helping to lift them.

His impulse was to bring the gun up to his shoulder immediately, but that would be a beginner's reaction. The pheasants were much too far away for a shot. They might fly anywhere,

76

and there was no point in mounting the gun until it was obvious that a bird was heading in his direction.

Holding the shotgun in a safety position, with the muzzle pointing down to the earth, he remained poised for action with his left foot advanced, balanced as though he were on the deck of a boat in a rough sea. Controlling his excitement he watched the pheasants' whirring approach. They were still rising. As they saw the line of guns below them, they accelerated.

Relax, Tait told himself. *Don't hurry or you'll miss.*

Choosing a target, he put his weight forward on his left foot, raised the butt of the gun to his shoulder, tucked the stock against his right cheek and snicked off the safety catch. Concentrating on the triangle made by the side-by-side muzzles and the bead, he swung the gun across the sky, matching its movement to that of the bird. His finger hovered over the trigger. Yes, good, follow *through* the target –

'Better leave it for your neighbour,' said Lewis Glaven quietly. 'It isn't coming over us, d'you see? Doesn't do to poach.'

Crestfallen, Tait lowered his gun. On either side of him, shots rang out. He watched enviously as his target, a hen, seemed to stumble in mid-air, a puff of feathers flying from its breast. Then it plummeted to the ground and lay still. The other bird, a cock, turned vivid cartwheels as it fell out of the sky.

Then someone shouted 'Over,' and Tait saw that a flurry of pheasants had got up from the kale. The leading birds were approaching high and fast. Wings whirred, shotguns cracked, and just in front of his expert neighbour a cock threw back its outstretched head and stopped, dead in the air. Another bird clattered earthwards somewhere on the right.

Now they were flocking over, a score of targets in the air at once. Maddeningly for Tait, though, most of them were curling left and right again, as though they were deliberately avoiding his peg. He could only stand watching while guns blazed on either side of him. Some birds managed to pass over unscathed, some were allowed to escape because they were unsporting targets, some planed down lightly wounded and ran for cover, but an enviable number hit the ground.

He was desperate to get in a shot of his own. And then, to

his joy, a hen that had passed the peak of its flight came gliding straight towards him. He raised his gun.

'A bit low, that one,' said Lewis Glaven in his ear. 'Too easy. I should leave it for another day.'

Tait's frustration mounted. The first drive was almost over and he hadn't yet squeezed a trigger. But a few late birds were rising from the kale, and he willed at least one of them to stay high and not to curl away.

The leading pheasant came strongly on. He watched it intently, found that it was doing exactly as he hoped, followed it through and fired his first barrel. To his delight the plump brown hen somersaulted out of the air, and bounced as it hit the ground.

Adrenalin pumping, oblivious to everything except the chance of achieving another kill with his second barrel, he swung his gun on to the last bird. It was flying to his right, past its peak and gliding, but still reasonably high. He fired. And, maddeningly, missed.

But what did that matter? He'd brought down a pheasant with his first shot! Dazed but exultant, in the sudden silence that followed the end of the drive, he glanced at Lewis Glaven expecting him to be impressed.

Instead, his host was bristling with disapproval.

'You realise what you've just done?'

'I've . . . er . . .'

Martin hesitated. His high spirits made a bumpy landing as he realised exactly where he'd gone wrong. In shooting at the second bird, he had swung to the right in a 45-degree arc and had fired above the heads of his neighbours. The falling pellets from his shot might well have hit one of them.

'Oh no . . .' He felt the blood drain from his face. 'I've shot across the line, haven't I? Is anyone hurt?'

'Seems not, thank God. Damn dangerous manoeuvre, though. An acquaintance of mine in Norfolk lost an eye last season, just because some new Gun wasn't shooting safely. Hoped I could rely on you to follow the rules.'

Martin was shaken. 'I really am sorry, sir. I'm afraid I got carried away in the heat of the moment. I do apologise.'

78

He fully expected to be told that he was no longer a welcome guest at Chalcot. But having calmed down, Lewis Glaven seemed prepared to give him another chance.

'Well . . . no harm done, so I'll overlook it on this occasion. Fact is, most of us have lost our heads at some time or other on a driven shoot. Damn difficult to remember the rules when your blood's up, eh?'

'A lot more difficult than I'd realised,' Martin admitted.

'Useful lesson to learn. No bad thing to have a chastening experience on your first time out. Should make you more careful in future.'

'It certainly will!'

'Glad to hear it. Oh, by the way – that first pheasant of yours. Good shot. Very good shot.'

His host's praise was welcome, of course. But as Tait followed the other Guns round to the eastern side of Long Spinney for the second drive, he still felt shaken.

He had always prided himself on his coolness in action. He had been absolutely confident that he would prove to be safe with a gun, and it appalled him to recall how easily he had lost control.

It wouldn't happen again, though! For the remainder of the shoot he was going to stick rigidly to the rules.

At least, that was what he intended. But he was uneasily aware that he couldn't guarantee it.

9

There were no pheasants calling from Long Spinney now. Those that had survived the flight from the kale must have warned the woodlanders to keep their heads down. All Martin could hear, as he rounded the end of the spinney on the way to his next peg, was an agitated rustling in the undergrowth.

Walking just ahead of him was Will Glaven – unfairly tall, cap tipped well forward in cavalry officer style, gun under arm, black labrador at heel. They had had time to do little more than exchange greetings up at the house. Now, glancing back and seeing Martin, Will waited for him to catch up.

'Any joy on the first drive?'

'Just one hen,' said Martin modestly. 'With my first shot.' Then, since his host's son was bound to hear what had happened, he felt obliged to add: 'But I'm afraid I put my second shot across the line. Criminally careless thing to do. No one's hurt, thank God, but your father isn't too pleased with me.'

Will grimaced. 'I can imagine . . . You should've heard what he said to me at a shoot last season, when I broke the "no ground game" rule.'

Martin's spirits rose. 'I'm not the only culprit, then?'

'God no. I was so cold and bored, waiting for the bloody birds to rise out of some sugar beet, that I shot at a bolting rabbit. Didn't stop to think – just fired instinctively. Trouble was, it was running along between me and the beaters. The old man bawled me out because this soil is so flinty that pellets ricochet off it. I might well have potted one of the beaters instead of the bunny.'

Will Glaven's admission made Martin even more determined not to offend his host again if he could possibly help it. But he liked Will's frankness, and immediately forgave the man his height advantage. He was almost prepared to forgive him for having misappropriated such a shyly beautiful girlfriend . . . But not quite.

The other members of the party were sauntering to their places. Lewis Glaven had said at his briefing that the Guns would as usual move up two numbers at the start of each drive. This gave most of them an excuse to indulge in convivial chat as they discussed which pegs they were supposed to be on, and to take warming nips from the hip flasks they all seemed to carry. But Joanna Dodd stood aloof, already at her peg with her gun under her arm, impatient to get on with the shoot.

Will took an audibly deep breath as he and Martin walked past her on their way to their own pegs.

'Better have a word with Joanna,' he said reluctantly. 'Excuse me . . .'

80

'Of course,' said Martin, watching as he moved towards her.

Will Glaven and Joanna Dodd were almost the same height and age, unmistakably from the same background and equally accustomed to muddy dogs and shotguns. They seemed ideally matched. Remembering what the Treadgold brothers had said about her and Will, though, Tait would have liked to overhear their conversation.

But here at Chalcot he was on his best behaviour. With regret, he walked out of earshot.

'Brilliant shooting at the first drive, Joanna – as always!'

Will had decided on a conciliatory approach. He didn't want to overdo it, but her haughty silence meant that he had to work hard to get a response out of her. 'Drink?' he offered, producing a flask from a pocket of his Barbour. 'It's sloe gin, your favourite.'

'I've brought my own, thank you.'

Joanna's voice was straight out of the freezer, and her long face was stiff with displeasure. Will couldn't decide whether she was hurt, or angry, or contemptuous. Possibly, he conceded, he'd given her cause over the years to be any or all of the three; but there was no sense in her holding a permanent grudge against him.

'Look,' he said, though he avoided making eye contact with her: 'why don't you get it out of your system and tell everyone what a bastard I am?'

'I wouldn't give you the satisfaction.'

'No . . . I s'pose not.' He nodded ruefully, then sighed. It was so bloody difficult to know how to deal with women. Besides, there was a far more pressing concern than Joanna on his mind. He'd done his best to appease her, and that was that. He could wrap up the conversation with a clear conscience.

'Glad you could join us today, anyway.'

She hitched the shotgun under her arm. 'I wouldn't have missed it for the world.'

'Good shooting, then. See you at lunch.'

'I shan't be with you for lunch. I have to go home to look at a lame horse.'

'But you'll be back this afternoon?'

'Oh yes,' she said. 'I'll be up at Belmont for the afternoon shoot, never fear.'

Darren Jermyn had found that being a beater was even worse than he'd imagined.

At first, as he went through the motions of his job, he thought only of Laura. But he soon realised that the other beaters were enjoying themselves, hollering and whacking the kale with their sticks, and he became aware of the pheasants' agitation as they scuttled ahead, bewildered by what was happening.

Some of the birds froze, as Arthur had said they would. Darren almost trod on one little brown hen that was crouched against the earth among the stalks of kale, hoping not to be seen. Cowering, she turned her head and looked up at him with one dark fearful eye.

He fancied that she recognised and was reproaching him. He willed her to stay put, pretending he hadn't noticed, but one of the rotten dogs came nosing along and pointed at her.

'Dog's found one for you!' called Arthur. 'Poke it out, boy.'

Darren made reluctant pushing motions with his stick. 'Don't move,' he hissed. 'Stay where you are!' But she was already up and scurrying forward with the others.

And then, as the leading birds emerged from the far edge of the kale and saw the Guns waiting for them, all hell broke loose.

'There they go!' shouted Arthur excitedly as the pheasants began to rise, screeching in alarm. A cock went up like a multicoloured rocket, its tail spread wide to give it lift, its heavy body carried up on valiant wings. 'D'y' see him, boy? He's a real Gabriel!'

The first shotguns cracked.

Darren had prepared himself for the sight of his birds being cleanly killed. What he hadn't taken into account was their being brought down injured. He was sickened to see the resplendent cock, mortally wounded, threshing in agony as it tumbled out of the sky.

'Keep in line, you bloody young idler!' bellowed the keeper from behind him.

Incensed, Darren turned to swear a reply. At that moment a hen bird tried to reach safety by flying back over the beaters. She was not much more than head high, a shamefully low target, but Len Alger didn't give her a chance. He swung his gun on to her as she passed to his left, and Darren saw the evil bastard grinning as his shot transformed her to an outburst of bloodied feathers.

The rest of the beaters had pushed on towards the edge of the kale, and a flurry of pheasants took to the air. Darren was dismayed by their cries of alarm, the frantic whirring of their wings, their evident terror as the shotguns clattered.

'Keep going!' he shouted, willing them to outfly the deadly pellets. He took no comfort from the fact that some of the birds, flinching and then planing down, were only lightly wounded. Even if they were able to drag themselves to cover when they landed, and evade the searching dogs, they would die a lingering death.

What he hated most of all, though, was to see pheasants badly injured. He recalled only too well the guilt and shame he'd felt when he picked up the jay that he had mangled with shot – and that was a predator, a bird that ate the eggs and chicks of others.

These pheasants were harmless. They trusted him. He'd fed them and cared for them, and he couldn't bear to watch them being slaughtered. OK, some of them escaped. Some of them were allowed to escape because they were flying low. But others were staggering in mid-flight and coming down in slow motion, sometimes somersaulting as they fell, sometimes beating the air in useless frenzy, still alive and suffering . . .

Laura was right. Killing creatures for sport was disgusting. This shoot would have to be stopped.

But he wasn't going to make another offer to help Laura stop it, not after the way she'd treated him. Somehow or other he was going to find a way of doing the job himself. And he'd do it this afternoon, when she was up at Belmont, just to show her that she wasn't the only one who cared about wildlife. Just to show her.

83

Darren flung down his stick. Ignoring the keeper's shouted threats, he set off on the long run back to the stable yard where he had left his mountain bike. Stopping the shoot wasn't going to be easy, but he'd already had an idea.

10

Martin Tait was travelling soberly to lunch. And that was more than he could say of the Treadgold brothers, with whom he was once again sharing the back of a Landrover.

'Good shootin'?' Tweedledum asked him, without waiting for an answer. They were discussing their own successes in tedious detail, while their muddy, panting dogs competed to lean against Martin's knees.

Tweedledee opened a vacuum flask and offered him a swig of their own concoction, a savoury drink with alcohol coming off it in steaming-hot wafts. Martin refused. He'd enjoyed the initial slug of whisky in his coffee, but that was all the drinking he intended to do while the shooting party lasted.

Privately, he had found it wretchedly cold standing about all morning waiting for the birds to be driven over. A drink would certainly have helped. But he'd had no hesitation in refusing Will Glaven's offer of a nip of sloe gin at the end of the second drive.

He had discovered that being a Gun at a driven shoot has several parallels with detective work. Both involve patient waiting, the identification of targets, observation, concentration – and then the tension and excitement of the final flurry of activity, which may or may not bring success.

But detective work doesn't involve the carrying of a gun. As a senior police officer he deplored any mixing of guns and alcohol, and he was astonished to find how casually it was done at Chalcot.

He wasn't going to be officious about it, of course, but he suspected that both Tweedledum and Tweedledee were well on the way to being drunk in charge of their shotguns. Barclay

84

Dodd, too. Tait had noticed him taking frequent nips from his flask, though it seemed not to have affected the precision of the old boy's shooting – not so far, anyway.

Martin himself hadn't had much luck during the rest of the morning. He'd found Long Spinney unrewarding because the tall trees demanded a different technique.

Lewis Glaven had stood with him again, for the first five minutes. They'd heard the distant tapping of sticks against tree trunks as the beaters approached, pushing their way through the undergrowth, and then one or two pheasants had come flying out from among the trees.

'Don't shoot at a bird unless you can see sky all round it,' his host had warned. 'Never shoot into trees. The pellets'll ricochet off the branches, d'you see. Can't risk injuring anyone.'

Inhibited by so many rules, Martin had had no joy at all at the spinney. He'd done a little better at the final drive of the morning, a field of sugar beet, where he had clipped at least two pheasants and brought down a high-flying cock for a crash landing. But on the whole he was dissatisfied with his performance.

Neither the spinney nor the sugar beet field had produced as many birds as the first drive, and Martin felt that he hadn't had a proper chance to demonstrate his skill with a shotgun. If he wanted to be invited again – and he certainly did, despite his reservations – he would have to improve his score during the afternoon. His last chance would be up at the big wood called Belmont, where the Treadgold brothers said there was sure to be plenty of action.

Meanwhile, there was an hour's lunch break to come. Martin would be glad to get some warming food inside him, but that was merely incidental. What he really looked forward to was the chance to impress that beautiful shy girl who had been misappropriated by Will Glaven.

In Chalcot tradition the shoot lunch was held in the gun room, where a blazing fire gave off the scent of apple logs, and photographs of long-gone shooting parties looked down from the panelled walls. A large table was laden with platters of cold ham, cold game pie, fresh fruit, salads, cheeses, and a variety of bottles.

Most of the party had assembled by the time Martin had washed the dogs' mud and slobber from his hands. The room buzzed with loud voices and laughter. He stood out in the flagged passageway for a moment, craning his neck in an attempt to see the girl, but she didn't appear to be there.

'Here I am, love!' said a familiar voice behind him.

'Ah – there you are!'

Martin turned, guiltily readjusting from his golden-haired dream to the dark-haired reality of his partner.

There was no denying it: Alison had neither the delicate beauty nor the vulnerability of the younger girl. She was lovely in her own way, certainly. He was still attracted by her smile, the glossy downsweep of her hair, and her eyes that were as green as peeled grapes. But she had never roused in him such a conflicting surge of intention, at once predatory and protective, as he had felt when he first saw the Glavens' guest.

True, Alison had a lot of other things going for her. Just at the moment, having lost his emotional balance, he wasn't quite sure what they were. But he didn't intend to lose her, so he quickly kissed her on the cheek to compensate for the fact that he'd hardly given her a thought since they'd got out of bed.

'Had a good morning?' she asked.

'Excellent.' He glanced with approval at the bracken-coloured casual clothes she had chosen to wear. 'You look very nice, darling. Absolutely right. Have you been here long?'

'About half an hour. I've been talking to Hope Meynell, Mr Glaven's son's girlfriend.'

'Oh, that's her name, is it? She appeared before we left for the shoot, but took fright and rushed off again.'

'So she told me. She says the gathering's a bit intimidating, and we're meeting here so that we can go in to lunch together. She's a beautiful girl, isn't she?'

There was no point in trying to pretend he hadn't noticed; Alison knew him too well for that. 'Yes, she is. Will Glaven's a lucky man. But I can't honestly see her fitting in here. This sporting country life isn't her style at all.'

'Excuse me, madam – '

'Sorry!' Alison moved quickly aside, out of the way of the smartly dressed housekeeper and her daughter as they brought hot food from the kitchen to the gun room. The mother carried a steaming casserole that left a mouth-watering smell of spiced beef and peppers in its wake. The girl, sulking furiously, carried a dish piled with foil-wrapped baked potatoes.

'*Madam* . . .' Alison scoffed in a low voice. 'This kind of life is hardly our style, either!'

'I don't see why not. We could soon get used to it.'

'I wouldn't want to. As for Hope, I don't think she realised what she was letting herself in for. Ah, here she comes . . .'

For Martin, the next few minutes passed like seconds. Hope Meynell was even more beautiful at close quarters than he'd anticipated. Everything about her – clear pale skin, tendrils of fine gold hair, lovely mouth, delicate figure – entranced him. She kept her eyes shyly lowered until they were introduced, but then she looked up at him with a half-smile that dazzled him with its blue brilliance.

Alison was saying far too much by way of introduction, making unnecessary references to himself as her partner, and to Will Glaven as Hope's. But Alison was somewhere out on the edge of his consciousness. He was focusing all his charm on Hope Meynell, aiming to convey to her that he understood her diffidence and that if she needed any support, preferably physical, he was her man.

Before Martin could win another smile from her, though, Lewis and Will Glaven emerged from the gun room in search of their guests. Will appropriated Hope immediately, putting his arm round her shoulders and steering the poor girl into the room to face their loud friends. Lewis welcomed Alison, gallantly recalling that he had previously met her at the County Show, and led her in too.

Martin was left to follow on his own. And the unsympathetic glance that Alison gave him in passing told him quite clearly that it served him right.

At first, he didn't much enjoy the lunch. The morning's activity – the noise of the shotguns and the acrid smell of cordite – had given him a headache, which wasn't improved by the volume of talk and laughter.

He was also having to come to terms with the fact that he'd made a bit of a fool of himself in Alison's eyes, and all to no purpose.

Martin was sitting almost opposite Hope. Lewis Glaven was at the head of the table, with Hope on his left, Will beside her, and then Tweedledum and Tweedledee. On Lewis's right was Mrs Wilson-Brown, with Martin next to her, then Alison, then Barclay Dodd.

If Hope had wanted to appeal to Martin for help, or at least register an interest in him, she could quite easily have caught his eye. But though he watched and waited, she never once looked in his direction.

There was no doubt that she was feeling wretchedly out of place at the shoot lunch. It was an informal, old-friends-together occasion. Conversation was general, and almost exclusively agricultural and sporting. Will was in high spirits and joined in, but though he tried to reassure and encourage Hope she seemed bewildered by the heartiness of it all. She rarely raised her eyes, and she ate hardly anything. Whenever the Treadgold brothers became too raucous, she flinched.

Lewis Glaven smiled on her benevolently, but spent most of the time roaming round the table, wine bottle in hand, attending to his duties as host. Dorothy Wilson-Brown addressed a few kindly remarks to Hope across the table, but she had to raise her voice in order to be heard and this made her sound so formidable that the girl was visibly alarmed. Martin offered one or two witticisms, trying to catch Hope's attention; but though Mrs Wilson-Brown was amused, the girl seemed not to hear him.

And the reason for that was plain to see. Despite her social unease at Chalcot, Hope Meynell was very much attracted to Will Glaven. When she raised her eyes, it was to no one else.

Martin observed them as they sat closely together and communicated in murmurs, sometimes becoming passionately entangled in each other's gaze. Will was clearly a man besotted – and who could blame him? The pair of them made Martin feel like a long-married man.

He was envious, of course. All the same, it was clear to him that there was an imbalance in their ardour. Attracted to Will though she was, Hope was definitely holding back; almost certainly unwilling to commit herself to the Chalcot way of life, Martin thought. And Will was aware of her problem. When they looked away from each other, they both had troubled eyes.

But intervention was out. Martin acknowledged that any further effort to interest Hope Meynell would be a waste of time. He'd regained his balance, and lost his headache, and so he turned to his right with the intention of being nice to Alison.

He found her deep in conversation with her neighbour on the other side. Or rather, since it was Barlcay Dodd, who couldn't hear her, she was listening with every appearance of interest as he told her in detail the sporting history of his Ashthorpe estate.

Tait could have set about rescuing his future wife, but he decided callously that she might as well get used to pretending not to be bored. It would be good practice for all the civic and social functions they would be expected to attend when he reached the rank of chief constable.

Instead, he turned back to Dorothy Wilson-Brown. He wasn't keen on becoming more closely acquainted with her dim brothers, but the old girl seemed to be well worth cultivating. She was the kind of doughty woman who would know and be known by everyone who mattered in the county; an invaluable contact.

It was a bonus to find that she was also an excellent table companion. Her conversation was wide-ranging, she had a fund of anecdotes, and she responded to Martin's wit with an agreeably dirty chuckle. Confident that he had made a good impression, he turned from her with the intention of going to Alison's rescue.

But Alison seemed perfectly at ease. She now had the attention not only of Barclay Dodd but of Tweedledum and Tweedledee. The brothers, having quietened down on black coffee, had clearly taken a shine to her. They were competing to entertain her, and Martin found himself registering both pride and affection as he saw how well she was dealing with them.

When he tried to cut in, though, she ignored him. Come to think of it, she'd been ignoring him all through lunch.

Perhaps she was peeved because of the way he'd gazed at Hope Meynell. A silly reaction, but he supposed it was understandable. He would have shrugged it off – except, he remembered wryly, that he still had some serious persuading to do.

Alison didn't yet know that she wasn't going to be allowed to wander about freely during the afternoon, or that the camera was banned. She didn't know that she was expected to stand with him, watching the shoot. And now he'd had some experience of what a driven shoot entailed, he certainly didn't want to have her with him.

Even he had felt a touch of shame and pity when he saw pheasants being brought down badly wounded rather than dead. How Alison would react, he dreaded to think. She'd be upset, of course – she hadn't the kind of country upbringing that would enable her to stand her ground stoically and look away. But tender-hearted though she was, she wouldn't burst into tears and run off, either.

Alison Quantrill could be as tenacious as her father when it came to putting right what she thought was wrong. Martin was sure that she would protest against the killing of the pheasants – and not discreetly, either. She wouldn't confine her complaints to him, she was far more likely to disrupt the whole shooting party, regardless of the fact that it would ruin his chances of being invited again.

It was a risk he wasn't prepared to take.

Alison had made a good impression so far, and he wasn't going to let her spoil it. It would be to everyone's advantage if she were to plead a headache and go home straight after lunch. He'd have to put it to her diplomatically, of course . . . not mentioning the pheasants, but laughing at the ridiculous country-house custom of women being expected to stand with their men, and saying that he refused to inflict it on her. Something like that.

But there was no time to speak to her at all. The lunch break was suddenly over, and everyone was on the move. Lewis Glaven immediately rounded up Alison and Hope.

'Now, my dears,' he said briskly, steering them out of the

90

room, 'as soon as you're ready, we'll be off. You must both travel with me in the Range Rover – host's privilege!'

That was it, then. Alison was being taken to the shoot and there was nothing Martin could do to prevent it. There'd be precious little he could do to stop her from making a conspicuous fuss when it started, either.

Scowling with frustration, he went to collect his shotgun for what would probably be his last appearance as a guest on the Chalcot estate.

11

'An excellent meal, Mrs Harbord, thank you!'

Lewis Glaven had appeared in the kitchen doorway, shooting coat on and cap in hand. He was clearly anxious to get away, but punctilious as always about showing his appreciation to his staff.

It had been a very busy morning for Ann Harbord. As well as making lunch for the shooting party and baking cakes for their tea, she had prepared a great panful of Scotch broth for the keeper's wife to heat up for the beaters. Her daughter was supposed to help when the Glavens were in residence, in return for her generous weekly pocket money, but Laura had been infuriatingly sullen and difficult all morning.

Lewis's thanks, though, made up for everything. Conscious that she was hot and looking less than her best, Ann hurriedly smoothed down her sharply cut black hair and assured him effusively that working for him was always a pleasure. He gave her an abrupt nod and turned away.

'And thank you, too, Laura,' he said, gruff behind his moustache. Ann was thankful that he'd evidently decided to forget her daughter's furious outburst yesterday evening. He produced his notecase from an inner pocket and took out an over-generous ten-pound note. 'Spoilt your Saturday morning, I daresay. We're obliged to you for your help – eh, Mrs Harbord?'

He made no attempt to hand Laura the money, but placed it on the table and went. Ann, calling out thanks on her daughter's behalf, almost ran down the passage after him, but he was already closing the back door.

Laura stared crossly at the banknote. She didn't *want* Mr Glaven to forget how angry she was about pheasant-shooting. And she certainly wasn't going to be bribed to keep quiet!

If only he'd tried to hand her the money . . . How she would've enjoyed refusing it, with pride and scorn! That would have shown him.

But if she rejected it now, he wouldn't even know she'd done so. Besides, leaving home for good was bound to be expensive . . . Half-ashamed, she snatched up the money and pushed it into the back pocket of her jeans.

Her mother was scolding her because she hadn't thanked Mr Glaven, but Laura had too much else on her mind to take any notice. She'd spent half the night and all morning worrying herself sick about the pheasants.

Dozens of birds had probably been killed already, and more would die this afternoon if she didn't soon get out there and put a stop to it. At least her favourites, Fitzroy and Francis and Fred, ought to be safe today, because they had no reason to roam as far as Belmont. But their turn would come later in the season, unless she could shame Mr Glaven into stopping the shoots for good.

Her insides were tight with anxiety. As she scraped the plates, the look and smell of the meaty remains almost made her heave. Swallowing her nausea, she loaded the dishwasher and banged it shut.

'That's my lot,' she snapped. 'I'm off – can I have my week's money now?'

'Do you call that finished?' exploded her mother. 'There's still the gun room to put straight, and this kitchen to clean – '

'That's your job, not mine. I've done everything I'm supposed to, and more besides. You heard what Mr Glaven said. He's grateful to me, even if you're not.'

Her mother gave way at the mention of Mr Glaven, as Laura had known she would, and reluctantly handed over the usual ten-pound note. Laura muttered a sarcastic 'Thanks a lot' – the last words she intended to say to her – slammed out of the kitchen and raced upstairs.

Packing to leave had been easy. First thing this morning she had rolled up as much as she could cram into her sports bag, and that was it. None of the details about running away – what to take, where to go, what to do – were important. All she could think about was how she was going to stop the shoot. What happened after that would have to take care of itself.

She pulled on her SHOOTING PHEASANTS IS WRONG sweatshirt, changed into her DM boots, picked up her sports bag and took a final look round her room. Grown up though she was, she felt sorry that she had to leave her toy animals – particularly the giant teddy bear that her father had given her.

But real live suffering pheasants are far more important than stuffed toys! She clumped out, shutting the door resolutely behind her.

As an embarrassed afterthought, she dodged back and pock- eted the smallest of the bears for luck.

Hers wasn't a mountain bike like Darren's, but an old wreck that had once belonged to her mother. It only had three gears, instead of his eighteen – but at least that saved her from having to keep making decisions. It had a rack which would hold her bag, and it would get her as far as –

Well, as far as she decided to go, once she had stopped the shoot.

Laura pedalled fast, scarf flying; out of the stable yard, over the slippery fallen leaves that carpeted the long tree-lined drive, through the open gates and on down to the village. She saw Reg Brunt's Daihatsu Fourtrak, parked outside his bungalow next to the butcher's shop, but fortunately there was no sign of Mr Toad himself. No doubt he was sleeping off a large lunch.

Laura hadn't intended to think about Darren, but she couldn't help doing so as she passed the house where he lodged. She was still angry with him, after the way he'd first mocked her for caring about the pheasants, and then had the nerve to offer to join her in stopping the shoot. She didn't want him, and she didn't need him. Her plan was made, and if he came out of the house now, this minute, and repeated his offer, she would still tell him to get lost.

She just wished that she hadn't begun to feel alone and slightly afraid.

At the far end of the village, the road forked. Instead of taking the familiar route to Breckham Market, Laura turned off to the right and pedalled as fast as she could along the narrow road that meandered towards Ashthorpe.

The road was bordered by verges of ragged, fading grass. Beyond the grass on the left was a ditch and a red-berried hawthorn hedge. On the right, overhung along much of its length by trees in their autumn colours, was the old wall that bounded the Chalcot estate. Everywhere smelled of damp earth and leaf mould.

Half a mile out of the village, the road rose steeply enough for Laura to need first gear. The trees behind the wall had thinned out, and through the gaps she could see Belmont wood, up on the highest part of the estate. That was where the afternoon shoot was going to be held, and that was where she was heading.

She remembered telling Darren the name of the wood, one amazing day in early summer when they'd biked up here to be alone together. It was before he'd taken his hateful gamekeeping job, of course. Laura found it difficult, now, to believe it, but at the time they were seriously in love.

Even though the dull November light and the falling leaves made everything look different, she could still recognise their private place. They'd raced each other up the rise in brilliant sunshine, dropped their bikes anyhow, and flung themselves panting on buttercuppy grass. This was where it had been, beside this hawthorn bush – then in blossom – where the newly opened leaves of the oak tree overhanging the wall had dappled them with shade.

This was where they'd proved their love, guiding each other's hands where they had never gone before.

Laura didn't want to think about it. It was a long time ago, and she knew now that Darren wasn't really the caring person she'd taken him for. All the same, she couldn't help remembering how gentle he had tried to be, though his big hands were shaking and she could hear the violent hammering of his heart.

She had trembled, too, with the newness and the shyness of it all. 'Belmont,' he had breathed as he touched her, and afterwards they had used the name as a private code word. For a long time she'd only had to hear it to shiver with secret pleasure.

But that was over, just as summer was. She'd finished with Darren Jermyn. The incident helped her to identify the place where the wood was nearest to the road, that was all. She had come back here to stop the shoot, not to go wobbly about a relationship that meant nothing to her any more.

There was no time to waste, either. Propping her bike hurriedly against the wall, she looked for a way to get into the Chalcot estate. She had no need to break in, of course. She could simply have left the house and followed the shooting party up the farm track to Belmont. But someone would have been sure to see her and that would have ruined her plan. For maximum effect, she had to take them all by surprise.

The wall was about six feet high, and built of greyish bricks discoloured by years of weather. In some places it was covered with ivy, in others badly cracked. She hurried along beside it, making for a place where bricks lay tumbled on the grass. But when she reached the gap, she found that it had been blocked by barbed wire. A large noticeboard said: PRIVATE LAND – KEEP OUT.

Within a few yards there was another gap, similarly blocked. Not wanting to tangle with barbed wire, Laura was about to try climbing up the ivy beside the gap. But then she noticed that the wire there had been cut and partially pushed back.

Grateful to the unknown poacher who must have done it, she scrambled over the fallen bricks. In front of her was rough pasture, with occasional parkland trees and the odd wandering pheasant. Beyond the pasture – about a couple of hockey pitch lengths away – was the edge of Belmont wood.

From a distance, Belmont always looked like a solid block of trees. But Laura had explored the estate when she first went there to live, and she knew that the wood was split in two by a wide grassy ride. She must have crossed the wall almost directly opposite one end of the ride, because in front of her were what looked like two separate woods.

She hadn't ever dared to go back to Belmont, after that first visit, because she'd been frightened by the vicious old game-keeper. He had come raging at her out of the trees, grasping by its bushy tail – she could never forget the horror of it – the limp body of a beautiful russet fox, with a mangled hind leg and with blood all over its muzzle.

Len Alger must have known who she was. He could see that she was doing no harm. But he'd sworn at her for being there, and swung the dead fox towards her, and told her that if she went in his woods again he'd set a trap for her as well.

Laura hadn't really believed that he'd set a trap for her. But he'd looked so cruel, and spoken so fiercely, that she had taken good care to keep away from the woods ever since.

She remembered Belmont and its centre ride well enough for her purpose, though. The centre ride was where the shooting party always stood for the first drive of the afternoon. Laura had discovered this yesterday, wheedling the information out of old Horace, the tractor driver who towed the game cart for the shoots.

The Guns always faced towards Ashthorpe, Horace had said. From where she was standing, Ashthorpe was somewhere over to the left. That was the direction the pheasants would be driven from, then – through the left-hand wood towards the guns in the centre ride. And judging by the number of *kurr-kuk* calls she could hear, that wood was full of victims.

She could also hear a vehicle, behind her, coming up the road from Chalcot village. It slowed to a stop not far from where she had left her bike and bag, and she hoped that the driver hadn't seen them and stopped to pick them up. It didn't really bother her, though. She was too concerned for the pheasants to worry about a little thing like losing her possessions.

Her plan was the simple one she'd first thought of. She would make for the wood they were going to shoot, and hide herself somewhere between the pheasants and the line of guns. That would be on the left-hand edge of the ride.

There she'd stay hidden while the beaters were driving the

poor birds forward. Then, just as the so-called 'sportsmen' were getting ready to fire, she would burst out in front of them shouting 'Stop the killing!' And she'd spread her arms wide to show them her SHOOTING PHEASANTS IS WRONG slogan.

It wouldn't be all that dangerous. She knew the guns would be aimed high. But it would certainly *look* risky, from the point of view of the shooting party, and that was what she wanted. If she showed them that she was prepared to defend the pheasants regardless of her own safety, they couldn't fail to respect her beliefs.

As soon as they saw her, they would lower their shotguns and give up the rest of the shoot. She felt sure of it.

Well, almost sure.

She didn't know whether she was frightened or excited by what lay ahead, but her breath seemed to be coming as fast as it had on that far-off day with Darren. This time, though, her feelings were completely different. There was no silly emotion now, and no self-interest.

Saving these pheasants was going to be her contribution to preserving the wildlife of planet earth. And if she could shame Mr Glaven into giving up shooting for good, then her life would really have been worthwhile.

She would be only just in time to do it. Already she could hear the shooting party's vehicles, over on the far side of the wood, drawing up at the opposite end of the centre ride.

Heart thumping, hardly noticing the weight of her Doc Marten's, Laura ran as fast as she could towards Belmont.

Martin watched as their host escorted Hope and Alison to the Range Rover. He took some pride in the fact that Alison was dressed appropriately, in boots and a waxed jacket she'd borrowed from a friend.

Hope, though, had emerged from the house looking delightful but conspicuously wrong, in a softly coloured town coat. Evidently she hadn't yet acquired a country wardrobe. But Lewis Glaven was a considerate host. Having complimented her on her appearance, he had sent his housekeeper to find her 'something that wouldn't take any harm from a bit of mud', and she was now wrappped in an old Barbour that was much too large for her.

Nothing could quench her loveliness, though. Martin's eyes were still drawn irresistibly towards her – as any man's would be, he told himself. Delicate beauty such as hers is too rare not to be gazed at. But he knew better, now, than to expect any recognition from Hope Meynell.

He no longer felt sorry for her, either. No doubt she would hate the shoot as much as Alison was going to hate it, but Will was too much in love with her to insist on her staying. She would be too shy to make any public protest, but if she said she wanted to leave he would simply take her away – and no one would think any worse of her for it.

As for Alison . . . Martin could only hope that being taken under Lewis Glaven's wing would make her realise her social responsibilities. Surely she'd understand that a guest had no business to object to her host's chosen sport?

Martin sighed. Knowing his partner as well as he did, he doubted it.

He was travelling again with the Treadgolds, knee-deep in dogs in the back of the Landrover. The brothers were gleefully discussing Joanna Dodd.

'Why wasn't she with us at lunch, eh?' said Tweedledum. 'Lame horse at home – ha!'

'Couldn't face the humiliation of seein' Will with his new girlfriend,' said Tweedledee, 'that's what.'

'But will she turn up for the afternoon shoot? That's the real question.'

'And if she does – will it be with or without intent to do him a mischief? Eh? Eh?'

They embarked on some ribald fantasies, and Martin's lip curled as he listened. The brothers were alleged to be old friends of the Glavens and the Dodds, and he didn't think much of the quality of their friendship. Nor of Tweedledum and Tweedledee themselves, come to that. They weren't half the man their sister Dorothy was.

What he found, though, was that their conversation wasn't so much distasteful as disturbing. He was appalled by their juvenile amusement at the idea of Joanna Dodd revenging herself on Will Glaven by taking a shot at him.

They were joking, of course. But Martin had investigated too many shotgun woundings and deaths to think it was funny. Once again – as with their alcohol intake – he deplored the cheerful insouciance with which they treated lethal weapons.

Didn't they know the sportsman's rules? he thought angrily. Didn't they know how easy it was for someone to be shot by accident? Even to be killed?

He went suddenly cold. He sucked in his breath as sharply as though an ice pack had been slapped against the back of his neck.

Alison, he thought.

Oh God – if Alison were to be so upset by the shoot that she rushed out and did something crazy, like trying to rescue a wounded pheasant, *she* could be accidentally shot!

The realisation came as such a shock that it cleared his head of all today's nonsense. Alison was the girl he loved, the one he intended to marry, and he regretted having eyed Hope Meynell in front of her. What's more, he regretted his trivial social aspirations. Alison meant far more to him (always excepting his career) than anyone or anything else in the world. Whether or not it offended their host, he was not going to have her put at risk.

He shoved the dogs aside and jumped out as soon as the Landrover stopped. The other vehicles had already arrived, at the end of a woodland ride that cut a wide, grassy, bush-grown swath through the middle of Belmont. Alison was standing beside the Range Rover, talking to Hope. Neither of them seemed entirely happy.

Martin went straight up to them, made an abrupt excuse, took Alison by the arm and drew her away.

'Look, darling,' he said. 'You're not going to enjoy this shoot, you know. Most of it's wretchedly boring – just standing about in the cold. I've had enough of it, I can tell you. Let's make our apologies and go home.'

Alison gave him a level look. 'I know I'm not going to enjoy it,' she said. 'Neither is Hope. We were discussing it before lunch. She has to watch the shoot because the Glavens expect it of her. And I've come to give her a bit of moral support.'

Martin tried to argue her out of it, but she refused to budge.

'Well, at least promise me this,' he insisted. 'However much you may hate the shoot, for God's sake don't do anything unsafe. I mean, don't run about or try to disrupt it. Just stay behind me the whole time – promise?'

Alison's lovely green eyes had become unaccustomedly cool. 'I see,' she said slowly. 'So that's what's worrying you? You're afraid I'll do something that will let you down in front of your county friends.'

'That's not true!' he protested. 'I'm concerned about your safety, that's all. Of course you won't "let me down . . ."'

Alison turned scornfully away.

'Don't bet on it,' she said.

12

Laura's plans were all going wrong.

She had reached Belmont, but not the part where she wanted to be. When she was half-way towards the wood on the left of the grassy ride, she had seen someone moving among the trees. Fearful that it might be her old enemy the gamekeeper, she had veered off to the wood on the right.

Panting after her run, she had reached the cover of the bushes that grew along the edge of the ride, between the grass and the tall trees. But this was the right-hand side of the ride – a useless place for stopping the shoot. Instead of being between the pheasants and the guns, she was going to be *behind* the shooting party.

She was about to run across the open grass to the other side when she heard distant voices. Peering round a bush, she could see a few members of the shooting party moving towards her up the single-vehicle mud track that ran along the middle of the ride. Guns under their arms, they were making for some conspicuous blobs of white, spaced out along the track.

The blobs, Laura realised, were labels, fixed to the top of tall sticks that marked where the shooting party would stand. She drew back, panicking for a moment. It was too late to change sides. The gunmen were almost in position for the shoot.

She took a gulp of cold damp air to steady herself. All right – she'd change her plan instead.

The important thing was to take the gunmen by surprise. She would have to stay deep in cover, and work her way along towards them without being seen or heard. When she was level with the gun positions, she could sneak up to the edge of the grass. Then, just before the firing started, she would have to run out through the line of gunmen, and turn to face them.

She took another gulp. She was afraid, of course . . . But she wasn't going to let that stop her.

Using a tall silver birch as a marker, she plunged into the autumn tangle of shrubs and bushes. Brambles clawed at her clothes and her hair and her hands, but she tore herself free and pushed on.

She'd quite forgotten that there would be pheasants on this side of the ride too, until she heard a rustling among the fallen leaves and saw birds scuttling away at her approach. These were the intended victims of the second drive of the afternoon. If all her plans went well they would have nothing to fear.

But though she was their friend, one of the pheasants took fright. *Kurr-kuk! Kurr-kuk!* it shrieked, blundering up through the bare branches of the silver birch.

Laura froze. Through a gap in the bushes to her left she could glimpse one of the gunmen. He seemed to be already in position facing the other way, but he turned his head immediately, obviously wondering what had disturbed the bird. She was sure he would see her.

But he faced front again. Praying that she wouldn't put up any more pheasants Laura moved as quietly as possible towards the open ride. She found a hiding place behind an evergreen privet and crouched down, scratched and sore. Cautiously parting the wood stems, she peered out through the dark green oval leaves.

She found that she was roughly half-way between two gunmen, both standing with their backs towards her. All the shooting party were similarly dressed, but she'd know Will Glaven's long legs, and the amazing way his thick hair curled at the back of his neck, anywhere. Her heart gave its familiar lurch in his presence, but she soon put a stop to that.

Will didn't care about her any more. Besides, he was every bit as bloodthirsty as the other gunmen. She was glad that she'd be making her protest right in front of him. That would just show him that the pheasants were a lot more important to her than he was!

She thought she was safely hidden, but suddenly she realised she'd been heard. Will's black labrador, Boris, sitting beside his master, had turned his head and was looking at her enquiringly. She held her breath.

She and Boris were old friends. Normally, the dog would run to greet her. But now, on gun duty, he merely gave his tail a token thump of recognition and looked to the front again. Like the rest of the shooting party, he was waiting to get at the pheasants.

And here was another problem for Laura.

Never having been at a shoot, she'd had no idea how the guns were spaced out. She'd imagined the gunmen would stand quite close together, and that as soon as she appeared in front of them they would all see her at the same time.

Now she realised they were much further apart than she'd thought. There were seven of them, she knew that, but even though she peered out as far as she dared she couldn't see more than three. The grassy centre of the ride was unevenly narrowed by bushes, some of which were so overgrown that they blocked the view along the track.

She had no way of telling whereabouts along the line of gunmen Will was standing. She was too far from the pegs to see the numbers on the labels. What was dismayingly clear to her, though, was that the men at one end of the line couldn't possibly know what was happening at the other.

Even if she could stop Will and the two on either side of him from firing, the rest of the party would carry on with the shoot. They wouldn't even know she was there. However hard she tried, a lot of pheasants were going to be killed.

102

A prickling sensation rose up behind Laura's eyes, but she swallowed it away. It wasn't defeat that had brought on the tears, it was frustration and anger. She was the only person who cared enough to help the birds, and she was determined to stop the gunmen somehow. One by one, if necessary.

But that was *another* problem. She sucked a bleeding scratch below her thumb, almost gnawing it in her perplexity. The men at the other end of the line would already be firing when she ran up to stop them. They'd be concentrating on high-flying birds, and probably wearing ear muffs. How was she going to make them see and hear her?

Kurr-kuk kurr-kuk.

A pheasant got up with a shocking clatter somewhere in the wood behind her, making her jump. And another. It crossed her mind that someone must be moving about there or the birds wouldn't have panicked. But she had no time to concern herself with who or why.

Like the gunmen, she was concentrating on the wood on the other side of the ride. She waited, with bat-sized butterflies lurching about in her stomach, ready to fling herself forward as soon as the pheasants appeared and Will raised his gun.

Martin didn't know exactly where Alison was. When she had turned her back on him, he'd immediately stalked away in a huff. Certainly he cared where she was. He cared very much. But he was determined, when he saw her, not to let her know it.

Impatient to get the shoot over, and Alison safely home, he collected his gun and cartridge bag from the Landrover and gave his mind to the afternoon's procedure. He knew which peg he would be going to for the first drive, of course: number five. He'd be disgusted with himself if he couldn't remember a simple instruction to move up two numbers at the start of each drive.

But some members of the party seemed to have lunched too well to remember their numbers. Barclay Dodd, who had been shooting with deadly expertise all morning on Martin's left and should now be making for number six, had already parked himself confidently on his shooting stick at the first peg, and no one had the heart to move him on.

As for Tweedledum and Tweedledee, they were in an amiable state of confusion as they filled their cartridge bags. Martin knew that one of them ought to be at number four, on his immediate right. Instead, they were bickering over which of them was going to number two and which to number three.

Unusually, Martin felt no urge to point out their mistake. Concerned as he was for Alison's safety, he was relieved to think that the neighbouring peg wouldn't be occupied by one of the gun-happy brothers.

All the same, he resolved to keep an eye on them throughout the afternoon. If they showed any sign of mishandling their guns, he would take Alison straight home whether she wanted to leave or not – though he would of course make some good excuse to their host. Whatever his feelings about the Tread-golds, he didn't want to be ruled out of any future men-only shoots at Chalcot.

The only other member of the party who seemed anxious to get on with the shoot was Joanna Dodd. She'd driven up in a hurry, exchanged a quick word with Lewis Glaven, patted her father's shoulder ('Eh? What?' the old man had said, waking from a doze and almost falling off his perch) and then crammed the pockets of her Barbour with cartridges before striding off up the ride.

Though she passed close to the Treadgold brothers she ignored them, her head held high under her tweed cap, her horsily handsome face proudly set. Martin, watching, saw to his disgust that they nudged each other slyly as she stalked past, her shotgun under her arm.

He couldn't believe that they seriously imagined she might take vindictive aim at Will Glaven; they were just mocking her, he decided, probably out of jealousy because she was known to be an excellent shot. Disapproving of them as he did, he found himself regarding Joanna with considerable sympathy.

Besides, her father's land at Ashthorpe was reputed to provide one of the best shoots in Suffolk. Hoping for a future invitation, Martin hurried after her and caught her up.

104

'How's your horse?' he asked.

It was obvious that she had some other preoccupation. She frowned at him as if she wasn't sure who he was. 'What?' she said.

'The lame horse.' He reminded her of her alibi: 'The one you had to miss lunch for – ?'

'I know which one,' she said irritably. Then she made an effort to be more civil. 'Sorry – good of you to ask.' She paused. 'He's very much on my mind.'

'I hope he'll soon mend.'

'Oh, I expect he will.'

It was only when they'd parted, and he was standing by his peg while she went on to number seven at the end of the line, that Martin realised she hadn't actually answered his question.

He watched with some misgiving as Will Glaven arrived at the peg left vacant by Barclay Dodd: number six, between himself and Joanna. Recalling her intense preoccupation, and the speculations of the Treadgold brothers, Martin wondered for a moment whether it really was her horse she'd been talking about.

But his thoughts were abruptly diverted. With a shriek and a clatter, a pheasant took off from the bushes just behind him. He turned his head immediately, wondering who or what had startled it.

Nothing else moved. Martin faced front again, and waited.

It seemed a long time since he'd had that argument with Alison, and he wished he knew where she was. Perhaps she and Hope had decided not to come to the shoot after all? He would have liked to ask Will, but he couldn't catch his eye. Besides, he knew better than to make loud conversation from one peg to another; it was important not to alarm the pheasants by giving away the presence of the Guns.

Anyway, Will Glaven seemed to be unapproachably deep in thought. His black labrador was gazing with interest at a bush behind them, probably having seen a rabbit, but it was too well trained to do anything that would distract its master.

Kurr-kuk kurr-kuk. That was another pheasant getting up, this

105

time from somewhere in the wood at their backs. And another. Martin turned with a sharp intake of breath. He hoped to God that Alison hadn't taken it into her head to do something utterly stupid on behalf of the pheasants, like lurking in the bushes with intent . . .

And then, with a rush of relief, he saw her. She and Hope – their body-language unmistakably reluctant – were being escorted up the track by Lewis Glaven and his dogs. Their host, one arm cradling his gun, was using the other to make enthusiastic gestures up and down the ride and towards the woodland. Evidently he was explaining the plan of the shoot before delivering them to the care of their respective partners.

Watching the girls' approach, Martin was glad that they would at least be safely out of range of Tweedledum and Tweedledee. In fact the brothers were so far away at the other end of the line that they were out of sight. The first four pegs, on Martin's right, were hidden from him by a thicket that narrowed the ride.

A pity, he thought – he wouldn't be able to check whether the brothers were shooting soberly. On the other hand, he remembered, their sister would be somewhere behind them with her dogs, waiting to do the picking-up. That was all right, then. He knew he could rely on Dorothy Wilson-Brown to keep the juveniles in order.

As for the girls, they would at least be on adjoining pegs now that Will had replaced Barclay Dodd on number six. That was another relief for Martin. Alison would be able to give Hope the moral support she needed; and having the younger girl to consider would, he hoped, curb Alison's impulse to *do* something about the shoot.

He breathed more easily. With luck, they might yet get away without any physical or even social damage.

'Hallo there,' he said as she joined him. Until he knew what her mood was, he intended to be friendly rather than fond. 'Nice chap, Lewis Glaven, isn't he?'

Alison was, if anything, more contemptuous than when they'd last spoken. 'If you think it's "nice" to enjoy killing wild creatures for sport . . . But then you do, don't you?'

It would be a waste of breath to argue.

Martin had always heard that girls mature to resemble their mothers, and that had bothered him at first because he thought Molly Quantrill a silly, fussy little woman. But Alison resembled her father; not only in colouring and features, but also in sheer obstinacy.

'The whistle's just gone,' he said, ignoring her protest. 'That means the drive's about to start. If you want to support Hope, the best thing you can do is to show her how to behave. You don't have to watch what's happening – just stand behind me where you'll be safe, keep quiet, and think of something else.'

He changed his grip on his gun, faced towards the wood and listened for the sound of approaching beaters. At his back, Alison's indignation simmered on: 'That's typical of you! All you care about is "behaving properly" – '

Kurr-kukkukkuk.

That was another pheasant taking off with a screech and a clatter from somewhere behind them. Frowning, Martin turned his head.

'What *is* going on in those trees?' he demanded.

'How do I know?' Alison snapped. Her cheeks were flushed, her eyes brilliant with on-going fury.

Martin shrugged. However annoyed with him she might be, temporarily, at least she should be safe for the duration of the drive. Reassured about that, he could now concentrate on his shooting.

The disturbances behind them still puzzled him, though. He gave a final glance in that direction but could see nothing moving. All that caught his eye, apart from Alison, were the golden-yellow leaves of a field maple at the woodland edge, blazing with colour before they died.

13

The clarity of the morning sky had dimmed. Rainclouds had begun to gather, shortening the already short November afternoon and darkening the wood. The air smelled earthy, a compound of decaying leaves, sodden hedgerow fruits and fleshy toadstools.

Silence had fallen all along the ride. Everyone there – Guns, dogs, pickers-up, reluctant spectators, would-be protestors – stood listening to the distant sounds of tapping that marked the beaters' progress towards them. There were occasional shouts, and eerie whistlings from somewhere deep in the gloom.

Minutes passed. The tapping sounds neared, and the wood seemed to rustle and stir. Agitated blackbirds scattered through the bushes. A disturbance of rooks got up from the treetops, wheeling and cawing. A jay screamed, and slipped out of cover and in again with a flash of its blue wing.

Then the pheasants began to call in alarm.

The first one got up high above the trees. It curled and went gliding off to the side, its long tail streaming out behind. Another rose and headed back, gliding down over the invisible line of beaters towards the safety of the far side of the wood. But then it staggered in mid-air and dropped, just a second before the watchers in the ride heard the echoing crack of the shot that had killed it.

'Bloody keeper, sneaking along behind the beaters,' muttered Will Glaven. 'He'll shoot more birds than I do.'

Martin Tait stood poised, ready to load, his mouth dry and his heart pumping with anticipation. But he controlled his excitement. This time he was going to prove that he was an asset to any shooting party. On this drive, with the Glavens on either side of him, Will on his left and Lewis somewhere on his right, he was going to shoot not only safely but brilliantly as well.

The tapping noises from the wood were louder now. The beaters were coming closer. Martin saw a movement on the ground at the woodland edge, and caught a glimpse of some of the pheasants that had been driven forward. Bunched together, their heads up, they were running about in bewilderment as they tried to decide which way to go.

He loaded his gun.

A flush of birds had got up on the right and were flying high over that end of the line. The guns on the first four pegs began to fire.

At Martin's end of the line, the beaters were making their final push. He could hear them trampling through the dead leaves and whacking the undergrowth with their sticks. The pheasants he'd been watching could hear them too.

Finding themselves trapped between the beaters and the guns, the birds took the only way out. Calling in alarm and powering their wings to gain height, they exploded out of the bushes, their long tails quivering with exertion.

Martin clapped on his ear muffs and raised his gun. With total concentration he swung on to the track of a fine cock pheasant, determined to get it at the peak of its flight. The bird rose high above him, gold against the darkening sky.

His gun almost vertical, he squeezed the trigger. The cock jerked and threw back its brilliant head. *Got it*! he thought exultantly.

Without pausing to watch its fall he swung his gun on to another high bird. *Don't shoot across the line*, he reminded himself, just in time. Watching the hen as it flew over, he turned with it, gun and arm and head moving as one, and dropped the pheasant into the bushes behind him.

A left and a right – excellent shooting! *And* he'd remembered the safety rules. High on success he reloaded, swung round again and took a snap shot at another bird that had just flown over him. Missing it, he gave it his second barrel. To his chagrin it flew on unharmed, gliding down into the wood behind.

But perhaps that was just as well, he thought, feeling slightly guilty. The bird was arguably low by the time it had crossed the line, and he was annoyed with himself for forgetting good sportsmanship in the heat of the moment.

He glanced to his left, hoping that Will Glaven hadn't seen him. But Will, his dog still at his peg, was already running towards him, carrying his broken gun and frowning heavily.

Martin pulled off his ear muffs and prepared his defence. 'Is there a problem?' he asked.

The shoot was going on all round them, with birds flocking over and the rest of the party banging away, the hidden four on the right, and Joanna Dodd on the far left. The air was filled with the noise of guns, with pheasants' cries and whirring wings, with the headachey smell of nitro-powder and the pattering of fallen shot.

'Young Laura – the housekeeper's daughter,' panted Will. He pointed towards the bushes in front. 'She suddenly appeared, waving her arms to disrupt the shoot. Now she's dived into cover to avoid being captured. Stupid kid – I'm afraid she'll be hurt. I'm going to warn Dad and the others to hold their fire. Can you go and fetch her out?'

Martin was concerned for the child, of course. But having had time to glance round, after the concentrated excitement of the last few minutes, he was far more worried about his girlfriend.

'Alison's disappeared! Have you seen her?'

Will answered over his shoulder. 'Hope couldn't face the shoot. She ran to hide in the wood behind us and Alison went after her. They're all right, it's young Laura who needs rescuing!'

He sprinted off along the track. Martin, still holding his unloaded gun, plunged into the bushes.

What he felt was an overwhelming surge of relief that it wasn't Alison who had put herself at risk. This wasn't a safe place to be, between the pheasants and the guns. Quite apart from the spent pellets, some of which came zinging down with a force that shredded twigs from trees, there was also the possibility of being hit by one of the falling birds. And four pounds deadweight of meat and feathers, coming straight down at speed, would certainly break bones.

'Laura!' he shouted, uneasy for his own neck as well as hers. He forced his way through the cover, using the butt of his gun to bash the brambles that reached out to snatch at him. There was no sign of the girl at first. Then he caught a glimpse of her, running from one clump of bushes to another, parallel with the ride.

'Laura! Stay where you are!' he shouted.

She ignored him and disappeared again, just as another flush of pheasants came over.

But fewer guns were firing now, thank God. Will Glaven was evidently doing a good job, because they fell silent one by one all along the right of the line.

Martin sighed with relief and returned to the open ride. The girl was no longer in danger, and Will would no doubt deal with her when she decided to show her face.

The firing hadn't stopped completely, though. Over on the extreme left of the line, isolated by her ear muffs and oblivious of what was happening elsewhere, Joanna Dodd was still bringing down birds with deadly accuracy.

Martin decided to tell her that the shoot had been stopped, at least temporarily. But as he approached her, he saw that they were about to be joined by unwelcome visitors.

Running towards the wood from the direction of the minor road came a scruffy, placard-carrying rabble. As they neared the ride, Martin could read their placards. BIG GUNS – TINY MINDS was one scornful message. MURDERERS! bawled another, unequivocally.

He groaned. It wasn't only the shooting season that had just begun, it was the anti-shooting season as well.

Martin had hoped that none of the antis would appear while he was at Chalcot. Shooting on private land is a lawful activity; so is peaceful protest. It would be his duty as a police officer to be impartial, and that was bound to cause difficulty between him and his host.

He anticipated no trouble from most of the protesters, genuine lovers of wildlife who minded terribly about birds being shot for pleasure. Like young Laura, they would make a nuisance of themselves – though hopefully they would be less foolhardy than she was. But their sole objective would be to end the shooting.

Regular saboteurs would be different. Just stopping the shoot wouldn't be enough for them, because they objected not only to the killing but to the people who did it. They knew their rights, and they enjoyed the exercise of power. What they came looking for was confrontation, during which they hoped to provoke at least some of the sportsmen into breaking the law.

They were not themselves breaking the law by trespassing on the Glavens' land. It was a provocative act, but as the law stood it was not a criminal offence.

111

Martin doubted the Glavens would see it like that, though. They would imagine the law was on their side because the land was theirs. Having a senior police officer as a guest, they would naturally expect him to get rid of the trespassers.

But no police officer had the power to do it. All Martin could offer his host was the standard advice for defusing a potential confrontation with saboteurs: *Don't argue with them – don't threaten them – don't try to force them to leave. Just call off the shoot, pack up and go home.*

Few members of this or any other shooting party were likely to accept such tame advice. Chances were that some of them would lose their temper and take the law into their own hands, and that was an alarming prospect. At best, they would thump a few saboteurs and end up being sued for common assault. At worst –

Bearing in mind that all members of the shooting party had a strong commitment to private property, that most of them had been drinking, and that they were armed with shotguns, the worst eventuality didn't bear thinking about.

Intent on preventing a confrontation, Martin raced the oncoming saboteurs and reached Joanna Dodd before they did. The drive was over – the beaters were just beginning to appear at the woodland edge – but Joanna was still firing at the last of the high pheasants. She was concentrating so hard that she didn't see him until he stood right in front of her.

With a three-inch advantage in height, she gave him a high-horse look from under her flat tweed cap.

'What *do* you think you're doing?' she demanded. As an afterthought, she pushed back her ear muffs so that she could hear his reply.

'We have uninvited visitors,' said Martin. He made a point of propping his gun against her peg. 'Would you mind unloading your gun and putting it with mine?'

Ingnoring his request, Joanna stared at the invaders. 'Oh God, it's the bloody antis,' she said with disgust.

She tightened her grip on her gun. Martin suspected that she meant to threaten the saboteurs with it.

'Put it down, please!' he said sharply.

Affronted, Joanna Dodd turned her contempt on him. 'I shall do nothing of the kind. Who the hell do you think you *are*?'

'Detective Superintendent Tait, county police,' said Martin, forgetting in the satisfaction of the moment that his promotion was still some weeks away. 'Your gun, please?'

He held out his hands for it. Speechless with astonishment, and looking at him as if for the first time, Joanna surrendered her shotgun. He unloaded it and propped it against the other side of the peg, just as the chanting, jeering saboteurs – fifteen or twenty of them – came skidding to a stop a few yards away.

At the front were two unmistakable regular saboteurs, tough customers in their mid-twenties in combat gear and heavy boots. They had shaven heads – one with a bristly crest, one as bare as a bullet – and their faces were perforated with ear and nose rings.

'Bloodthirsty bastards!' they snarled, their faces distorted with hatred as they jabbed their fingers at Martin and Joanna.

'Posh scum, posh scum – '

Another man of the same age, taller, paler and pony-tailed, stood unobtrusively to one side and kept silent. He was carrying something heavy. Martin couldn't at first see what it was, but he could guess. Saboteurs who know their rights come with an essential piece of high-tech equipment.

The rest of the crowd were of student age, and they were fired with indignation and dismay.

'Killers!' they cried.

'Save our pheasants!'

'Murderers, murderers!'

The intrusion had infuriated Joanna Dodd. Her strong-boned cheeks red with anger, she raised her voice and attempted to wither the saboteurs with words. Martin tried to defuse the situation.

'Don't speak to them,' he advised her quietly. 'It'll only encourage them. What we're going to do now is to pick up our guns – without being threatening – and walk away.'

She turned to glare at him, her contempt renewed. 'Walk away? I don't *believe* this! Why aren't you *doing* something – Superintendent?'

113

Martin picked up his own gun by the barrel and put it under his arm. 'There's nothing I can do,' he explained patiently. 'They're being thoroughly objectionable, but they're not breaking the law. They'll clear off, just as soon as we leave. Come on, let's go.'

But Joanna stood her ground. The saboteurs, targeting her, moved nearer with slow deliberation. The bullet-headed one picked up a cock pheasant she'd killed, holding it by its claws. Snarling, he shook it at her so that drops of blood, dripping crimson from its dangling green and scarlet head, splattered on her clothes.

'Bloodthirsty bitch!' he screamed.

Joanna didn't flinch. She was used to dead birds and blood. She'd already demonstrated that when it came to expletives she had a larger vocabulary than his, and now she wasted no more words.

'I'll give you ten seconds to turn and start running . . .' she said grimly. She reached for her shotgun, only to find that Martin had already taken charge of it.

'Ignore them, Joanna,' he insisted. 'They're trying to provoke you into breaking the law.'

'To hell with that! It'd only be their word against ours.'

'No, it wouldn't, they'll have evidence. One of them's using a video camera. Just pick up the rest of your gear and we'll make a dignified retreat.'

'But if we do that, they'll have won!'

'No, they won't. They'll only win if they can sue you for threatening behaviour or assault. Come on, we're going. *Now.*'

He turned and walked away, hoping that she would follow. But Joanna was reluctant to retreat. She took her time over collecting her gun case and cartridge bag, while the saboteurs jeered and jostled her. Martin watched from a short distance, ready to extricate her if she insisted on getting herself into trouble.

Most of the protesters had begun to scatter. Uninterested in confrontation, and unsure of their purpose now that the shooting had stopped, they had thrown down their placards and were running about among the bushes on either side of the ride.

Martin thought they seemed agitated. Then he realised, from

their cries of distress, that they must be finding and trying to rescue wounded pheasants.

It was a hopeless cause. Exactly the kind of thing he'd feared that Alison might do during the shoot. He wondered whether she was doing it now, having emerged from the safety of the wood at their back when the shooting stopped. Hoping to see her, he glanced over his shoulder.

But the only people in sight were the Glavens. The other members of the shooting party were masked by the bushes further along the ride. The beaters had already made themselves scarce, and the pickers-up and their dogs hadn't put in an appearance. Will's labrador still sat by his peg, its domed forehead creased in puzzlement at the goings-on, but totally obedient.

Lewis Glaven was approaching hurriedly. Some way behind him, Will was running up from the far end of the track. Both carried their guns under their arms.

Martin went to meet his host. 'Saboteurs, I'm afraid,' he reported. 'They're doing nothing illegal, but they're being provocative. I suggest we walk away from trouble. Would you mind calling off the shoot, sir?'

He'd expected Lewis Glaven to explode with fury, but he seemed almost indifferent. Martin wondered if he felt unwell. His normally pink complexion had greyed to the colour of his moustache, and hurrying had made him lose his puff.

Lewis paused to regain his breath. He surveyed the saboteurs with exasperation.

'Unprepossessing lot . . . Ignorant, too – they've no under-standing of the countryside. Good God, if they had their way there'd be no pheasants at all . . .'

Then his colour began to return, and he continued in his usual clipped, unemotional style: 'Not surprised they've appeared. Increasing problem in every rural area. We've discussed it at the Landowners' Association. Nothing you police-men can do, in the present state of the law, eh?'

'Except keep the peace,' said Martin, thankful that Lewis was so reasonable. 'I've been trying to persuade Joanna to walk away, but she's determined to argue with them. At least I've disarmed her, though.'

115

'Quite right – she's too quick with that gun. Can't have any law-breaking. I'll send Will to fetch her.'

Will Glaven was nearing, his handsome face fired with annoyance. Evidently he'd made an appraisal of the situation, without having any idea of its legal delicacy, and intended to take gung-ho command.

'Leave this to me, Dad,' he ordered. 'Get out of the way, Joanna!'

He advanced on the two leading saboteurs, still carrying his shotgun under his arm.

'Put your gun down, Will,' urged Martin. His host's son ignored him.

The two front men, eager for a confrontation, folded their arms and stood squarely in Will's way. The pony-tailed man hovered behind them, keeping his camera out of sight.

'Call yourself a sportsman?' taunted the crested saboteur.

'Makes you feel big, does it, killing birds?' enquired bullet-head.

Will's annoyance increased to anger, but he made an obvious effort to contain it. 'This land is private,' he said, his jaw set, 'and you are trespassing. Now get out.'

They mocked him with grins. 'If you want us to leave, you'll have to make us,' said one.

'How're you going to do that?' tempted the other.

Rattled, and conscious that he was being watched by Joanna, Will Glaven resorted to bluff. 'Don't worry, I shall do it!'

Martin saw with alarm that his hand was tightening on his gun. He could also see that there were no cartridges in the breech; but that wasn't the point.

'Put it down!' he called. But Will was so wound up that he was oblivious of everything except the taunts of the saboteurs: 'You reckon?' 'You and whose army?'

There was a second's ferocious pause, and then their provocation worked. Will lost his head. Seizing his gun in both hands, he cocked it menacingly.

'*Move!*' he roared.

It was Martin who did the moving. He leaped forward, grabbed the barrel of the shotgun and forced it upright. 'Don't be an idiot, Will! You're playing right into their hands.

116

They've got a video camera. They're filming us – don't you understand?'

Whether Will Glaven understood or not, his father certainly did.

'*Filming?*' His face was as angry as his son's. 'The hell they are!'

Lewis Glaven pushed Will aside. Before Martin had a chance to stop him, he went straight for the pony-tailed man with the camcorder, who filmed him every inch of the way.

'Give me that!' he bellowed, seizing the camera by the lens.

There was a brief, undignified scuffle in the fading November light. It had begun to rain; the track was slippery with mud, and the pony-tailed man suddenly fell down with a yelp and a bloody nose. His assailant wrenched the video camera out of his hands.

And then the unthinkable happened. Lewis Glaven – hereditary landowner, chairman of a major insurance group, respected public figure, churchwarden – pulled open the camera in a fit of rage and snatched out the film. Then he threw the whole lot to the ground and jumped on it, his heavy leather boots trampling the smashed components into the mud.

The saboteurs cheered him on ironically. Even the cameraman was grinning, despite the blood running down his upper lip, as though the destruction of the camcorder was some kind of victory.

'Oh my God . . .' groaned Martin. A girl saboteur in a bobble hat had produced a pocket camera, and was busily taking photographic evidence. He looked on helplessly, envisaging charges of criminal damage and affray against Lewis Glaven, and the court case that would follow.

Will Glaven, having failed to see the girl, was trying to bluff away the incident. 'I didn't see a thing!' he asserted. He gave a heavy hint to their guest: 'And you didn't either, did you, Martin?'

A sudden commotion saved Martin from rejecting the suggestion. The noise came from somewhere along the ride behind them. One of the protesters, a gangling lad, had leaped out of the bushes and was running up the track with long strides, his arms and legs pumping frantically.

As he approached them, with spectacles so splodged with rain that he could hardly see, he was yammering something. It was impossible at first to hear what he said, but the shrill pitch of his cries chilled Martin to the bone.

'A girl – a girl – ' he gabbled. 'Lying there – blood all over her face. I think she's been shot. I think she's dead – '

14

The next few minutes were the worst in the whole of Martin Tait's life. He knew without doubt that it was Alison who had been shot. And he was convinced that it must have been his own last shot, the one that missed the lowish bird behind him, that had hit her.

– that hadn't killed her, though – that please God hadn't killed her –

He wasn't conscious of flinging down his gun, or of hurling himself along the track and plunging in among thorns to find her. All he was aware of was the piercing ache of love and the gouge of impending loss.

'*Alison!*' he cried as he fought his way through rain-dark thickets in search of her. And the pheasants he disturbed seemed to mock him with an echoing *kurr-kuk*.

When he found her, it was quite by accident.

Tripped by brambles that snaked out from a bush, he stumbled and almost fell; and where he almost fell, there she lay.

Face down on wet grass, her legs ensnared by the same brambles, Alison lay with her head turned to one side. He could see the long lashes of her closed eye, and blood oozing down her cheek.

'Oh my love – '

He dropped to his knees beside her, and put out a shaking hand to touch her face. As he did so, her eyes flew open.

'I thought you'd never come,' she groaned.

Relief that she was still alive washed over Martin like a

breaker on a summer sea. He came up for air, his spirits buoyant.

'Of course I've come! You're going to be all right, darling . . .'

Still on his knees, heedless of the mud, he lifted her shoulders so that she could rest against him. The movement made her draw in her breath with pain, and he took an apprehensive look at her facial wound. What with the dim light, and the mingling of blood and rain on her cheek, he couldn't tell how badly she'd been hurt.

It was clear, though, that the gangling lad had exaggerated when he reported blood all over her face. Gently dabbing it with his handkerchief, Martin realised thankfully that the wound was only superficial.

Alison groaned again, but this time with a hint of asperity. 'Never mind my face, that was just where a bramble clawed me. It's my ankle that hurts like hell.'

'Is that where you were shot?' he asked, anxious again.

'*Shot*?' She sat up with an 'ouch'. 'I wasn't shot anywhere – I was tripped by the blasted brambles and I've wrenched my ankle. I've been struggling to free myself, but I'm entangled worse now than when I started. I called and called for help . . .'

'My poor love.' Light-headed with relief, Martin took his Swiss army knife from the pocket of his Barbour and began to cut away the vicious growths that trapped her. 'When I saw you lying there so still, I was convinced you'd been shot.'

'I was just plain exhausted . . . Where's Hope?'

All Martin could think of was that the girl he loved was safe and well. 'What?' he said, forgetting for a moment that Hope was the name of another girl.

'Have you seen her? She couldn't bear to watch the shoot, so she ran for the wood behind us. I followed to keep her company, but lost sight of her when I fell.'

'I expect she's found Will, now the shooting has stopped,' Martin reassured her. 'I'm afraid your ankle's badly swollen, love. You'll have to have your boot cut off.'

'Oh no! My favourite boots . . .' she mourned.

'Stop complaining, when I'm ruining these expensive trousers on your behalf! Come on, let's get you up on your good foot.

119

I'll help you as far as the ride and then I'll fetch some transport. As soon as we get back to the house, I'll operate on that boot. I've always fancied myself as a surgeon . . .'

Half-carrying her, he began steering her out of the bushes by a route that avoided the worst of the thorns. But though he was making jokes to cheer her, Martin was no longer feeling light-hearted.

Something was wrong. Badly wrong.

Where was everyone else? Why hadn't Will and Lewis Glaven, and Joanna Dodd, and every protester who had at least a spark of concern for human as well as bird life, come running to help? Why hadn't the gangling lad shown him where Alison was lying, instead of leaving him to find her by himself?

In fairness to the lad, Martin had to acknowledge that he hadn't given him a chance to help. Terrified by what he thought had happened to Alison, and knowing that she must have disappeared into the bushes somewhere behind his peg, he'd gone rushing off on his own.

And why hadn't anyone followed him?

Because Alison hadn't been shot, that was why.

And how did they know that?

The logic was irrefutable: they knew, because it wasn't Alison who had been shot. Because the gangling lad had seen another girl lying in the bushes with blood all over her face.

Martin could hear a commotion going on, somewhere not far away. That was where everyone had run to.

But who was lying there? Was it Hope? Or was it young Laura?

15

It was just after six in the evening, wet and cold. The lights were on all round the yard at the back of Chalcot House, illuminating the rain as it drummed down on the shooting party's vehicles, still standing where they had been left at the start of the tragic shoot.

Most of the members of the party were gathered in the gun room, their tweeds and their dogs steaming as they dried. The panelled room had an almost festive look, with a blazing log fire and the table laid for a traditional shoot tea of scones and rich fruit cake; but most of the food was untouched, and everyone needed a stronger drink than tea. Little was said, and the atmosphere was one of gloom and anxiety.

Will Glaven was absent, and so was Hope Meynell.

With the gangling lad as a guide, Will and his father and Joanna had found Hope lying among the trees at the edge of Belmont wood. She was unconscious, and bleeding copiously from a shotgun wound to the head. They had taken her back to the house in the Range Rover, and sent for an ambulance. Will had followed the ambulance to Saintsbury hospital, from where he had rung his father to say that she was in the intensive care unit, in a critical condition.

Everyone was now waiting apprehensively for further news. That included Barclay Dodd, even though he was asleep. What with age and the exertions of the day, and whisky and the heat of the fire, Barclay was well away, his legs outstretched and the cake crumbs on his tweed waistcoat rising and falling with his snores. But before his eyes had closed, he had mumbled an instruction to his daughter to wake him when there was any news from the hospital.

Joanna herself had withdrawn to a window seat. Set-faced, she gulped gin and tonic while she flipped without interest through a pile of back numbers of *Horse and Hound*.

Dorothy Wilson-Brown and the Treadgolds were all at the table, with a bottle of Islay malt conveniently to hand. Dorothy was absently breaking up scones and feeding them to her dogs. Her brothers, slightly ashamed to be doing so but not knowing how else to pass the time, were playing poker dice.

Unable to settle anywhere, Lewis Glaven was roaming grey-faced between the gun room and the estate office, just across the kitchen corridor. He spoke to no one, but every now and then he gave an anguished mutter:

'Never forgive myself . . .' 'First time there's ever been a serious accident at a Chalcot shoot . . .' 'Never forgive myself . . .'

121

Martin Tait, uneasy in his conscience, and aware of being an outsider in a distressed gathering of old friends, was patrolling the lower end of the corridor. As soon as he'd brought Alison back to the house he had rung Douglas Quantrill, who had made it his priority to collect his daughter and have her ankle attended to. Tait was now waiting for Quantrill to return, in his capacity as head of Breckham Market CID rather than as Alison's father.

Tait had already explained to Lewis Glaven that Detective Chief Inspector Quantrill would be coming back to begin the enquiry into the shooting. He'd been half-apologetic about the intrusion, but Lewis was evidently expecting it.

'Yes, of course there must be a police investigation. Essential after a serious accident. Do we have to wait for your colleague, though? You're a senior man, aren't you?'

Tait had no intention of admitting that he didn't yet out-rank Doug Quantrill, and that until his promotion took effect he had no authority here in the Breckham Market division. But even if he were already a superintendent, he still couldn't take charge of the investigation.

'I'm also one of the witnesses, as a member of the shooting party,' he'd explained. 'I shall have to be interviewed just like everyone else.'

Lewis Glaven gave him a sharp blue-eyed stare. 'Did you see how it happened?' he demanded. 'Damned if I did . . . Nor any of the others.'

'Nor I,' said Martin, with complete truth but rather too much haste.

His last shot, though arguably unsporting, had been nowhere near low enough to hit Hope directly. But he remembered how apprehensive he'd felt when he was searching for young Laura, and found that spent pellets were zinging down all round him with twig-shredding force. That could well have been how Hope was hit. He didn't want to believe that the pellets were from his gun, but it was a worrying possibility.

Fortunately, his host suspected nothing. 'Chief Inspector Quantrill . . .' Lewis Glaven was muttering. 'Know of him, of course. Met him once or twice. Recognised him as soon as he came to pick up his daughter. A good sound countryman, I thought. Does he shoot?'

'Never has done, to my knowledge.'

Lewis shook his head. 'Pity . . . A man who doesn't shoot can't possibly understand the concentration that's required. Or the emphasis we place on safety. But at least you know that now, eh? No doubt you'll make it clear to him.'

'Of course,' said Martin, with a sick feeling of culpability.

'It's these interviews I'm concerned about, d'you see?' Lewis confided in a lower voice. 'Concerned for my guests, I mean. God knows how this terrible accident happened, but trying to apportion blame will serve no useful purpose. My friends are distressed enough already. I don't want them upset by a police grilling.'

'There's no question of a "grilling",' Tait had protested, quick to defend the reputation of the Suffolk constabulary.

'You know what I mean. Ask your colleague to make it as much of a formality as possible, eh?'

Lewis Glaven had clapped him on the shoulder and returned to the estate office without waiting for a reply. Tait paced up and down the corridor, pulled two ways. As a senior police officer, he deplored his host's request for a token investigation. But a thorough investigation might well show that he had fired the near-fatal shot.

If the responsibility were his, there would be no way of ducking it. Quantrill would have photographs taken of Hope Meynell's injuries, showing the spread of the pellets. These photographs would enable the forensic lab to calculate the angle and distance of the shot. Together with photographs of the scene, with measurements from each peg, they would reveal exactly which of the Guns had fired it.

It was an accident, of course. Everyone knew that. If the shot had been his, no one would openly blame him.

But how could he live at ease with himself, with that careless shot on his conscience? How could he look the Glavens and their friends in the eye, when the victim was Will's girlfriend? And how would Alison react?

She was already furious with him for shooting wildlife in

pursuit of his social ambition. So how was she going to feel about him if he'd shot a human being – particularly a girl she'd liked and was trying to take care of? Would she ever forgive him? Would she still be prepared to marry him?

Martin was sweating out possible scenarios when the telephone rang in the estate office. Lewis Glaven answered it instantly. Anxious for news, Dorothy Wilson-Brown appeared in the gun-room doorway, looking old and drained. Martin moved away down the corridor, every bit as anxious but not wanting to seem to be listening.

When Lewis emerged from the room he was visibly shaken. His normally straight shoulders sagged and even his trim moustache seemed downcast. Mrs Wilson-Brown hurried to put a sympathetic hand on his arm.

'My dear . . .?'

He patted her hand absently. 'That was Hope's father. I'd left a message on his answering machine to call me urgently. I've just broken the news to him.'

'Poor Lewis . . .'

'Poor Meynell . . .' He gave a heavy sigh: 'How d'you tell a man that the daughter he'd entrusted to your care for a weekend has been shot? Frankly, I couldn't. Told him there'd been a bad accident, that's all. He's going straight to the hospital tonight, and he'll hear the details from Will. I'm meeting him there in the morning.'

'That was the best thing to say, for his sake as well as yours.'

'Was it? I don't know . . . I feel so guilty, Doffy.'

'It was an accident, my dear. We all know that accidents happen at shoots.'

'Country people know it. Suburban dentists can't be expected to. Besides, it was my fault she was at the shoot. She hated the idea of watching pheasants being killed. Will would have let her off, but I insisted on her going.'

'For the best of reasons. And I agreed with you, so don't reproach yourself.'

'You're a great support to me, Doffy. Be a dear and come with me to the hospital tomorrow? Don't think I can face Meynell on my own.'

As the old friends disappeared into the gun room, Martin

124

heard a vehicle crunching to a stop on the gravel outside. He pulled on the Barbour he'd left in the lobby, and his cap, and splashed across the illuminated yard to meet Douglas Quantrill.

'Thought you might like a quick briefing before you go indoors,' he said, sliding into the passenger seat of Quantrill's car. 'How's Alison?'

'She'll be fine. The casualty department's having a precautionary X-ray taken, but they don't think any bones are broken. Her mother's with her, and Peter's going to drive them home when the ankle's been dealt with.'

'Good. You didn't tell her how seriously Hope Meynell was injured?'

'No. As you said, Alison's concerned for the girl and there's no point in upsetting her tonight. But as for you . . .'

Quantrill's voice had hardened. He turned in his seat and stared at Martin across the half-dark interior of the car. The hostility that came from him was almost palpable.

'It's just as well for you that their injuries weren't the other way round. If it were Alison who'd been shot, I'd have broken your bloody gun over your head. You've been totally irresponsible.'

'That's not true!' said Tait.

After all, it wasn't necessarily his shot that had caused Hope's injuries. He didn't intend to be caught out by forensic evidence, so he planned to cover himself when he gave Quantrill his formal statement. He would say quite frankly that he'd turned round to fire at a pheasant that had flown over him, and that he'd missed. But at the moment he was admitting nothing.

'*I* didn't want Alison to come and watch the shoot,' he went on. 'I advised her not to. Lewis Glaven insists on safe shooting, but even so I told her it was a dangerous place to be. I begged her to stay away, right up to the last minute. But she takes after her father – she's every bit as obstinate as you are.'

Deprived of his righteous anger, Quantrill was reduced to a peeved retort: 'D'you think I don't know it? The times I've told her she must be out of her mind to partner you . . .'

'Our relationship is no one's business but our own,' said Tait loftily. Then, remembering with pleasure that he would shortly become Douglas Quantrill's boss, he decided to be magnanimous: 'Now, do you want any help from me in this investigation?'

Quantrill accepted with a bad grace. 'I suppose it'll save time. You already know the names and addresses of the shooting party, I take it?'

'Of course. And I imagine you'll want me to show you where the shoot took place?'

'Tomorrow morning, if you can make it. I don't intend to do the interviews tonight – shooting talk won't mean anything to me until I've had a look round. If you'll just give me a general idea, now, of what happened, I'll have a word with Lewis Glaven and then call it a day.'

Quantrill paused: 'Unless of course you already know, or suspect, who fired the shot?'

Martin was slightly ruffled. 'No idea.'

'No one's admitting responsibility?'

'No.'

Quantrill nodded thoughtfully. 'But then,' he said, 'considering it's their host's son's girlfriend who's been critically wounded, who'd be prepared to admit it?'

Douglas Quantrill took it very kindly that Lewis Glaven's first words to him were an enquiry about his daughter's injury.

'Thank you, but it's probably just a sprained ankle,' he said. 'Painful, but nothing to worry about.'

'Good. Charming girl. We were delighted to have her with us at lunch.'

Lewis Glaven led the way into the estate office. Like the gun room it was panelled, but it contained modern, functional equipment more appropriate to Glaven's role as a company chairman than as a gentleman farmer; as well as filing cabinets there was a computer, a fax machine and a shredder. But the walls were dominated by two large-scale maps of the Chalcot estate, a yellowed one from the nineteenth century, and a modern one with a write-on wipe-off overlay. A number of silver cups and trophies stood proudly on a shelf, and the panelling was hung with framed photographs of individual

126

pale-coloured beef cattle, each frame decorated with prize-winner's rosettes.

The men sat down on opposite sides of the large desk. Quantrill had remembered Lewis Glaven, from previous brief encounters, for his healthily pink complexion and his decisive manner; but now his face was as grey as his hair, and his hands fiddled restlessly with a fountain pen.

'I'm sorry to intrude at such a time,' said Quantrill. 'It's a distressing situation for all of you. My daughter's upset too – she particularly liked Miss Meynell. What's the news from the hospital?'

'They give her less than a fifty-fifty chance of surviving.'

Lewis Glaven stood up abruptly, went to a corner cupboard and fetched two glasses and a bottle of Laphroaig malt. He began to pour for both of them.

'Not for me, thanks,' said Quantrill. 'I've never acquired the taste, and it'd be a pity to waste it.'

'Please,' insisted Lewis Glaven. 'I need one, and I don't want to start drinking alone.'

Quantrill took a reluctant sip, identifying tar and seaweed. It confirmed his unashamedly philistine opinion that, for all its expense, malt whisky tastes medicinal. Certainly it cleared his sinuses, but if he needed to do that he could suck a Fisherman's Friend lozenge.

'You've got a lot on your mind this evening – I'll leave my questions until tomorrow,' he said. 'Except that I need to know whether you yourself have any idea how Miss Meynell came to be hit?'

'None at all, I'm afraid. Fact is, when a drive's in progress we're all too busy concentrating on what we're doing to be aware of other people. We're looking and firing high, d'you see? We're safety-conscious, mind. Always follow the sportsman's rules.'

'So Martin Tait tells me. But when you're pumping out shotgun pellets, there's always the possibility that some unfortunate person will get in the way. It happens somewhere every shooting season.'

'But not at Chalcot. Nothing as serious as this, in a hundred and fifty years.' Anguished, Lewis Glaven stood up and paced about his office. 'That it should happen to a watching guest, to my son's girlfriend . . . Never forgive myself, never.'

He came to an abrupt halt in front of Quantrill and resumed his decisive tone.

'Well, Chief Inspector. You must do what you can to establish how it happened. But it was clearly an accident and I must ask you, please, not to apportion any blame.'

Quantrill, already on his feet, raised a heavy eyebrow. 'Why do you say that, sir?'

'Because it would be damned unfair, don't you see? With birds coming over thick and fast, no Gun can be sure where his shot is going to land.'

'I realise that. But the facts will speak for themselves – we can't consider collective responsibility.'

'Nor do I suggest it!' The colour had returned to Lewis Glaven's cheeks. He straightened his shoulders, a country gentleman bristling with honour.

'I am the host of this tragic shooting party,' he said. 'Miss Meynell is my guest, and I hold myself responsible for what happened to her. Solely responsible, you understand?'

16

Martin Tait had made his farewells to the other members of the shooting party. It hadn't taken long. Barclay Dodd and all the dogs had snored at him, Joanna had ignored him, Tweedledum and Tweedledee had merely nodded at him over their dice.

Dorothy Wilson-Brown, though, had treated him almost as a friend. She was evidently glad to talk, discussing her anxiety over Hope Meynell's condition and the shattering effect the accident would have on Will and Lewis. But this made Martin even more uneasily aware of his possible involvement, and he escaped as soon as he decently could.

As he went down the corridor, he caught sight of Lewis

Glaven's housekeeper through the half-open kitchen door. Like the rest of them, she was hanging about waiting for news.

And that reminded him: before Hope was wounded, before Alison was injured, and before the episode with the saboteurs, he had been concerned for young Laura's safety at the shoot.

He raised his voice. 'Is your daughter all right, Mrs Harbord?'

'Laura? Oh yes, thank you, sir.' Eager to talk, Ann Harbord darted out into the corridor, her gypsy ear-rings swinging. Smartly groomed as always, she hadn't a hair out of place; but she seemed almost excited by the drama of the day. Her cheeks didn't need their artificial colour and her eyes were hard and bright.

'Any news of Miss Meynell?' Her voice, respectfully low, emerged almost as a hiss. 'Is she going to make it? Will she live?'

'We can only hope so,' said Martin formally.

'Yes – yes of course, for everyone's sake. Poor Major Will, just as they were going to get engaged . . . Not that she was right for Chalcot, Mr Glaven said so himself. But who'd have thought she would meet with such a terrible accident, poor girl – '

Martin didn't intend to discuss it. 'I was asking about Laura,' he reminded her. 'She watched the shoot this afternoon, and I wanted to be sure she'd got home safely. Is she here now?'

Ann Harbord was instantly evasive. 'Ah, well, she's not actually at *home*. The little madam has been in one of her moods lately, and she went off after lunch taking some clothes with her. She'll be staying with a friend.'

'You mean you haven't seen her since lunch time?' Remembering the shotgun pellets that had been zinging down when Laura disappeared into the bushes, Martin was chilled with concern. 'Has she telephoned? Do you know where she's staying?'

'No, but I see no need to fuss. We had a few words last night, and the silly child's staying away to punish me. That's all.'

That's all?

Martin's mind reeled with anxiety. God, what had happened to the girl? Suppose she'd been lying out there at Belmont all this time, wounded?

He should never have left the ride without checking that she was safe. Was this going to be another tragedy for which he'd feel forever responsible?

But he was too experienced a police officer to panic. There was nothing he could do tonight to ease his conscience over Hope Meynell, but at least he could take immediate action to find Laura Harbord.

'We have to know where she is. Telephone all her friends,' he ordered the startled housekeeper, 'and don't give up until you've spoken to Laura herself. I'm going back to where I last saw her.'

He'd intended to commandeer the first available four-wheel-drive vehicle, but fortunately there was no need for an after-dark expedition. The gamekeeper had just driven up to the back door in the Landrover, and was about to unload it in the illuminated rain.

'Just the man I wanted to see!' said Tait.

Taken by surprise, Len Alger creaked upright. 'Why? What for?' he asked suspiciously.

The fact was that Martin wasn't at all sure he could identify the place where he'd last seen Laura. Not in the darkness, anyway. Besides, all he needed to do was to reassure himself that she was *not* lying hurt out there.

'Have you seen young Laura, since the drive finished?' he demanded.

Len Alger was instantly defensive: 'Who?'

'The housekeeper's daughter. You must know her.'

'What if I do?'

'She was running about in the bushes during the drive, between the beaters and the Guns. You were following the beaters, weren't you? Did you happen to see her, after the shooting stopped?'

'No, I didn't!' Len Alger turned truculent. 'I've got more to do than take notice of bloody kids. She'd no business to be at the shoot anyway. If . . .'

'If what?'

130

Alger, his craggy face half-shadowed by the peak of his cap, seemed not to hear. But evidently he was thinking.

'Tell you what,' he said, in a much more co-operative voice. 'I reckon I *did* see her. When the shooting finished I could hear them poxy saboteurs hollering, and I went to help Mr Glaven get rid of 'em. On the way, I happened to see these two, messing about with each other behind a tree. The Harbord girl and her boyfriend.'

Tait's spirits rose. 'Do you know him – the boyfriend?'

'I know him all right.' The keeper's voice was vicious. 'He's the idle young bugger who's supposed to help me with the pheasants. Darren Jermyn.'

'And you're sure the girl with him was Laura?'

''Course I'm sure. Here, wait a minute . . .'

Len Alger bent stiffly into the Landrover and emerged holding a loop of thick string from which hung a brace of pheasants, a cock and a hen. Each end of the loop was fastened round the neck of a bird, just below the head. Alger smiled an ingratiating smile and held up the pheasants in his left hand, their finely feathered necks elongated by their dangling weight, their long claws extended. Paired by the string, their limp bodies seemed to snuggle together in death.

'Yours, sir,' he said with smarmy civility.

Tait was taken aback. 'Did I shoot these?'

'Don't matter who brought 'em down, sir. It's shooting party tradition, the keeper always hands a brace to each of the Guns at the end of the day.'

The man's horny right hand hovered, half-outstretched for a farewell shake and the hoped-for receipt of a good tip.

Tait looked with repugnance at the birds. Their feathers were still beautiful in death but their heads, flopping down over the string, were cruelly bloodied.

He thought again of Hope Meynell.

'I trust you enjoyed the actual shoot, sir?' the keeper was saying pointedly, thrusting the dead birds towards him. 'Apart of course from the very unfortunate accident – '

Tait curled his lip and turned abruptly away.

'Stuff 'em,' he said.

Next morning, a low sun shone out of a sky washed blue by days of rain. The countryside glowed with the last of the autumn colours – hawthorn berries crimson, bramble leaves rose-pink, oak leaves buff as chamois leather, field maples incandescent.

Douglas Quantrill was in good spirits as he drove through these splendours on his way to Chalcot House. He would have hated to waste such a day as this on paperwork in his office. And though the wounding he was going to investigate was tragic, at least the victim was still alive.

He was sorry for the Glaven family, of course. His over-whelming feeling, though, was relief that it wasn't his daughter who'd been shot. Considering the gravity of Hope Meynell's condition, he took no satisfaction in having been right about the dangers of shooting parties. But Martin Tait had been very subdued when he came to visit Alison last night, so perhaps the arrogant prat had learned something from the experience.

There was a further reason for Quantrill's good humour that morning. His sergeant, Hilary Lloyd, was with him; and just as Alison brightened his domestic life, so Hilary's presence lit up his working hours.

He was no longer infatuated by her, as once he'd been. Her thin dark elegance and occasionally dazzling smile no longer disturbed his dreams. To be honest – he was embarrassed to recall it – he'd probably made a bit of a fool of himself over her. But now, though he still felt a secret joy when he was with her, he prided himself on treating her with nothing more revealing than a slightly rueful affection.

As he drove, he told her what he knew about the shooting.

'Let's hope there's enough forensic evidence to make it clear who fired the shot,' he said. 'If we have to rely on information, we're going to get very little out of the Glavens and their friends.'

'Bloodthirsty lot,' said Hilary. 'Yes, I know – shooting on private land is a lawful activity. I'm a police officer, so I have to uphold their right to do it. But I'm seriously prejudiced against people whose idea of entertainment is to go out and kill birds.'

'People like Martin Tait?'

'*Especially* Martin Tait.'

They shared a snicker at the expense of their future boss. As a countryman, though, Quantrill wasn't prepared to let his sergeant get away with her blanket prejudice against people who shoot.

'Sporting landowners do a lot more for the environment', he said firmly, 'than those who don't shoot. Take the land on either side of this road . . .'

On their left was the outer edge of the Chalcot estate, with its traditionally farmed patchwork of smallish fields bounded by tall old hedges and overtopped by high autumnal woods. It was the kind of countryside Quantrill had grown up in, not only a pleasure to the eye but teeming with wildlife.

On the right of the road, a thousand newly drilled acres sprouting a green designer stubble of winter barley extended towards the horizon. This land was part of the empire of a faceless agri-business company, and the local manager's brief was clearly to maximise profits. Hedges had long since been ripped out, ditches replaced by drainage pipes, ponds filled in and most of the trees felled. Resident wildlife was restricted to whatever worms and insects could survive regular drenchings with pesticide.

'Intensive farming's been the ruination of Suffolk,' Quantrill pronounced, giving his own prejudices an airing.

He saw no reason to admit that traditional farming doesn't pay. He could have explained to Hilary that the only people who can afford to farm organically are those like the Glavens, who don't need to make their living from it. But there was no point in spoiling his argument.

'Is that what you'd prefer for the whole county?' he demanded, jerking his thumb at the unnaturally flattened earth. 'Because that's how it'd be, if it weren't for farmers and landowners who shoot. They're the ones who maintain woods and ponds and hedges. They're the real conservationists. If

133

saboteurs understood anything about wildlife, they'd support game-shooters instead of trying to stop them.'

'Conservationists? How can you say that, when they kill birds for pleasure?' objected Hilary. 'That's what gets to the saboteurs – well, to the protesters, the idealists, anyway. It gets to me, too. I don't understand how you can condone killing of any kind, not when you see the reality of it in our job. You say you hate shotguns, but here you are applauding the people who use them.'

'It's their land management I'm applauding, and their interest in wildlife. They don't shoot because they're bloodthirsty. They simply enjoy exercising their skill with a shotgun.'

'That must be a great comfort to the pheasants . . .'

Quantrill sighed, knowing he could never make her understand. 'Look, I'm in favour of game-shooting because it's traditional. It's part of the pattern of country life. If shooting and hunting and fishing were made illegal, that would be rural England gone.'

Then he added, to tease her: 'Beats me why a townie like you ever came to work in this division.'

'Beats me, too,' said Hilary crossly. 'It's not fondness for country life that keeps me here, I can tell you.'

She had always guarded her privacy but it was rumoured at the nick that she was involved with a doctor from Saintsbury hospital. Quantrill would have liked to know something about the man, preferably to his disadvantage; but as long as she continued to work with him at Breckham Market, he wasn't going to push his luck by making enquiries.

'Now if it had been one of the Guns who was wounded at the shoot,' Hilary meditated aloud, 'there'd have been some justice in it. It's all wrong that it should have been a girl onlooker – but at least it wasn't an innocent young protester.'

They had reached Chalcot village, and Sunday morning bells were ringing out from the church tower. The graveyard wall was overhung with almost-bare lime trees, and the quiet road was slippery with decaying leaves.

Quantrill slowed to a stop, waiting patiently for some elderly church-goers to make their way across from the opposite side

134

of the road. Not all drivers were so considerate, though. A chromed-up Daihatsu Fourtrak backed out abruptly from the driveway of a bungalow next to the butcher's shop, and one old lady almost lost her footing as she scrambled out of its way. The thick-necked driver accelerated off without giving her a glance, to a muttering of police disapproval.

'According to Martin Tait,' said Quantrill, resuming their theme, 'Hope Meynell was as much of an innocent as the youngest protester. It was her first time at a shooting party, and she hated the idea of watching pheasants being killed. She wouldn't have been there at all, if Lewis Glaven hadn't insisted.'

'Oh no!' Hilary was indignant. 'That was downright cruel. Why would he do that?'

'I don't know. It's one of the things we need to find out.'

Quantrill had arranged a rendezvous at 10 a.m. at the gates of Chalcot House, and he was there almost exactly on time. Two members of the scenes-of-crime team, Ed and Mick in their police Landrover, had caught him up in the village and followed his car. Of Martin Tait there was no sign.

Typical, thought Quantrill. He wouldn't put it past him to be lurking round the next corner so that he could emphasise his status by arriving last.

Sure enough, the four detectives had hardly had time to exchange greetings and sniff the crisp air before Tait rolled up. He was wearing his country gentleman outfit, and driving a Range Rover.

Quantrill went to meet him. 'Tired of your BMW, were you? Or is this your second car?'

Tait seemed impervious to the jibe. ''Morning, Doug,' he said. He nodded a greeting to the other men and then went straight to Hilary – they'd known each other since he was a sergeant fresh from police college – and gave her an affectionate off-duty peck on the cheek. It was more than Quantrill had ever presumed to do; but then he didn't belong to the cheek-pecking social classes.

'Good to see you again, Hilary!' said Tait, not at all put off by

135

the coolness of her greeting. 'I've borrowed a four-wheel drive because the track across the estate's too muddy for cars. Of course, if Doug insists on being independent . . .'

Doug didn't insist. He wasn't best pleased to have arrangements made for him, but he had more sense than to risk getting his own car bogged down and having to accept a tow. He drove as far as the yard at the back of Chalcot House and then he and Hilary transferred to the Range Rover for the rest of the journey. The Landrover bumped along the track behind them.

Quantrill had never before been on the Chalcot estate and it was exactly as he'd imagined it – a time warp, a small piece of leafy, traditional England, hidden away behind its high enclosing walls. It was full of pheasants, their copper and bronze and red and green colours echoing the sunlit landscape as they wandered and pecked about.

'Stupid birds,' complained Martin, braking just in time as a cock pheasant decided to strut handsomely across the track in front of his wheels. 'They've no traffic sense at all. I know you disapprove of shooting them, Hilary, but you must have seen plenty of feathered corpses on the roadside. Pheasants are much more likely to get themselves killed playing last across than they are to be shot.'

Martin had had a bad night. He was sure that all the other members of the shooting party were holding him to blame for Hope Meynell's wounding. He would be their natural suspect. For one thing, he was an outsider; for another, he wasn't an experienced game-shooter.

But he'd spent the night going over the scene of the shooting in his mind's eye, and he was sure that his last shot couldn't possibly have reached the place where Hope was found. What was needed, to clear his own conscience as well as to quell rumours, was proof. And thankfully, he could rely on the position of the pegs to provide it.

He'd already explained the theory of a pheasant drive to his passengers, and had just told them how invaluable the pegs were going to be to their investigation. They had reached the edge of Belmont wood, and he had stopped at the entrance to the main ride. It was where the vehicles had been parked the previous afternoon, and the leaf-strewn grass was churned by tyre marks.

He could see some distance up the open ride, to where the hawthorn thicket, its berries bright in the sun, put a bend in the track and blocked the view. The track itself was much more heavily scored than when he'd first seen it, because of the rescue activity that had followed the shooting. Otherwise the ride looked much the same, except that the encroaching shrubs that narrowed the grassy centre had lost a lot of leaf overnight.

And except that the pegs were missing.

His own number five peg, and those of Will Glaven and Joanna Dodd, would be out of sight from here anyway. But numbers one to four ought to be in full view, measured out along the track; and there was no sign of them.

Did that mean his own peg was missing too?

Martin put his foot down and roared along the ride, sending up agitated flocks of fieldfares and redwings from the berried bushes where they were feeding. A few wary pheasants, survivors from yesterday, rocketed up in alarm as he passed.

Ignoring his passengers' complaints about his driving, Martin did a controlled slide round the bend in the track and stopped abruptly.

Ahead of him, the ride stretched at least two hundred yards to the far side of the wood. The bushes where young Laura had hidden were on the right, and the bushes where Alison had tripped and Hope had been shot were on the left. But the pegs that should have been in the centre were missing.

Martin jumped down from the driving seat, ran along the track and tried to discover where his peg had stood. But last night's rain had washed away his footprints, and he couldn't find a single empty cartridge case. It was as if the shoot had never been.

His colleagues, including Mick and Ed, joined him. He was explaining the problem when a bellow of rage issued from the woodland edge.

'What the bloody hell d'you think you're doing? This is private property – you're trespassing. Get out!'

The gamekeeper, rigid with anger, was striding stiffly

towards them out of the bushes. He was carrying a shotgun in both hands, and as he came he cocked it.

Martin waved back the others. 'I know him. I'll deal with him.' He advanced towards the oncoming keeper. 'Put up your gun, Alger,' he called.

The keeper hesitated in mid-stride, peered short-sightedly, and at last recognised him.

'Oh – it's you . . .' He didn't bother with yesterday's 'sir', but he lowered his gun. "T'weren't loaded,' he grumbled, breaking it as proof.

'Just as well,' said Martin. 'I'm Detective Sup – ' He remembered not to advance his promotion within earshot of his colleagues. '. . . Detective Chief Inspector Tait. We're here to examine the scene of the shooting. And what I want to know is, what happened to the pegs?'

Len Alger gave a creaky shrug. 'Same as always. I took 'em up after the shoot and put 'em back in my shed, ready for next time.'

'On your own initiative? Or did someone tell you to?'

'I don't need telling how to do my job!'

'And what happened to the spent cartridges?'

'I collected them an' all, same as usual. Mr Glaven likes the estate to be left clean after a shoot.'

'Look,' said Martin in a more conciliatory tone, 'we need to know exactly where the pegs were sited. Mine was number five. Can you show me where you hammered it in?'

'No, I can't. Mr Glaven said whereabouts he wanted number one, and I stuck the rest in forty yards apart, same as we always do at Belmont. I can't be expected to point out the bloody *spot*.'

Martin made a last attempt to gain the man's co-operation.

'We've got a bit of a problem,' he said. 'Unless we know exactly where the pegs were, we're not going to be able to work out how Miss Meynell came to be shot. And we all want to know that, don't we?'

'Makes no odds to me,' said the keeper. 'You were standing on the peg for half an hour – if you can't remember exactly where it was, how the hell d'you expect me to?'

'Chippy bastard,' muttered Martin as the gamekeeper sloped

138

off. He returned to his colleagues, who were trying not to look amused.

'That's all right,' he said confidently. 'I know how to work out where the pegs were. But first I'll show you where Hope was shot.'

He wasn't sure how far along the ride it was, but he knew he'd have no difficulty in identifying the place. In order to rescue the wounded girl, Lewis Glaven had called up the beaters to slash a wide path through the bushes.

Martin led the others up the path, their boots scrunching on broken branches and through drifts of leaves. Near the woodland edge he pointed out where he had pushed through a shocked mingling of Guns, beaters, pickers-up and saboteurs and had seen Hope Meynell lying in Will's arms. For a moment he fell silent, recalling how her beauty had been masked by blood.

Ed and Mick, in their scenes-of-crime overalls, were already unpacking their equipment and starting work. Shaking his head to clear it, Martin led Quantrill and Hilary back to the ride and up towards the far end. His abortive conversation with Len Alger had reminded him that even though he couldn't locate his own peg, he had a good chance of finding the last one in the line.

He scoured up the ride, and found what he was looking for: an area of grass that had been trampled into mud.

'This is the site of the number seven peg, Joanna Dodd's,' he said. 'The saboteurs crowded round, provoking her, and then I joined her and so did the Glavens. She'd have been standing just about here.'

He marked the spot by sticking a hazel twig into the earth and flagging it with a page torn from his pocket diary.

Hilary was walking round the trampled area. For all her elegance, she was dressed for the job in trench coat and boots. 'Is this from the wrecked video camera?' she said, picking up a chunk of black plastic casing that had been half-trodden into the mud.

'That's it,' agreed Martin. 'No doubt the sabs removed the rest of it, as evidence against Lewis Glaven. He really was an idiot. He could have got away with destroying their film, but not the camcorder as well. He seemed to lose his head completely.'

'Pity about that film,' said Quantrill, 'it might have been useful to us. You didn't by any chance take your own camera to the shoot?'

'I did, but I knew I'd be busy with the gun so I asked Alison to take the photographs. Lewis Glaven wouldn't allow it, though.'

'Sensible man,' said Quantrill. He sounded as though he might be about to make one of his disapproving-prospective-father-in-law comments, so Martin cut him short.

'Shall we get on with the job?'

Impatient to check his own peg, he paced out the distance as the gamekeeper would have done. He flagged Will's peg at forty yards, and his own forty yards further on.

His markers were only estimates, of course: the scenes-of-crime team would be able to identify the peg sites accurately. But as he stood facing the wood the pheasants had flown from, he was confident that he'd got it right within a yard or two. Certainly the landscape seemed familiar enough, given that some of the trees had shed their leaves by the bucketful overnight.

Taking up his shooting stance, he recreated the shot that had been worrying him ever since he'd fired it. Raising an imaginary shotgun at an imaginary pheasant as it overflew the line – arguably low – he swung round to his right and took an imaginary shot. Missing it, he fired the second barrel as the bird went gliding down, and missed again. Then he held his stance.

He had transferred his weight to his right foot and he was now pointing his imaginary gun towards the trees that had been directly behind him. He shifted his gaze to the right, searching the bushes to identify the place where Hope Meynell had been shot.

When he finally caught a glimpse of blue police overalls, up near the trees, they were much further over to his right than he'd realised. He sighed with relief.

He didn't need any measurements to reassure him: his shots would have gone nowhere near Hope. Even if he'd been pointing his gun in that direction, she would have been well out of range. He was in the clear, and forensic science would prove it!

For a moment he felt elated. But then he sobered. As far as he could judge, Hope would have been somewhere opposite pegs six or seven when she fell. The nearest Guns were therefore Will and Joanna; one or other of them would have to bear the responsibility, and that was going to be hard.

It had been quite bad enough for him, an outsider, to feel that he was responsible for accidentally wounding Hope Meynell. But it was going to be a hell of a lot worse either for Will Glaven, who loved her, or for Joanna Dodd, whose social circle would forever suspect her of having taken a jealous shot at her rival.

18

At the back of Chalcot House a breeze was stripping the last of the leaves from the shrubbery, twirling them round the stable yard and bundling them into corners. There were two vehicles in the yard, and both of them had been parked there long enough to be littered with dead leaves.

Chief Inspector Quantrill had arranged that he and Hilary would call on Lewis Glaven, before they left Chalcot, to take his statement. Tait went with them, to enquire after Hope before he went to see Alison. Quantrill had left his own car in the yard, and he was interested that the vehicle parked beside it was the one whose driver they'd disapproved of earlier that morning.

'Ah, the shiny Daihatsu Fourtrak,' said Hilary. She walked round it, amused. 'It doesn't look as though it ever goes off-road, but there are enough extras on it for a safari.'

'D'you know who it belongs to, Martin?' asked Quantrill.

'A man called Brunt. I saw him here yesterday morning. He's a self-important butcher who thinks he's a crack shot. He turned up in shooting gear just as Lewis Glaven was briefing us, and offered to pay to join the shoot. Lewis sent him off with a flea in his ear. He was furious, so red and puffed-up I thought he'd burst.'

'He doesn't seem to have taken permanent offence, anyway,' said Quantrill. 'Go on, Martin, you're the one who's known round here: we'll let you ring the door bell.'

The housekeeper, though gypsy-smart as always, was clearly in a state of some anxiety. Her neck was flushed, her eyes were over-bright, and she fussed conspicuously over the expected visitors.

'Is there any news from the hospital?' asked Tait, as she darted ahead of them to the gun room and threw an unnecessary extra log on the fire.

'Not yet – but no news is good news, isn't it?' Ann Harbord gabbled, attacking the logs with a poker and sending up a shower of sparks. The panelled room was mellow with sunlight, tidied but not yet thoroughly cleaned, with a lingering morning-after scent of cigars, doggy tweeds and whisky.

'Mr Glaven . . .' She paused to take a deep breath in a conspicuous effort to calm her voice. 'Mr Glaven went to the hospital first thing this morning, and he said he hoped not to keep you waiting. Can I offer you coffee? Or something else . . .'

'Coffee will be just right, thank you,' said Quantrill. And then, curious to know more about the Daihatsu driver: 'I'm sure I recognise that Fourtrak out there . . .'

Mrs Harbord was no longer merely flushed, she was definitely flustered.

'It belongs to a – er – a local man. He called to ask after Miss Meynell, so I offered him a cup of coffee. Of course, I wouldn't normally entertain him when Mr Glaven's at home. But in the circumstances, with all the worry . . .'

'It helps to talk to a friend,' supplied Hilary.

'It does indeed!'

The housekeeper gave the sergeant a grateful smile, regained her composure and darted off, ear-rings swinging. When she returned with the coffee tray Tait asked, 'Is Laura home yet?'

It was clear that her daughter's whereabouts were not Ann Harbord's chief consideration. For a second she looked blank.

'Oh – not yet,' she said, elaborately casual. She pushed down the plunger of the cafetière. 'I'm expecting her tonight. Or perhaps after school tomorrow.'

'Have you spoken to her?'

'No . . . But – '

An alarm bell began to ring in Tait's head. Quantrill and Hilary looked up; he stood up: 'Do you know where Laura stayed last night? Have you spoken to anyone who's seen her?'

'No, but – '

'For God's sake, Mrs Harbord,' Tait snapped. 'Your daughter's – what – fifteen years old? Don't you *care* where she is?'

'Of course I care!' The housekeeper's flushed neck darkened from pink to angry red and she poured the coffee with a shaking hand. 'But it's been a dreadful time for Mr Glaven and I've been doing all I can to support him. You told me Laura had been seen with Darren Jermyn after the shoot, so I knew she must be all right.'

'Didn't you do as I said, and ring round Laura's friends?'

'No, not after you'd told me she'd been seen.' Aggrieved, the housekeeper put down the cafetière and appealed to Hilary.

'Laura was being extra difficult, and I finally lost my patience with her. I know what she's doing, she's staying away for the weekend to punish me. Well, I wasn't going to humiliate myself by ringing round after her – you can understand that, can't you?'

Hilary calmed her. 'Do please sit down, Mrs Harbord. Tell us about Darren Jermyn. Is he Laura's regular boyfriend? Would she have spent the night at his house?'

No longer on the defensive, Ann Harbord suddenly seemed to realise that Laura's absence was potentially serious. For the first time, she sounded shaken.

'Laura wouldn't be with Darren – he lodges in the village, and his landlady's very strict. Anyway, their silly affair's finished, and a good thing too. They were all over each other in the summer, but then Laura went off him. He sometimes hangs about looking hopeful, but she's not interested.'

'It was Darren she was seen with yesterday afternoon,' Tait reminded her.

'Well, she still *talks* to him. I saw them talking outside here

143

yesterday morning. But there's none of the lovey-dovey stuff. All she cares about these days is pheasants.' Ann blew her nose resentfully.

'You've been very helpful, Mrs Harbord,' said Quantrill. 'I'm sure there's no cause for alarm, but we'd all like to know exactly where Laura is. Will you please ring round her friends right away, while we're still here? Just to check.'

All three of them smiled reassuringly at Ann Harbord as she retreated. As soon as she'd gone, Quantrill and Hilary looked uneasily at Tait.

'That information about her being seen with the boy after the shoot,' said Quantrill. 'No doubt there's more to it than you let on?'

'Yes. It was the gamekeeper who saw them, and he said they were "messing about with each other".'

'Oh my God . . .' sighed Quantrill, contemplating the worst possible outcome.

But Hilary deplored his inclination to gloom. 'They've been in love before and they could be in love again,' she said. 'Let's be positive for once. Mrs Harbord will find that Laura's been staying with one of her friends, Hope Meynell will make a good recovery – and we shall drink this coffee before it's cold. Now, can we get on with taking Martin's statement?'

As they did so, they heard low voices in the corridor and the opening and closing of the back door. The gun room overlooked the yard, and they saw a squat figure climbing up into the driving seat of the Fourtrak. Mr Brunt the butcher was evidently on his way home.

Half an hour later, when the statement and the supplementary questions and the coffee were all finished, they heard a vehicle crunching up over the gravel. Lewis Glaven's Range Rover came to a stop and he eased himself out wearily, looking as though he'd aged a decade overnight. His two labradors stepped out after him, as subdued as their master.

There could be no doubt about the news he was bringing to his housekeeper. Martin felt his insides knot with dread as he

144

hurriedly opened the door of the room, so that they could all hear.

Lewis Glaven spoke heavily, without any preliminaries.

'Miss Meynell has died.'

'Oh, Mr Glaven . . .' There was a deep and scarcely disguised affection in the housekeeper's voice. 'I am so very sorry . . . And poor Major Will – how has he taken it?'

'Thank you, Mrs Harbord.' Lewis Glaven's own voice was flattened by weariness. 'Will's gone straight to the stables – riding's the best therapy for him. Police still here, are they?'

'Would you like me to send them away? I'm sure you don't want them bothering you at a time like this.'

'No, no, I must talk to them. Might as well get it over. Ask them to bear with me for five minutes. And then coffee for anyone who wants it, please, and perhaps some sandwiches . . .'

'Of course, Mr Glaven!'

The detectives stood tactfully out of sight as he walked on past the open door of the gun room. But Quantrill, glancing back down the corridor towards Mrs Harbord, was greatly intrigued by what he saw.

The sadness in her voice was belied by her expression as her eyes followed Lewis Glaven. It was a shining expression such as Douglas Quantrill had once seen on Molly's face, a very long time ago. He recognised its components immediately.

He was then an over-sexed young fool of twenty-one, in an antique world where condoms were as difficult to come by as willing girls. Telling Molly he loved her had produced the desired effect, but he hadn't reckoned on making her pregnant. The expression was the one she'd worn when Douglas, cornered by her father, had finally agreed to marry her.

That was exactly how Ann Harbord was gazing after Lewis Glaven: with great relief, with love, with happiness, and with an unmistakable gleam of triumph.

When Lewis Glaven entered the gun room, followed by his dogs, he was freshly shaven and brushed. His eyes were heavily

145

bagged and his face was almost as grey as his moustache, but he was clearly making an effort to appear normal. He accepted their condolences and then, a good host as always, offered them a choice of drinks. His housekeeper had already put fresh coffee on the table, and an attractively presented platter of cold roast beef sandwiches.

'To be frank,' Glaven said, standing with his back to the fire beside his recumbent dogs, and swallowing whisky and water, 'Hope's death came as something of a blessing. She'd have been permanently brain-damaged if she'd survived. That doesn't lessen our distress, of course. Nor my son's grief. Nor her father's, poor devil . . .'

'Wasn't her mother there?' asked Hilary.

'Her mother's dead.' Glaven reached absently for one of the crustless sandwiches, filled with thinly sliced rare beef. 'Naturally, I told Meynell that I take full responsibility for what happened. Never forgive myself . . . And I'll never hold another driven shoot at Chalcot. Told the keeper so last night.'

He finished the sandwich, poured himself a second drink, and agreed with Quantrill that he was ready to give his statement. Hilary turned to a new page in her pocket-book. Martin, remembering reluctantly that as a witness he could take no further part in the investigation, made an excuse and got up to go. His host accompanied him to the door of the room.

Martin was badly shaken by Hope's death. Such beauty . . . Such a waste . . . And what must Will Glaven be feeling? What would he himself have felt if the victim had been Alison?

He began to express his sympathy to Lewis Glaven by way of farewell, but his host cut him short.

'Thank you. Thank you, I'll pass on your message to Will.' Glaven gave Martin a penetrating look and a brisk handshake, and told him to see himself out.

It was an anti-climactic departure from Chalcot House, after the hopes Martin had arrived with yesterday. But until he'd been officially cleared of blame for the accident, he could hardly expect a cordial invitation to return. And even then . . .

He drove away feeling low. The recollection that he was going to see Alison didn't cheer him, because he would have to break the news of Hope's death to her and she was bound to be distressed.

It cheered him even less to think that he would then have to endure Sunday lunch with his prospective mother-in-law.

Lewis Glaven's account of the circumstances leading up to the shooting tallied with Martin Tait's, given that he had witnessed them from a different peg.

'And you all stay on your pegs, do you?' asked Quantrill. 'You don't move away to get a better shot?'

Glaven looked shocked. 'Certainly not. That's one of the principles of shooting driven game. Besides, it's a question of safety. If people move about, they're liable to be hit.'

'I'd have thought that was a good reason', said Quantrill bluntly, 'for *not* taking an inexperienced young woman to watch a shoot at close quarters.'

Lewis Glaven sighed, as if despairing of making him understand. 'It's traditional, d'you see. A traditional part of English country house life.'

Hilary was trying not to look amused at this reversal of Quantrill's authority on country matters. He declined to meet her eye.

'It's also traditional, I believe,' he said, 'for the Guns to drink alcohol during a shoot.'

'Certainly. Damn cold, waiting about. Need something to warm you up. Besides, alcohol's a relaxant. It makes for better shooting.'

'But not for safer shooting.'

Lewis Glaven's voice took on an irritated edge. 'We pride ourselves on safe shooting, here at Chalcot. All the Guns yesterday were experienced shots.'

He said it with complete conviction. There was nothing in his tone or his look to suggest that he was excluding Martin Tait from his warranty. But Quantrill realised well enough that the exclusion was implied.

To state it would of course point to Martin as the Gun most likely to have been careless enough to shoot Hope Meynell.

147

Lewis Glaven was clearly too courteous a host to suggest any such thing. Even so, the unspoken suggestion floated in the air of the room, as tenuous and pervasive as smoke from the log fire.

Whatever Quantrill himself felt about Martin, this was an occasion for closing ranks.

'Chief Inspector Tait is well aware of the importance of safe shooting,' he said. 'He's an excellent shot on the police firing range – but as you know, he'd never before been to a shoot. I can't help wondering why you invited him to a private shooting party.'

'Not for his own sake,' said Lewis Glaven promptly. 'Perfectly presentable and agreeable, of course. But it was his girlfriend I particularly wanted here this weekend.'

'My daughter?'

'Didn't know who she was at the time, but yes. I'd met them together at the County Show, d'you see. Charming girl, and rather like my son's girlfriend – not used to shooting, either of them. That's why I asked Tait to bring her, to keep Hope company. Your daughter did an excellent job. Very grateful to her.'

'Thank you – now I understand.' Quantrill sighed: 'Alison will be grieved that it's ended like this. She was saying last night that if only she hadn't tripped, she would have caught up with Hope and possibly saved her.'

'She mustn't blame herself in any way,' said Lewis Glaven. 'Thank God she wasn't caught by the shot, too.'

'We're all thankful for that,' said Hilary. She had been checking through her notes, and now she came up with another question.

'Did you change the placing of the Guns for that last drive, Mr Glaven? Chief Inspector Tait said that Mr Barclay Dodd should have been at the peg on his left, but your son arrived instead. Did you arrange that for Hope's benefit?'

'Yes, I did. Didn't think she'd enjoy the shooting, d'you see. By putting Will on the peg next to Tait, I ensured that the two young women would at least be neighbours. Moral support, and so forth.'

Hilary smiled at him with apparent appreciation. 'That was

148

very considerate. Obviously you did all you could to make the shoot less unpleasant for her.

'But what I don't understand,' she added, losing the smile, 'is why you thought it necessary to take Hope Meynell to the shoot at all. You say you "didn't think she'd enjoy" it. Our information is that she was dreading the shoot. Wouldn't it have been even more considerate of you to let her stay away?'

Lewis Glaven stared at the sergeant for a moment, his jaw tightening, his moustache bristling with annoyance. Then he turned to Quantrill. 'That,' he said stiffly, 'is something more easily explained by one father to another.'

Hilary closed her notebook and stood up. 'I have to talk to Mrs Harbord,' she said. 'Excuse me.' She walked quickly to the door of the room, but Glaven reached it first and held it open for her with a distant courtesy.

Quantrill eased the tension by helping himself to one of the housekeeper's sandwiches, and found that they were as delicious as they looked. Molly's cold roast beef was cardboard-brown and in desperate need of pickled onions; Mrs Harbord's rare pink beef was a revelation, tender and juicy and full of flavour. The sandwiches almost tasted of loving care, as though she expended on her employer all the emotional energy she failed to give her daughter.

Lewis Glaven poured coffee for both of them. 'Tricky young woman, your sergeant,' he commented with disapproval.

'She's very good at her job,' said Quantrill. 'And her question is mine, too. Tradition's all very well – I'm in favour of it myself – but neither of us can understand why you wanted Hope Meynell to go to the shoot when you knew she would hate it. As one father to another . . .?'

'Ah yes.' Lewis Glaven looked keenly at Quantrill. 'Tell me,' he said, 'are you entirely happy about the relationship between your daughter and young Tait?'

Quantrill hesitated for a moment. They were sitting on either side of the table, and he decided to put his cards on it.

'Professionally,' he said, 'I respect Martin Tait. But does a father ever feel that any man is good enough for his daughter?'

'My own feelings exactly. Wouldn't have chosen either of my sons-in-law. Different with a son, of course. No question of

149

Hope Meynell not being "good enough" for Will – charming girl. But not right for Chalcot, d'you see. It wouldn't suit her. Will needs a wife who understands country living, a young woman who can handle dogs and horses, and doesn't mind a bit of muck.'

'So what were you trying to do? Frighten Hope Meynell off?'

'Not "frighten" her, good God no. That would be indefensible. Didn't want Will to persuade her to marry him under false pretences, though. Unfair to the girl, to let her think that life at Chalcot was going to be all country walks and cosiness.'

Quantrill nodded, half-convinced. 'Even so, a shoot was bound to be a horrifying experience for her. Wasn't it a cruel way of making your point?'

'Possibly,' conceded Lewis Glaven. 'Being cruel in order to be kind, perhaps . . .'

He stood up and walked restlessly about the room, a frown of distress on his face. 'Wish to God it hadn't ended like this, of course. Can't tell you how bitterly I regret it. But that's all hindsight. At the time, it seemed an ideal way of showing the girl that she wouldn't enjoy living at Chalcot.'

He stopped pacing and looked straight at Quantrill, his frown replaced by a challenging look.

'Now then. As one father to another, if you had an equally effective way of sorting out your daughter's boyfriend, wouldn't you take it? Eh?'

'Like a shot,' Quantrill admitted.

In the circumstances, as he realised immediately afterwards, that hadn't been the most tactful way of putting it.

19

Sergeant Lloyd, calling on Mrs Harbord in her kitchen, had found the housekeeper in a strange mood. Her eyes had an exultant shine but her expression, as she stood riffling through the telephone directory, was a mixture of worry and anger.

'No luck with Laura's friends?' asked Hilary.

'Not so far. I've spoken to one girl I know of, in the village, and she's given me some other names. But either they haven't seen Laura, or there's no reply.'

'What about Darren Jermyn?'

'I rang his lodgings. His landlady says he didn't sleep there last night – she hasn't seen him since yesterday morning. She thinks he might have gone to his own home for the weekend, though he hadn't said anything about it. I've been ringing his home, at Brocklesford, but there's no one there.'

Hilary's insides took an apprehensive dip, but she spoke reassuringly. 'Families often go out for the day on Sundays, don't they? There'll be a better chance of catching them this evening. But don't bother with Darren any more, I'll contact him.'

'Ooh, will you?' Ann Harbord, her gypsy ear-rings swinging, turned to Hilary with eager relief. 'Oh, I shall be so grateful. Look, here's a list of Laura's friends' names, with question-marks where I couldn't get through. Thank you *ever* so much for taking over.'

Hilary stared at the woman in astonishment. Ann Harbord was transformed. Her worried frown had disappeared, her lips were no longer tight with annoyance. It was beyond belief, considering that she had no idea where her daughter was, but she looked almost happy.

'*Mrs Harbord*,' said Hilary, trying to get through to her. 'Laura is only fifteen – you can't just abandon your concern.'

Ann Harbord flushed, all the way up from her neck to the sharp-edged fringe of her black-dyed hair. 'Of course I'm still concerned,' she protested. 'I've done everything possible to find her – what else can I do?'

'Most mothers,' said Hilary in a carefully controlled voice, 'regardless of what the police were doing, would want to go on ringing round their daughters' friends until they'd spoken to all of them.'

'Most mothers', retorted Mrs Harbord, 'live in their own houses and are at liberty to use the telephone as much as they like. This is Mr Glaven's house. My job is to look after his interests, not my own.'

Hilary looked at her in disbelief. 'Do you mean that you haven't even told him your daughter's missing?'

'I didn't want to bother him.'

'For Heaven's *sake*,' Hilary protested. 'The feudal system's finished, even on an estate like this! When Mr Glaven knows that Laura's missing, he'll expect you to drop everything else until she's found. Haven't you any transport? Can't you go and call on her friends?'

'Yes, I've got transport. Mr Glaven kindly gives me the use of a car. But I can't just go out, not when he and Major Will are so upset. I don't yet know whether they'll want lunch, or whether there'll be any guests for supper . . .'

Her voice was querulous with self-justification. Despairing of getting any action out of her, Hilary spoke more kindly.

'Would it help if *I* told Mr Glaven about Laura?'

'Oh no!' Mrs Harbord became agitated. 'I don't want him disturbed in any way, not when he's got Miss Meynell's accident on his mind. He's a wonderful employer – I'm so lucky to work for him.'

'I see. So what you're telling me,' said Hilary, 'is that your job is more important to you than your daughter.'

Ann Harbord considered the matter.

'In the long run,' she said simply, 'yes, it is.

'Laura will be back,' she explained, 'I'm sure of it. The fact is, though, she'll be leaving home in a few years' time anyway. But with Major Will not getting married after all, he and his father are going to need me. I'll be able to stay here now, and look after Mr Glaven for the rest of his life!'

Her eyes were exultant. Even when Hilary made the requests that chill the hearts of most parents – to look at the missing child's room, to be given last-seen-wearing details, to take away a photograph – Ann Harbord seemed insulated by happiness.

Lewis Glaven already knew that his housekeeper's daughter was missing. The chief inspector had told him, at the end of their discussion.

'Good God,' said Glaven with concern. 'Hasn't the child been seen since she tried to stop the shoot?'

'Your gamekeeper saw her, immediately after the shooting stopped. He told Martin Tait that she was with his assistant, Darren Jermyn.'

Lewis Glaven's face cleared. 'Ah, that's all right, then. Thought for a moment that you meant she could be lying shot, somewhere up at Belmont. Couldn't bear a second tragedy.'

'Even so,' said Sergeant Lloyd, who had quietly re-entered the gun room, 'we're concerned to know Laura's whereabouts. Her mother hasn't been able to get any telephone information from her friends.'

'Has Mrs Harbord spoken to Darren?' said Quantrill.

'He seems to have disappeared, too. That may be a good sign, of course. Some of Laura's clothes are missing, as well as the old bicycle she uses, so she must have planned to go away. Darren might have decided to go with her.'

'Quite possibly,' said Quantrill, for the benefit of Lewis Glaven. 'But until we're sure of that . . .'

He had been thinking back to the domestic murder he and Hilary had dealt with earlier that week, when a jealously possessive husband had fired a shotgun at his disaffected wife. *I loved her so much*, the man had said as he wept over her body. And Quantrill hadn't doubted it, because every experienced detective knows that assault and even murder are often powered by love.

True, they didn't yet know anything about Darren Jermyn's character. Perhaps, like Quantrill himself, Darren wasn't possessive. Perhaps his love for Laura wasn't strong enough to drive him to desperation when she no longer returned it.

But there were those other statements to be considered. *They were all over each other in the summer*, Mrs Harbord had said. *Then Laura went off him.*

Yet, according to Tait, the gamekeeper had seen them just after the shoot, *messing about with each other behind a tree.*

Was that 'messing about' voluntary, on Laura's part? Or was it a preliminary to a second tragedy, more horrific than the accidental shooting that Lewis Glaven had feared?

Quantrill stood up. There were routine procedures to be gone through, and the sooner the better.

'With your permission, Mr Glaven, we'll make a search of the

153

area where Laura was last seen. I'll raise as many police officers as I can, but we're going to run out of daylight before they've finished. Sorry to ask for your help, when you've your own tragedy to contend with, but – '

'You'll need more searchers, eh?' Lewis Glaven stood too, gladdened by the prospect of useful activity. 'I'll tell my game-keeper to round up yesterday's beaters. Ideal men for the job. I'll come as well, of course – only too glad to be able to help.'

Quantrill had planned, as he drove through Chalcot village first thing that morning, that he would give Hilary a proper Sunday lunch at the Dun Cow. It was an attractive old pub, its grey bricks crimsoned at this time of the year with Virginia creeper. It had as good a reputation for food as any in the area, and he'd been looking forward to sharing a long leisurely meal with her.

In the event, by the time he had organised the setting up of the search party, and Hilary had interviewed Darren Jermyn's landlady, all the restaurant tables at the Dun Cow had already been taken. But Hilary said – enigmatic as always – that she'd promised to cook a meal that evening, anyway, and she'd be perfectly happy just to eat a bowl of soup in the bar. It wasn't Quantrill's idea of Sunday lunch, with or without her company. But at least it gave him a retrospective justification for having eaten more than one beef sandwich at Chalcot House.

Hilary found a vacant bar table for two, and Quantrill fetched a glass of wine for her, and a pint of his favourite Adnams bitter. Space under the small round table was cramped. As he fitted his long legs under it, his knee accidentally pressed her thigh, sending his pulse-rate leaping.

'Sorry!'

He moved immediately, and she gave him a disturbingly complex half-smile. It acknowledged that the contact hadn't been deliberate, but it also recognised with wry appreciation that he wasn't sorry in the least. He was sure, too, that he detected a reciprocal spark in her eye. But then she looked away, and wasted the rest of her smile on the assistant barman who brought their soup.

Quantrill's knee was still tingling, in imagination anyway,

from the contact. But the assistant, an amiable amateur, had omitted to bring any spoons. In the business of signalling to him and being provided with what he seemed to consider a novel requirement – 'There y'go,' he said, humouring them. 'Chiz.' – Quantrill had time to recover his breath and his wits.

'Did you get any useful information from Darren's landlady?' he asked.

'Not much that Mrs Harbord hadn't already told us. The boy biked to work yesterday morning, as usual, but he doesn't seem to have taken any spare clothes so he can't have planned to stay away. There's still no reply from his home telephone number. I thought I'd go there this afternoon.'

'I'd like us both to have a word with Will Glaven first,' said Quantrill. 'Until we get the forensic report on Hope Meynell, we can't usefully do much more about the shooting. But though I can understand, now, why Lewis Glaven wanted Hope to go to the shoot, I'm damned if I can understand why Will inflicted it on her.'

'According to Martin, there seemed to be some kind of question mark over their relationship.'

'That's why I want to talk to Will as soon as possible. He should have finished his ride by the time we get back to the house.' Quantrill looked at his watch and then – mindful not to slurp – polished off his soup.

'After we've seen Will Glaven,' he said, 'we'll concentrate on young Laura. I'll go over to Belmont wood and check the progress of the search party, while you track down Darren Jermyn. When you find him, bring him in.'

The original stables at the back of Chalcot House had been replaced in the late nineteenth century by a larger block, built on the far side of the shrubbery downwind of the Glavens' residence.

That was where Quantrill and Hilary found Will Glaven, mucking out the brick-walled stable yard. For a few moments they stood at its entrance, watching him as he forked up a reeking pile of straw with manic energy.

He was no longer a laid-back cavalry officer in perfectly cut sporting tweeds, but a dishevelled stable hand in a battered cap, dirty old sweater and breeches. His clothes were dark with sweat, his own and the horse's. As he worked, head down, steam rose from his body and mingled in the cold air with steam from the heap of muck.

His black labrador lay outside a half-open loose box, from which came the occasional clop of a hoof as a weary horse shifted on clean straw. The dog, nose on tired paws, was watching Will, who was himself clearly exhausted.

'Once he stops working, he'll collapse,' said Hilary.

'I'll steer him into that tack room over there,' said Quantrill. 'He'll have leathers to clean, but at least he can sit down on the job.'

He walked across the yard in full view of Will Glaven, but even so he had to touch the man's arm to gain his attention. Looking dazed, Will stood rocking on his feet as the chief inspector introduced himself and his sergeant.

'You have our sincere sympathy,' said Quantrill. 'My daughter Alison's, too. But what I reckon you could do with at the moment,' he added, holding up a four-pack he'd brought from the pub, 'is a beer.'

Will Glaven blinked in surprise, and then muttered his agreement. He sluiced his hands and his handsome sweat-streaked face under an outside tap, wiped his face on the sleeve of his sweater and his hands on the seat of his breeches, and shambled wearily where Quantrill led.

The tack room was a shadowy, cobwebby place where saddles and bridles and reins belonging to past generations of the Glaven family hung, slowly mouldering, from the roof trusses. Standing on the grimy brick-paved floor were racks that held the tack in current use, as well as saddle cloths and rugs. There was a good smell of hide and saddle soap, overlaid by pungent horse sweat on the tack that Will had just been using.

He sat down abruptly on a low bench and took the can of beer the chief inspector handed him. Hilary pushed aside a dusty rug to make space for herself on another bench, and Quantrill leaned against a rack. They both watched Will as he emptied the can with long thirsty gulps.

'Thanks,' he said, 'I needed that.'

He crumpled the empty can in his hands and stared, unseeing, at the brick-paved floor. His labrador, which had padded in after him, put its head on his knee and gazed up at him with concern.

'Most of the time,' Will went on, absently fondling the dog's ears, 'I can't believe Hope's dead. It's as though I'm having a terrible nightmare – but I survive it by clinging to the thought that when I wake up, everything will be all right. Then I realise I *am* awake, and I know it's true . . .'

The dog whined softly, put its paws on his knee and licked his face. Will seized it in a great hug. 'Oh, Boris,' he groaned, burying his face in its ruff, 'you old fool . . .'

Quantrill waited for a few moments while master and dog comforted each other, and then cleared his throat.

'Another beer?'

Will Glaven gave a long shuddering sigh. 'Sorry,' he said, releasing the dog and reaching for the proffered can. 'Good boy, Boris – lie down.'

'Don't let us stop you from cleaning your tack,' said Hilary. Will sighed again, this time with more composure, and took another drink. Then he got up to collect a tin of saddle soap, rags and brushes, and began to work on a sweat-dark bridle. As he worked, he talked.

'Hope was actually *afraid* of Boris, you know. Can you believe it? He's such a soppy dog, with the gentlest mouth for picking up pheasants, but she couldn't bring herself to touch him. And when I brought her down to the stables, she wouldn't even come into the yard.'

If the situation hadn't been so tragic, Hilary would have laughed at his puzzled incomprehension. For a detective, encounters with stenches are part of the job; in comparison with a decomposing body, say, she found the smell of the stables positively healthy. But their ammoniac reek was powerful, and it was hardly surprising that Hope Meynell hadn't wanted to linger.

'It sounds as though she simply wasn't used to animals,' said Hilary tactfully.

'I s'pose not,' Will conceded. He sighed once more. 'Every girl I've ever known has loved animals. I grew up with Joanna

Dodd, who exercises my mare for me when I'm away, and she's passionate about dogs and horses. She's the kind of woman I expected I'd eventually marry. I never imagined I'd fall in love with someone who knew nothing at all about country life. But Hope was so *beautiful*, you see . . . I wish to God I'd never taken her to that bloody shoot.'

'As a matter of interest,' said Quantrill mildly, 'why did you take her to the shoot? Wasn't it a bit hard on the girl?'

'It was my father's idea, not mine. I brought Hope here for the first time at Easter, and Dad and I had a row about her afterwards. He had nothing against her personally, of course, but he said she wouldn't be right for Chalcot.'

'Wasn't that fair comment?' said Quantrill, with fellow-feeling for a beleaguered father.

'At the time, yes . . . but I was sure she'd fit in when she got used to our way of life. Anyway, I was in love with Hope, so it didn't matter what the old man thought. As it happened, when I told him I was going to marry her he was surprisingly reasonable. He invited her for this weekend, and said he'd arrange a shooting party so the neighbours could meet her. I agreed to it just to humour him.'

'Didn't it occur to you that a shoot might put Hope off country life for good?' said Hilary.

Will Glaven took a swig of beer while he considered the matter.

'Not really,' he said with baffled honesty. 'I thought she'd accept it, you see, just as I was sure she'd eventually get to like the animals. I knew Hope was worried, yesterday, but I thought it was because of the problem over her mother.'

'Her mother?' Quantrill was puzzled. 'I understood she was dead.'

'Yes. Hope told me, before I met her father, that her mother died last year. No details. But on the way here on Friday, she said there was something she wanted me to know before we became engaged. Apparently her mother had some kind of mental illness, and she died in a psychiatric hospital. Hope hadn't told me before because she was afraid I'd be frightened off. Not that I was, of course – '

Hilary quickly intervened.

'I used to be a nurse, before I joined the police,' she said. 'I spent six months on a psychiatric ward. Hope was brave and honourable to tell you, but mental illness is much more common than she probably realised. There's no stigma attached to it now.'

Will gave a bleak laugh. 'My father wouldn't have seen it like that. Not that I had any intention of telling him, because Hope and I . . .'

He paused, his eyes tightly closed and his fist pressed hard against his mouth. His other hand, going out to grip the edge of the bench, knocked over the half-empty beer can. It fell to the floor with a clonk and the remains of the beer frothed out, washing the bricks and carrying dusty debris in runnels along the cracks between them.

Will swallowed his emotion. 'We both very much wanted children,' he continued in an uneven voice. 'If my father had known about Hope's mother, he would've assumed her illness was hereditary. He'd have made one hell of a fuss about our getting married, and I wasn't going to put up with that.'

'The news must have come as a bit of a shock to you, even so,' said Quantrill.

'It did threaten to put a cloud over the weekend,' Will admitted. 'But only because Hope wouldn't be convinced that I truly wasn't bothered by it. She was so . . .'

The handsome contours of his face crumpled, ageing him instantly. 'Oh God . . . I can't understand how she came to be shot. If she had to bolt anywhere, the woods behind us ought to have been perfectly safe. We had a new Gun with us, of course . . .'

Then his frown cleared and he stood up, the well-mannered cavalry officer surfacing. 'I'm sorry,' he said: 'Martin Tait's one of yours, isn't he?'

He hung the cleaned bridle on a hook and set to work on his saddle. 'I'm not trying to blame Martin,' he said, 'or anyone else. I should have been looking after Hope, and I failed her. I blame no one for the accident except myself.'

'Your father says the same thing,' said Quantrill. 'That he blames himself, I mean.'

'Of course he does,' said Will Glaven.

He used the superior everybody-ought-to-know-it tone that never failed to annoy Quantrill when Tait used it. But coming from the heir to the Chalcot estate, it had an authentic ring. Will's response was simply an inbred acknowledgement that privilege entails responsibility.

'I ought to have been watching Hope's reaction,' he said, 'instead of trying to impress her by shooting high pheasants. I didn't realise she'd bolted, until she was half-way to the wood. I should have gone after her, of course. But I saw young Laura deliberately putting herself in danger and I knew I had to stop the firing. Is the child all right, by the way?'

'As far as we know,' said Hilary quickly. Will Glaven had enough grief already, without being burdened by Laura's disappearance.

When they returned to Quantrill's car, his radio indicator was flashing. The operations room was trying to contact him with a message.

Two police officers, driving along the minor road that skirted the Chalcot estate on their way to join the search team, had found a woman's bicycle. It was an old model, propped up against the wall of the estate not far from a gap which had once been blocked by barbed wire. The wire, though, had been cut and pushed back.

Fastened behind the saddle of the bike was a sports bag containing clothes and a few personal possessions. And written on the bag with a green felt-tipped pen was the name Laura Harbord.

20

It was no longer a kindness to conceal Laura's disappearance from Will Glaven.

Quantrill returned to the tack room to tell him. Will – instantly anxious, and as glad as his father to have something positive to do – volunteered to help in the search. He took Quantrill up to Belmont wood in one of the estate Landrovers, while Hilary drove the chief inspector's car to Darren Jermyn's house.

Up at Belmont, the search for Laura was under way in the waning light of the November afternoon. Vehicles of every kind were parked in the muddy ride, and the line of searchers included police officers, estate workers, and yesterday's beaters with their dogs.

They were working from the far end of the ride, where the saboteurs had made their entry, and taking in the places where Laura had last been seen. The line extended from just inside the woodland edge, down through the bushes to the open grass of the ride. Movement was necessarily slow. Progress was marked by curses from searchers snared by brambles, the eruption of flocks of fieldfares disturbed yet again while they were feeding on berries, and an occasional exasperated *kurr-kuk* from a harassed pheasant.

Will Glaven immediately joined the line of searchers. His father was there already; so was Martin Tait.

Martin had asked to be kept informed, and Quantrill had rung home to let him know that he was setting up the search. He knew that Martin would join him, if only to avoid the after-lunch tedium of keeping Alison company in the presence of her mother.

What Quantrill had expected was that as soon as Martin arrived, he would be his usual exasperating self and rehearse the role of deputy head of the county CID. But it seemed that he'd done the man an injustice. Martin was greatly concerned for young Laura, and was now fighting his way anxiously through the bushes with the rest of the searchers. And alongside Martin was Quantrill's lanky eighteen-year-old son, Peter.

He's only trying to notch up a bit of credit, thought his father irritably. Molly had always spoiled the boy, and more so since the motor-bike accident that had smashed his legs and nearly cost him his life. In Quantrill's experience, any offer of help from Peter was a signal that he was about to ask for something, usually money. *He'll be wheedling a tenner out of Martin before the afternoon's over*.

But though he wouldn't admit it, he was both pleased and

161

touched to see his son giving up a free afternoon in order to join the search. Peter was handicapped in the rough by his reconstructed legs, but he was struggling gamely to keep up with the others. Perhaps, conceded Quantrill, it wasn't only Martin he'd done an injustice to.

The uniformed sergeant in charge of the search joined him to report: as yet there was no sign of Laura.

One of the problems was that the undergrowth at the woodland edge, and in the ride, had already been disturbed during yesterday's shoot. The beaters, having worked their way through the wood during the drive, had emerged from it when the shooting stopped and had pressed on through the bushes to reach the open ride. There had been a lot of trampling about, all over the area.

Today, said the sergeant, the gamekeeper had been in no doubt when he'd pointed out the place behind a tree where he had seen Laura with Darren Jermyn. But then, he knew the woods inside and out. There was certainly enough in the way of broken twigs and crushed vegetation to indicate that someone had been in that place. But there was no evidence to link it with Laura.

The search would soon be halted because dusk was already gathering among the trees. Out in the ride, though, there was still enough light for Quantrill to cross to the other side and take a thoughtful look at the place where Hope Meynell had fallen.

Was it simply a coincidence that one girl who was staying at Chalcot House had been shot yesterday, while another had disappeared? Or was there some possible connection between the two incidents?

Certainly there had been a lot going on at that shooting party. It seemed to have drawn together a great many people – approaching fifty in total, by all accounts – with a diversity of aims and intentions. And that in itself was curious, considering that it was a private party held on a small estate in deepest Suffolk.

It was the presence of the protesters that puzzled Quantrill. Hunting, whether of fox or hare, is liable to attract saboteurs because the date, time and place of every meet is published in the local newspaper for the benefit of genuine followers. But shoots are always private occasions and are never publicised.

Perhaps some of the young protesters, the idealists, were friends of Laura Harbord. But if she'd asked for their support, why hadn't they joined her when she ran out in front of the guns?

As for the saboteurs Martin Tait had encountered, Laura was most unlikely to have known them. But this shoot had been arranged at only two days' notice, so how else had they heard about it?

Someone connected with the Chalcot estate must have spread the word. But was it done purely out of concern for wildlife – or out of malice? And did the invasion have any bearing on either the shooting of Hope Meynell or the disappearance of Laura Harbord?

The only way to get any answers would be to interview everybody who was present at the shoot. And that meant not only the Guns and beaters and pickers-up, but every single protester and saboteur as well.

Sergeant Lloyd, meanwhile, had driven to Darren Jermyn's home in Brocklesford, a village on the other side of Breckham Market.

The Jermyns lived near the village centre, in one of a haphazard row of dwellings dating from the sixteenth to the eighteenth century. After what must have been a great deal of hard work they had modernised their home so that its age and original construction were completely obscured, and they were clearly proud of the result.

Both of Darren's parents worked in the town, Mick Jermyn as foreman at a builder's yard, Brenda as a check-out operator at Sainsbury's. When Hilary arrived, the two of them had just returned from a Sunday morning visit to a car boot sale. The smell of crispy roast duck, fried rice, sweet and sour pork and beansprouts wafted out of the living-room as soon as Mrs Jermyn opened the front door, indicating that they'd come home via Breckham Market's Chinese takeaway.

A homely couple, with no reason to think that their youngest son was not at Chalcot, they had just settled down to eat their late lunch in armchair comfort. Mick, trying to conceal his vexation at being disturbed, stopped eating and muted the television programme as soon as his wife brought in their caller. But they were both so rattled by the news that Darren hadn't returned to his lodgings the previous night that Mick put aside his tray, with its foil dishes and beer can, and got up to switch off the set completely.

Hilary saw no point in alarming them at this stage, and suggested that Darren had probably stayed overnight with a friend. She was looking for him, she said, simply as a possible witness to an incident on the Chalcot estate.

'Please don't let me spoil your meal,' she added, accepting Brenda's offer of a mug of tea and a piece of prawn cracker. 'There's nothing worse than a cold Chinese, is there?'

Between mouthfuls, the Jermyns explained that they hadn't seen their son for at least a month. But that hadn't worried them, said Brenda, because Darren's temporary gamekeeping job kept him hard at work seven days a week. And no bad thing, either, Mick pronounced. Far better for him to be doing an honest job rather than mooching about the streets unemployed, like a lot of boys his age.

Darren had been lucky, too, in being found lodgings in Chalcot village. They'd visited him there a couple of times, and though it wasn't exactly comfortable – his landlady was a terror for tidiness – he was being looked after well enough. A bit of discomfort would do him no harm, said his father; make him appreciate his home.

He was a good lad, but not where keeping in touch was concerned, so his mother rang him once a week. She'd last spoken to him the previous Sunday evening. He hadn't said anything to her about planning to visit a friend.

But then, what with working so hard and being stuck out at Chalcot with only his mountain bike for transport, he hadn't much chance of seeing his mates. To tell the truth, he hadn't bothered with them since last spring, when he'd found a girlfriend. Yes, Laura Harbord. He'd brought her home once or twice during the summer, and she seemed a nice girl.

They were much too young to be serious, of course, but there: they were in love, the pair of them. Darren was so taken up with her that he'd stuck photographs of her all over his newly decorated bedroom. When he left home he'd pulled off the photos and ruined the emulsion, and his mother had told him sharply that he needn't think he could do that kind of thing at his landlady's.

It was solely on Laura's account that Darren had wanted the job at Chalcot. Brenda didn't know what, if anything, had happened between them after he'd gone to live there. Darren usually sounded depressed when she rang him, but she'd put it down to hard work and homesickness. He didn't tell her much, except what a slave-driver the old gamekeeper was.

He did like the pheasants, though. He certainly sounded happier when he talked about them. And he seemed to enjoy going after pigeons and carrion crows with the shotgun he'd been given for his work. But his mother hadn't liked him having a shotgun at his age, and she'd told him to be careful what he was doing with it because accidents could so easily hap –

Mick Jermyn looked up, a forkful of crispy roast duck half-way to his mouth. 'I'd forgotten about that blasted shotgun,' he said slowly.

They stared at each other, appalled by their imaginings. Hilary stared too, equally appalled, though for a different reason.

Brenda rose to her feet, clutching her tray for support. She was totally unconcerned that her plate slid off it and deposited soggy beansprouts on the carpet.

'If my Darren is missing,' she said to Hilary, her voice rising with panic, 'he could've been in a shooting accident. He could be lying out there in the woods, now, bleeding to death!'

Hilary stood too, and put a reassuring hand on her arm.

'No,' she said firmly, 'Darren is safe. There was a shooting party at Chalcot yesterday, but he was seen *after* the shooting finished. It was stopped by a crowd of young protesters – perhaps he knew them and decided to go off with them. He'll turn up in his own good time. Don't worry about him, I'm quite sure he's unharmed.'

165

But that, thought Hilary as she left, was more than she had reason to feel about Laura Harbord.

Sergeant Lloyd went straight back to Chalcot village, where Darren Jermyn lodged in one of the grey brick Victorian dwellings that had been built for workers on the estate. Mrs Flatt, his elderly widowed landlady, was disapprovingly concerned when she heard that the boy was missing. Hilary reassured her as she had reassured his parents, and then asked if she could take a look at Darren's room.

The afternoon had almost gone and Mrs Flatt had to switch on the light, which was provided by one shaded bulb dangling from the high ceiling. The room was grudgingly heated, and furnished with more emphasis on polished wood than comfort. There was very little evidence of occupation except a portable television set, which could well have been brought by Darren himself.

'It's very . . . tidy,' said Hilary. She was looking for some evidence of an obsessive affection for Laura, but there was nothing at all on display, let alone any photographs of the girl.

'I won't have untidiness,' said Mrs Flatt. 'That's what I told him and his parents when he arrived. There's plenty of room in that wall cupboard, I said, and if he doesn't put everything away before he goes out to work I shall want to know the reason why.'

'May I?' said Hilary, quickly opening the door of the cupboard before Mrs Flatt could object. The interior was crammed with a jumble of clothes and teenage male belongings, but while Darren's landlady tutted over them, Hilary found what she was looking for.

Darren had simply transferred his picture gallery from his bedroom walls at home to the inside of Mrs Flatt's white-painted cupboard door. Some of the photographs were school groups, formal and informal, but most of them had been taken individually.

From all of them, a girl of about fifteen with a waterfall of fair hair looked out at whoever opened the cupboard door. The

166

season was always summer. Sometimes posed, sometimes unaware, she expressed a range of attitude and emotion: here she was pensive, there she was alert, here she clowned, there she was tired of being photographed; but more often than not she was either laughing or smiling directly at the photographer, and her eyes expressed an unequivocal love.

'Just look what the dratted boy's done!' Mrs Flatt complained. 'That sellotape will ruin my paintwork.'

But Hilary was studying the inner page of a birthday card that had been stuck on the door in the middle of the photographs. On the card was printed 'To My Darling' and an excruciatingly sloppy verse. There was also a handwritten message in large capital letters.

'When was Darren's birthday, do you know?' asked Hilary.

'His mother told me he was sixteen last May,' said Mrs Flatt resentfully, 'and if I'd known he was going to cause all this trouble I'd never have had him in my house.'

Ignoring the printed verse on the card, Hilary looked again at the handwritten message. Having since been dumped by Laura, the boy could only have tormented himself by reading it over and over.

MY DARREN –
THOUSANDS OF KISSES FOR YOUR BIRTHDAY – AND MORE!!!
LOVE YOU LOVE YOU LOVE YOU
ALWAYS AND 4 EVER
YOUR LAURA XXXXXXXXXXXXXXXXXXXXXXXXXXXXXXXXXXX

ps Remember BELMONT???

Up at Belmont it was almost dark, and Quantrill had called off the search until the following day.

He was in the floodlit stable yard at the back of Chalcot House, in discussion with Martin Tait and Lewis Glaven, when Hilary returned and joined them. Will Glaven, having thrown himself into the search for Laura, had been overwhelmed with grief for Hope when the activity stopped and had taken refuge in the house.

'Young Jermyn probably knows some of the protesters,' Lewis Glaven was saying, unaware of the police interest in the boy. 'Hardworking lad, very promising I thought. Too squeamish to drive the birds over the guns, though. The keeper tells me he ran away after the first drive. Wouldn't be surprised if he then stirred up some local friends to come and make nuisances of themselves.'

'He was at Breckham Market High,' Hilary told Quantrill. 'I thought I'd go there tomorrow and see what I can find out. That won't account for the older sabs, though . . .'

'In my opinion,' said Tait authoritatively, 'they're rent-a-mob students from Yarchester. They couldn't have come from far, because of the time factor, but they've obviously done this sort of thing before. They know the law and how to manipulate it, and they're probably being subsidised. I'd certainly try the university for the pony-tailed man who just grinned when his video camera was smashed.'

Lewis Glaven cleared his throat. 'Ah yes . . .'

He turned, honourably straight-backed, to Quantrill.

'Regret to say that I was the one who destroyed their camera. With hindsight, that film could have been useful to you, so I was doubly stupid. Moment of anger, I'm afraid.'

'No doubt you were provoked,' said Quantrill.

'No excuse, for a man in my position.'

'No excuse at all. If the saboteurs lay charges, you'll find a copper on your doorstep asking you to accompany him to the police station. On the other hand, if they *do* lay charges, they'll save us the trouble of finding them. There must be over a thousand students at the university, and then there's the City College . . .'

The chief inspector's eye fell on his tall son, who had propped himself against his father's car while he waited for a lift home. Despite his air of boredom, it seemed that Peter had enough of the detective in him to be listening avidly to the discussion. His ears had pricked at the mention of the City College, where he was in his second year as a woodwork design student.

At least the lad hadn't immediately made himself scarce, and that was a good indication that none of his own friends went

168

sabbing. Quantrill went over to him, and tried to enlist his help without offending his sense of student solidarity.

'D'you think Martin's right about the sabs being students?' he asked.

Peter was non-committal: 'Could be.'

He was leaning back nonchalantly against the car, but his father could see that he was rubbing one foot against the calf of the other leg, as though it was aching intolerably.

'Not that I want to involve you,' said Quantrill. 'I'd rather you concentrated on your classes. But sabbing's perfectly legal, and I just wondered whether there's any publicity about it at your college?'

'On and off. I've seen notices on the Greenpeace board in the students' union.'

'Good. All I need is a contact name and telephone number, from your place and from the university. Oh, and I want our "Missing" posters, with Laura's photograph, put up on the Greenpeace boards too. I can't spare anyone to go over to Yarchester and do it, though, because of the search. Trouble is, I'm short of manpower.'

Peter perked up. 'I can do the City College, no problem. But the university campus is miles away . . . Trouble is – ' he gave a wickedly accurate imitation of his father's ruminative tone of voice – 'I'm short of petrol.'

Quantrill knew perfectly well that the distance involved was less than two miles. But it was such a relief, after Peter's accident, to know he was zooming about in the comparative safety of an old banger rather than on two wheels, that he was prepared to indulge him.

He gave the expected heavy sigh. 'Supposing I forget that you still owe me for the last repair job. Will an extra tankful be enough?'

'Just about,' said Peter, infuriatingly offhanded. But then he gave the engaging grin that no doubt attracted more than his fair share of girlfriends: 'Chiz, Dad.'

Before leaving the Chalcot estate, the three detectives drove along the track that led to Keeper's Cottage. As they approached the walled and gated back yard they were met by an outburst of barking, and a bellowed *Quiet you bloody dogs*! from the gamekeeper.

The yard was illuminated, but considerably less well than the stable yard at Chalcot House. In the shadowy light, Len Alger was heaving sacks of grain into the back of his Landrover, ready for the morning's work of feeding the pheasants.

'Where's that bloody boy got to, that's what I want to know?' he greeted the detectives angrily. 'He's left me with both rounds to do, just at the busiest time o' the year. I'll half kill him when I get my hands on him!'

'We'd be interested to know where he is, too,' said Tait. 'You're the man who saw him last. My colleagues would like to hear about it.'

Alger seemed reluctant to answer. It was difficult to know whether he was being deliberately surly with Tait, or whether he couldn't hear. He continued his work, making no reply until Quantrill raised his voice.

'Tell us about seeing Darren Jermyn with the housekeeper's daughter.'

'What else is there to tell?' grumbled the keeper. 'I told him – ' he jerked a contemptuous thumb at Tait – 'what I saw, and I told that sergeant in uniform where I saw it. Young Jermyn and the girl were together behind a tree, and that's all I know.'

'Were they standing up, or leaning against the tree?' asked Hilary.

'Leaning, I reckon. The girl had her back against it.'

'You told me they were "messing about" with each other,' said Tait. 'What exactly did you mean by that?'

'Eh?'

'What were they *doing*?' said Quantrill impatiently. 'Were they making love, or were they arguing?'

'How do I know what they were doing?' snarled Alger. 'I didn't stand there gawping at 'em, I was hurrying to get rid of the bloody intruders. All I know is that they'd got their arms round each other.'

'In a loving way?'

'How should I know? I didn't look, I tell you. They could have been at each other's throats for all I saw of 'em.'

170

'But did you hear their voices?' said Tait.

'No, I didn't,' the keeper snapped. 'I've told you all I know, and I've got work to do even if you haven't.'

'Just one more thing, Mr Alger,' said Hilary. 'Did Darren have his shotgun with him yesterday?'

The keeper stared at her blankly. 'No. No reason for him to have it. He was supposed to be beating, only the idle young bugger ran away.'

'So if he didn't take his gun, it would still be where he usually kept it. Where's that?'

'Why, here o'course. It's not his own gun, it's an old 20-bore Mr Glaven loaned him. I couldn't let the boy have charge of it outside working hours, he's too unreliable. It's kept in one o' my locked sheds, hanging up on the wall. You can see it if you like.'

Len Alger walked stiffly over to a range of brick-built sheds that formed the back wall of the yard, unlocked one of the doors with a key from a ring he kept in his pocket, and switched on the light. The detectives, following him, stood blinking just inside the door, dazzled by the single unshaded lamp.

The shed contained the gamekeeper's ironmongery, neatly stowed. On the floor were bundles of metal stakes, coils of barbed wire and rolls of netting. There were hooks all round the walls, and from them hung a variety of evil-looking traps, most of them with old dark blood encrusted on their spikes.

But Darren Jermyn's shotgun wasn't there.

21

Late on Sunday afternoon, Detective Chief Inspector Quantrill authorised two low-key press releases.

On Monday morning the *East Anglian Daily Press* carried the front-page news that Miss Hope Meynell (22), of Ware, Hertfordshire, a weekend guest at Chalcot House, had died on Sunday in Yarchester hospital from a gunshot wound to the head. The wound had been sustained the previous day, when she was a spectator at a shoot on the estate.

On an inner page it was reported that Laura Harbord (15) and Darren Jermyn (16), both of Chalcot although Darren's home was at Brocklesford, had been missing since Saturday afternoon. Their heights were given, and the clothing they were wearing was briefly described.

'Anyone who might have seen either of them, together or separately, or who knows their whereabouts,' the report concluded, 'should contact Sergeant Hilary Lloyd, Breckham Market police.'

There had been a ground frost overnight, and Monday morning was bright and crisp; one of those days, thought Quantrill as he surveyed the unwelcome pile of paperwork on his desk, when it was all wrong to be stuck in the office. But the routine enquiry work involved in the search for the missing youngsters was in progress; and nothing further could be done about the shooting until the forensic report arrived.

When it was delivered to him, in mid-morning, Quantrill skimmed through the details, studied the diagrams, read the conclusion and reached for his car keys.

According to the report, the shot that had fatally wounded Hope Meynell was fired from a 12-bore shotgun.

Calculated from the angle of entry of the pellets, the shot was a direct hit.

Calculated from the spread of the pellets, the shot had been fired from a range of ten yards.

The place where Hope Meynell had fallen was approximately thirty yards from the nearest peg, which was number seven, at the far end of the woodland ride.

The fatal shot was therefore inconsistent with a shooting accident.

'Martin Tait', said Quantrill with satisfaction as he drove Hilary towards Ashthorpe, 'is going to be really peeved if we can pin this on Joanna Dodd. After all, he'd been told she was jealous of Hope Meynell. I don't know why he didn't suspect her right away.'

'You're being unfair to him, as usual,' said Hilary. 'I'm no fan of his, heaven knows, but I'm sure he'll regret that he didn't keep an eye on Joanna. If she killed the girl, Martin is bound to feel guilty.'

'So he should,' said Quantrill callously. 'It'll teach him to remember that landowning families have the same failings as the rest of us.'

'And the same virtues, if it comes to that.'

'True,' he admitted. 'I can't believe that it wasn't Joanna Dodd who shot the girl, but we've yet to prove that she did it.'

'I really can't see that it would have been feasible,' said Hilary. 'Joanna would've had to leave her peg when she saw Hope bolt, then run twenty yards – partly through bushes – before she fired. Then she'd have to run back to her peg. I don't know how she could have done all that without being seen by one of the other Guns.'

'But we heard Martin going on about the way they have to concentrate when they're shooting,' said Quantrill. 'Besides, the Guns were facing the other way, and watching for high birds. If Joanna had psyched herself up to shoot her rival, I reckon she'd have thought she could risk it.'

'We shan't be able to prove it, though, unless someone else saw her. One of the beaters, perhaps . . .'

'Or a saboteur. Their video film could well have been useful to us. It's a thundering nuisance it was destroyed.'

They had arrived at High Ash, Barclay Dodd's farm. The Dodds had lived there a century longer than the Glavens had lived at Chalcot, and their farmhouse proclaimed its well-preserved age. It stood among gardens on a wooded rise just off a minor road, a gabled and dormered sixteenth-century dwelling topped by a cluster of massive chimneys. Its ochre-coloured walls glowed warm in the November sun.

'Don't be fooled by the traditional appearance,' said Quantrill. 'Old Barclay Dodd owns four times as much land as the Glavens, but there's no more than a hundred acres of woodland and meadow where he shoots and his daughter rides. All the rest is intensive arable, run commercially by a nephew.'

An unpretentious lane led up from the road, past the garden gates and round to the left, to the back of the old house. On the right was a range of traditional farm buildings. They were unused except for the stables, where half a dozen horses looked out from their loose boxes. In the yard outside, two teenage girls in skin-tight jodhpurs and Pony Club sweatshirts were forking steaming muck, joyfully working their socks off in return for the chance to ride.

Joanna Dodd, tall, big-boned and handsomely horsy from her face to her boots, had been speaking to the girls. She broke off as the detectives got out of Quantrill's car, and strode across to meet them.

'I've been expecting you,' she said, in what would have been a ringing voice if she weren't so clearly subdued.

'Has Lewis Glaven been in touch with you?' asked Quantrill.

'He telephoned yesterday about Hope's tragic death. We're all appalled, of course . . . I won't take you into the house, because I don't want to disturb my father. He's desperately upset about the accident, as we all are.'

She led the way to a loose box that had been supplied with coat pegs, an electric kettle and some old garden chairs for the use of the stable girls. On the whitewashed walls were Pony Club and Riding for the Disabled notices, and large-scale posters illustrating the bone and muscle structure of the horse.

The detectives elected to stand, and declined the offer of instant coffee.

'Miss Dodd,' said Quantrill formally. 'You referred to an accident. I have to tell you that the forensic report has ruled that out. The shot that killed Hope Meynell was fired directly at her from a distance of ten yards.'

Joanna Dodd's long face seemed to lengthen, and her healthy complexion paled. She stared at him wide-eyed.

'Good God,' she said slowly. 'That's – that's incredible. I simply don't *believe* it. Who could possibly have done such a thing?'

The detectives allowed her to go on in the same vein a little longer. Then Hilary said: 'Have you any other comment to make?'

'Yes, I have.'

The ring of self-confidence had returned to Joanna Dodd's voice. She looked at them challengingly. 'I'm very sorry the girl

174

is dead, but I'm not sorry to hear she was murdered. From my point of view, it's "Thank God."

'I can guess what's being said by some of Saturday's Guns,' she went on. 'Everyone knows that I've always expected to marry Will Glaven. If Hope's death were to be officially declared an accident, I'd never live it down. Some people would always wonder whether I hadn't arranged it. But a deliberate shot from ten yards? No one will suggest *that* was fired by me!'

It was the detectives' turn to stare. 'Why not?' said Quantrill bluntly.

'That's obvious. I couldn't have fired the shot because my peg was at least twenty-five yards away from where she fell.'

'Thirty yards, actually,' said Hilary. 'But if you'd wanted to fire at Hope Meynell, you could simply have left your peg.'

'Left my peg at a driven shoot?' Joanna Dodd looked pained. 'One doesn't do that kind of thing.'

'Someone did,' said Quantrill. 'And as you admit, you're the natural suspect.'

Joanna Dodd leaned back against the door, her riding boots elegantly crossed at the ankle, her arms folded, a tolerant smile on her face.

'You're *completely* wrong, you know. I met Hope when Will first brought her home, and I was so sorry for the poor child. She was totally out of her depth at Chalcot. She had nothing in common with country people like us, who love dogs and horses. If she'd married Will, she would have been wretched. It would never have worked.'

'Possibly not,' said Hilary. 'But you couldn't be sure of that, could you? You couldn't rely on being able to gloat over her misery.'

'I'm not vindictive. If I were . . .' Joanna thought about it briefly, and a grin twitched the corner of her mouth: 'If I were, I wouldn't have been at all sorry if Will had been lightly peppered with shot – by accident, of course. But I certainly didn't shoot Hope Meynell.'

Quantrill tried a different approach.

'Tell me,' he said, '*why* did you accept the invitation to that shooting party? I believe it was specially arranged to celebrate the engagement. You didn't join them at lunch – understandably, in the circumstances – but I'm surprised you could face the happy couple at all. Unless of course you had some other reason for being there . . .?'

Joanna Dodd straightened. She was nearly six feet tall, not far short of being able to look him right in the eye.

'It's called pride, Chief Inspector,' she said. 'I was damned if I was going to let everyone see I was hurt. It's what children are always taught when they learn to ride – if you're thrown, you get straight back in the saddle.'

Quantrill returned her unwavering look. 'But if you're the only suspect in a murder enquiry, Miss Dodd, you don't get away with a denial. We'd like you to come with us – '

'Wait a minute, please!' Her confidence slipping, Joanna Dodd held up her hand as if to ward him off. She sounded shaken, as though the seriousness of the interview had only just occurred to her. 'Why do you say I'm the only suspect? There was someone in that wood behind us, you know. While we were waiting for the drive to begin, someone was putting up the odd bird. I turned to look at a rocketing pheasant, and it was very close to the place where Hope was shot.'

'But you're not claiming to have seen anyone?' said Hilary.

'No – but someone must have been there! Why don't you ask the other Guns? Ask Will Glaven, he must have heard the disturbance. Ask Detective Superintendent Tait.'

'That wretched Tait's got a nerve,' fumed Quantrill as he waited for a call to be put through to the DCI's office at Saintsbury divisional police headquarters. 'Passing himself off to his county friends as a Super already . . .'

'Don't tell me about it,' said Hilary, 'tell him. You'd better not blast his ears off, though, because we're going to need his help.'

'Fat chance we'll have of keeping him away, once he knows Hope Meynell was murdered.' Then, over the telephone: 'Out, is he? All right – as soon as you can get in touch, ask him to ring me.'

They had returned to Breckham Market with Joanna Dodd, having first cautioned her and allowed her to telephone her family solicitor. The senior partner in an old-established firm, he was clearly astonished by the turn of events and unaccustomed to accompanying his clients to a police station. But he had gallantly provided moral support as she made her statement, and afterwards he had insisted on driving her home himself.

Having failed to contact Martin Tait, Quantrill headed for Chalcot to break the news of Hope's murder to the Glavens. As he and Hilary drove up to the gates of the house, a shiny Daihatsu Fourtrak was just nosing out of them.

'Ah – Mr Brunt the butcher's been visiting his lady friend again,' observed Quantrill as the driver turned his almost hairless head to stare at them.

'At least he's someone for Mrs Harbord to talk to,' said Hilary. 'She's probably lonely – and worried sick about Laura, whatever she likes to pretend. I'll have a word with her while you talk to the Glavens.'

Lewis Glaven, though, had gone to London for the day on business. The housekeeper took Quantrill to the gun room where Will, weary from riding and unable to raise the energy to pull off his muddy boots, was glumly drinking coffee in the company of his dog.

Quantrill told him, as sympathetically as he could, what he had told Joanna. Like her, Will was incredulous; he couldn't imagine who would have done such a thing, or why. And then, when he'd recovered from the immediate shock, he expressed much the same opinion as hers.

'You know what? I'm glad it wasn't an accident. I couldn't have borne it if you'd discovered that I'd fired the shot. And I didn't want it to be pinned on Joanna – or your colleague, either.'

'The Guns aren't necessarily excluded, just because their pegs were too far away,' said Quantrill. 'One of them could have moved.'

Will Glaven sat up and stared at him, affronted. 'Of course they didn't move! Guns always stay on their pegs.'

'But if anyone had moved, would you have noticed?'

Will said nothing, except 'Boris' as he fondled his dog's ears.

'If it wasn't one of the Guns who fired the shot,' said

177

Quantrill, 'someone must have been in that wood just behind you. Was there any legitimate reason for anyone to be there?'

'No – not at that stage in the shoot.'

'Did you hear any sounds from that direction, when you were waiting for the drive to start?'

Will frowned. 'I don't know, I can't remember. I was thinking about Hope, and what she'd told me about her mother's illness. Wait a minute, though – yes, I did hear a pheasant rocketing up somewhere behind me.'

'Would it have done that unless it was disturbed?'

'No, only if something or someone spooked it. But that was probably Laura, when she was creeping through the bushes before running out and trying to stop the shoot.' Will looked up, heavy-eyed: 'Is there any news of her?'

The man had such a burden of grief that it would be wrong to add to it. 'Not so far – but I'm sure we'll soon find her,' said Quantrill, sounding a good deal more positive than he felt.

22

Quantrill had been looking forward to having a go at Tait about his premature claim to the rank of superintendent. But when they met, they had more important things to discuss.

'Any news of young Laura?' Martin said immediately. And he spoke with such genuine anxiety that Quantrill almost forgot how much his daughter's partner annoyed him.

The three detectives had met for a late lunch at the Royal Oak, an old inn on the former turnpike between Breckham Market and Saintsbury. It provided a log fire, Adnams beer and crusty ham rolls for the men, and fresh orange juice and a salad for Hilary who was feeling dehydrated after too much wine the previous night. Tait offered to pay, and no one argued.

'I don't believe Joanna Dodd would have shot Hope Meynell,' he announced. 'Yes, I agree, it would have been possible for her to do it. And she was certainly hurt and angry. But I never thought she was unbalanced enough to take a shot at Will

178

Glaven, despite what the Treadgold brothers said about her. Besides, what could she possibly gain from killing Hope?'

'What about her claim of a mystery gunman in the wood behind you?' said Quantrill. 'You didn't mention anything about it in your own statement.'

'That was because of Laura. I'd heard the odd pheasant taking off behind us – in fact I mentioned it to Alison – and afterwards I assumed that Laura must have spooked them. That was when we were thinking in terms of a shooting accident. But now it's obvious that someone else was up among the trees with a shotgun.'

There was a confidence in the way he said it that invited the next question.

'All right,' said Hilary, 'who's your candidate?'

Martin Tait paused, his blue eyes sharp under his springy fair hair, alert as a terrier about to pounce on a woodpile and produce a rat. He'd always been good, thought Quantrill sourly, at attention-getting pauses.

'How about Reg Brunt, the Chalcot butcher?'

His colleagues stared at him, astonished. Tait sat back, glass in hand, looking intolerably pleased with himself.

'What possible motive could the butcher have for killing Hope Meynell?' demanded Quantrill.

'Ah, well.' Tait was enjoying their wonderment. 'Having been a member of the shooting party gives me a great advantage, of course. Though something you've since told me,' he added hastily, 'confirms my theory.'

'In my view, Reg Brunt had two strong motives for killing Hope Meynell. One was social resentment against the Glavens. The other was love for their housekeeper.'

Hilary screwed her eyes shut. 'Wait a minute,' she said. 'I've got a headache, and this doesn't help.'

She drew breath, and opened her eyes again.

'Yes,' she agreed, 'we know Reg Brunt makes frequent visits to Mrs Harbord. I'll certainly believe his attachment to her, though she doesn't return it. And you told us he wanted to join the shoot on Saturday morning, and how furious he was when he felt they were putting him down. But that doesn't add up to a reason for shooting Hope.'

'It does, you know,' said Tait. 'Will Glaven is leaving the army next year, and coming back to Chalcot to run the estate. If he were to bring Hope here as his wife, they'd have no need of a housekeeper. Mrs Harbord would be out on her ear, and Reg Brunt would lose her. His only way of keeping her at Chalcot is to get rid of Hope.'

'Oh, come off it!' scoffed Quantrill, breaking apart his ham roll with such vigour that he scattered crusty crumbs all over the table. 'Hope Meynell isn't the only girl in the world. Will Glaven's devastated now, of course, but sooner or later he'll meet someone else. Are you suggesting that Reg Brunt intends to pick off every girl Will thinks of marrying?'

'I'm not suggesting he's thought it through,' said Tait. 'There's no logic in love, you know that as well as I do. Anyway, it wouldn't necessarily have been Reg Brunt's own idea. He could well have been put up to it by Mrs Harbord.'

Quantrill took a long, thoughtful drink. Remembering the housekeeper's look of relief and triumph after Lewis Glaven had told her Hope was dead, he could almost believe that aspect of Tait's theory. He wasn't prepared to swallow it whole, though, because he and Hilary had been working on a theory of their own.

'So where's your evidence?' he demanded. 'Have you got any proof that Brunt was anywhere near Belmont on Saturday afternoon?'

'No, of course I haven't!' Tait was visibly annoyed. 'Good grief, I've presented the solution to you on a plate – it's not my job to go grubbing around finding evidence to support it. Surely you can do that for yourself?'

Irritation was zinging between the two men like an electric current. Hilary decided to intervene.

'I don't know about anyone else,' she said, 'but I'd love some coffee. Are you still buying – "Superintendent" Tait?'

Martin sloped off to the bar. 'Slip of the tongue, that's all,' he was heard to mutter as he went. Quantrill and Hilary grinned at each other.

'All the same,' Quantrill admitted, 'he could be right. I can imagine Mrs Harbord stirring up Brunt, and him doing anything at all to please her.'

'She's certainly besotted with Lewis Glaven,' agreed Hilary,

180

'and a very happy woman now Hope Meynell's dead. But I still think we're on the right track. Besides, we've got evidence to support our theory – circumstantial, perhaps, but coherent. Are you going to tell Martin now?'

'I hadn't intended to, not before we've visited Hope Meynell's family. Still – why not?'

'*Lewis Glaven?* Don't be ridiculous . . .'

'What's ridiculous about it?' said Hilary. 'Surely it's the fact that he's a landowner, and concerned for his family and the estate, that makes it believable. He'd already told his son that Hope wasn't right for Chalcot, but Will was too much in love with her to care. The only way to stop him marrying Hope was to get rid of her.'

'Rubbish! Absolute rubbish. However much a father may disapprove of his prospective daughter-in-law, he doesn't go after her with a shotgun. Does he, Doug?' Tait added with a flick of mockery. 'Not even if it's a prospective son-in-law he'd like to get rid of . . .'

Quantrill ignored the gibe.

'The point is,' he said, 'that Lewis Glaven's behaviour changed completely when he realised that Will intended to marry Hope. He stopped objecting, and invited her to Chalcot for the weekend. And he arranged a shooting party, ostensibly for her to meet the neighbours. After that, his behaviour was all of a piece. He cleverly set up a situation in which Hope Meynell could be killed, but everyone would assume it was a shooting accident.'

Tait shook his head with scorn. 'Look, I know Lewis Glaven, and I've never met a more honourable man. You don't know what you're talking about.'

'Not at first hand, no. A lot of it's based on what you told us – but you were so much Lewis Glaven's guest that you couldn't see its significance.'

'Let's take it bit by bit,' said Hilary, intervening again. 'First, Hope didn't want to watch the sport. She was quietly terrified by the whole thing, only Will was too unimaginative to see it. You'd agree with that, wouldn't you, Martin?'

181

'Yes . . .'

'But if Hope had been the only female spectator, it might have seemed cruel of Lewis Glaven to insist on her being present. That was where Alison was useful to him. Lewis specifically asked you to bring her, didn't he? She didn't want to watch the shoot either, but Lewis insisted that both girls had to be there. Right?'

'More or less . . .'

'In fact,' said Quantrill, 'he made sure of it by driving them to Belmont himself and taking them to their places. He didn't say anything to Alison about an escape route. But she heard him tell Hope that if she felt she'd had enough, the safest place for her to go would be the wood behind them.'

'That's perfectly true, actually,' said Tait. 'That wood ought to have been the safest place.' But he had begun to sound subdued.

'It's significant, though,' said Quantrill. 'And didn't Lewis Glaven rearrange some of the places for the last drive?

'He and his friends were out of sight of the rest of you, weren't they? As a result, we've never suspected them of shooting Hope, either accidentally or deliberately. But because Lewis was the host, he could leave his peg without comment. And because he knew his own woods he'd be able to move through them, unseen, until he could get a shot at her.'

Martin sat silent, frowning at his glass.

He was still on his original half-pint. He didn't much like beer, but he was always sparing with wine and spirits because they had contributed to his father's early death. The midday drink he really preferred was lager. But how could a man with his aspirations drink that now, when everyone associated lager with louts?

'What you say may sound plausible,' he said, 'but there's a rational explanation for everything Lewis Glaven did.'

'Not for his apparent phobia about cameras,' said Hilary. 'Didn't he refuse to allow Alison to take photographs at the shoot? And then later, when he saw the sabs making a video film he went berserk and destroyed both film and camera. I'd say that was totally irrational. Unless of course he had a reason for not wanting anyone to make a record of where people were and what they were doing at the shoot.'

Tait raised an eyebrow. 'You aren't trying to dispute Lewis Glaven's sanity, then? Good – because no sane man has been known to kill his prospective daughter-in-law simply because he didn't consider her suitable. Do bear that in mind before you think of barging in on Lewis, won't you?'

He looked at his watch. 'Sorry, but I really must go. I do have rather a lot to do in my own division.'

Quantrill raised a magisterial hand. 'Now hold you hard,' he said, sounding more Suffolk than usual. 'What you don't know, Martin, is that Hope Meynell's mother died in a psychiatric hospital. Hope told Will, but he didn't want his father to know. He reckoned Lewis would assume the disease was hereditary, and oppose the marriage. But what we suspect is that Lewis did already know, and . . .'

His confidence wavered. The construction he and Hilary had been working on was still several planks short of a bridge, and he found himself teetering on the edge of the drop. Martin Tait knew it, and was looking superior.

'That is the most unlikely argument I've ever heard. Even if Lewis already knew, and even if the disease *were* hereditary, he wouldn't reach for his gun! What kind of a man do you think he is?

'Oh, I agree: in those circumstances he would certainly oppose the marriage. But the natural thing would have been for him to tell Will as soon as he found out, and do everything he could to talk him out of it. He would never have kept such serious information from his son – let alone killed the poor girl.'

'Well, we shall find out,' said Quantrill. 'If betting weren't a mug's game, I'd – '

'I wouldn't take your money,' said Tait loftily. 'Even though I'm shortly getting married – with or without my prospective father-in-law's approval.'

He stood up, and collected his Barbour and country gentleman's tweed cap from a nearby peg.

'The thing is, Doug,' he said in a more conciliatory tone,

'you've completely overlooked one crucial point. Lewis Glaven invited me to join his shooting party, knowing who I am. If he'd intended to kill Hope, the last person he'd have wanted at the shoot was a senior detective.'

Hilary smiled at him. 'We did notice that point, actually. But we put a different construction on it. In fact, it reinforces our argument.'

'Oh yes?' Tait looked at his watch again, sighed and propped a shoulder against one of the exposed timbers of the ancient inn. 'Go on, then.'

'Just let's assume for the moment', said Quantrill, 'that Lewis Glaven had decided to kill Hope Meynell. And let's assume that he set up the shoot as we've suggested. What he's hoping to do is to pass off her death as an accident.

'Now, he knows there's bound to be a police investigation. And what he doesn't want at Chalcot is some cynical, bolshy detective, who's got no time for the upper classes anyway, sniffing round saying *What's been going on here?*'

'Someone like Ian Wigby,' suggested Hilary, naming a detective constable who had done his best to cut Tait down to size when he was a sergeant at Breckham Market.

'Exactly,' said Quantrill. 'Far better, from Lewis Glaven's point of view, to have a socially ambitious senior detective already there, as his guest at the scene of the crime.'

Tait straightened immediately. His ears reddened with anger. 'Are you suggesting that I'm an accessory?'

'No, of course I'm not. But Lewis Glaven might well have thought it would be no bad thing to have you there. At best – from his point of view – you might have been prepared to short-circuit the investigation. At worst, he knew he could rely on you to refuse to believe a word against him.'

'Just as you've been doing for the past half-hour,' pointed out Hilary.

They both smiled at Tait.

'What we reckon,' said Quantrill kindly, 'is that Lewis Glaven set up the murder – and you as well.'

*

184

They were still feeling pleased with themselves as they watched Martin Tait's BMW disappear rapidly down the road to Saintsbury. But as soon as they were in Quantrill's car, they sobered.

There were two radio messages for the chief inspector.

One was that Darren Jermyn had been found, but he denied all knowledge of Laura Harbord's whereabouts.

The other was a report from the enquiry team that had been doing a house-to-house in Chalcot village. Several ageing vehicles – a minibus, two small vans and the odd car – had assembled outside the Dun Cow at about two thirty on Saturday afternoon. They had apparently contained a crowd of teenagers, with one or two older men. Later, the vehicles had been seen parked on the verge of the minor road between Chalcot and Ashthorpe, beside the wall of the Glavens' estate.

A different vehicle had been seen, earlier on Saturday afternoon, parked in much the same place. The witness had recognised it as the Daihatsu Fourtrak belonging to Reg Brunt. But when the enquiry team called at the master butcher's bungalow, and at the next-door shop, he could not be found.

23

Darren Jermyn had made a voluntary reappearance when he was down to his last thirty pence. His mother was working the Monday morning shift at Sainsbury's when a solitary packet of smoky bacon crisps sailed along the conveyor towards her till, and a sheepish voice muttered, 'Hallo, Mum.'

The Jermyns had spent a very worried night. Brenda had been further distressed, and embarrassed, to arrive at work and find that her colleagues knew from the local newspaper that both Darren and his girlfriend had disappeared. Asking to finish her shift early, she took her son firmly in hand.

Brenda was of course thankful to see him. But she was angry with him for causing so much trouble, and shocked by his dishevelled appearance and his unwashed smell. She sent him to clean himself up and then have a hot meal in the coffee shop, while she rang Breckham Market police station to report that he was found.

Sergeant Lloyd interviewed Darren as soon as she returned.

She had seen his school-leaving photograph when she visited his parents, but the Darren who sat opposite her in the interview room was no longer curly-haired and confident and happily in love. His eyes were downcast under his cropped head, his face was sullen, his fingernails were filthy, and a rash of spots had broken out beside his mouth. Whether it was the withdrawal of Laura's love that had brought about the change, Hilary reflected, or the change in him that had made her withdraw her love, the lad's pain was evident.

'You've been sleeping rough, haven't you, Darren? What made you do that?'

'Trouble,' he muttered.

'Trouble because of Laura?'

'No, because of the sabs. Nothing to do with Laura. At least . . .'

He knew he'd be in trouble with Mr Glaven, he said, because he'd deserted from the shoot and then called in the sabs. He wanted to stop the killing, that was all. Same as Laura wanted, only he hadn't told her what he was going to do.

He'd biked down to the village and rung an old mate from school, who now went to Yarchester City College and had done a bit of anti-hunt sabbing. Darren had told him how to get to Belmont, across the broken wall from the back road. He'd asked him to spread the word and bring in as many protesters as possible.

But Darren hadn't reckoned on experienced sabs coming. He hadn't reckoned on serious trouble. When the protest turned nasty, and there was a fight between Mr Glaven and one of the sabs, Darren had decided he'd better disappear.

'You were there protesting with your mate, were you?' asked Hilary.

'No – I didn't want anybody from the Chalcot estate to see me. I was watching, that's all.'

186

He couldn't go back to his lodgings, or home, he said, because everybody was going to blame him for what had happened. So he'd biked to Breckham Market and he'd been there all weekend, sleeping in a shed in the builder's yard where his Dad worked. But then he'd run out of money . . .

'Why did you go back to the shoot, if you weren't going to join the protest?' asked Hilary. 'Was it because you knew Laura would be there?'

Darren picked at his spots. He was concerned for Laura, he said. He knew she intended to make some kind of risky solo protest, and he wanted to find her and stop her doing it.

Yes, because he loved her.

Yes, because he wanted to get back with her.

Yes, all right: because he couldn't accept that she didn't love him any more.

'Laura's missing,' said Hilary. 'But then, you know that, don't you?'

Darren muttered that his mother had told him.

'When did you last see Laura?'

He had finished the coffee he'd been given, and now he fiddled with the empty polystyrene mug, squeezing it and cracking it in his big raw hands. Sergeant Lloyd repeated her question.

It was at Belmont, Darren said. But all he'd seen of Laura was one distant glimpse, when she'd run out from the bushes to try to stop the shooting. She was in the wrong place, that was why he hadn't seen her earlier.

He'd expected Laura to be hiding in the bushes between the driven pheasants and the shooting party, so she'd be facing the Guns as soon as she jumped out of cover. That was where he'd been searching for her, before the drive started. But then, after the Guns were standing by their pegs, somebody spooked some birds *behind* them. No wonder he couldn't find her, if that was where she'd been hiding.

Hilary sat back, easing the pressure on the boy. Though she was interviewing him about Laura Harbord, there was always the possibility that he'd seen something relevant to the murder enquiry.

'Where exactly were you when you saw the birds being spooked?' she asked.

'Far end of the ride, on the edge of the trees,' he said. 'I'd worked my way all along, looking for Laura. I ended up opposite the horsy woman.'

'I see . . . Tell me, Darren, did any of the Guns move away from their pegs while the shooting was going on?'

Now that his own actions weren't in question, he looked up and became more co-operative.

'Everybody moved,' he said. 'Major Will's girlfriend got upset and ran for the wood at their back. The other man's girlfriend went after her. Then Laura jumped out from behind them, shouting and waving her arms, and ran down the ride the other way. I didn't have a chance to rescue her, I wasn't near enough. Major Will and the other man were rushing about like headless fowls – '

'And Joanna Dodd? The horsy woman?'

Darren almost smiled at the recollection, and for a few moments Hilary could see the attractiveness of the lad.

'She didn't take a blind bit of notice,' he said with admiration. 'She just stayed put and went on firing at high pheasants until the sabs surrounded her.'

'You're sure of that?'

"Course I'm sure. I was watching her. I wouldn't mind some of the pheasants being shot, if every Gun was as good as she is. Every bird she hit was dead in the air.'

'That's nice to know,' said Hilary. She had believed Joanna Dodd's denial, and so she was glad to be able to cross her off the list of murder suspects.

'And talking of birds, Darren – you notice what they're doing, don't you? You said that some of them were being spooked, behind the Guns, before the drive started. Do you think it was just one person who was doing the spooking?'

'Couldn't have been,' he said, confident now that his own expertise had been called on. 'I could tell that somebody was moving along through the bushes by the way the fieldfares and redwings were taking off. That must have been Laura. But there were pheasants rocketing up from a lot further back in the wood, at the same time. That must have been somebody else.'

188

'Any idea who?'

He shrugged, evidently tired of being questioned. 'No idea. Can I go now?'

'Sorry,' said Hilary firmly. 'You've been helpful, and I'm grateful to you for that. But you haven't finished telling me about Laura. What did you do when you found her, after the shooting stopped?'

Darren scowled, sullen again. He *hadn't* found her, he protested. He'd caught that one glimpse of her, when she ran out from behind the Guns, and that was all.

'That's not true,' said Hilary. 'You were seen together, behind a tree. "Messing about with each other", so we've been told. Were you trying to make love to her?'

Darren's face flared up, as red as his acne.

He denied that he'd spoken to Laura on Saturday afternoon, let alone touched her. He had no idea where she went after the shoot – he'd assumed she'd gone home. He hoped to God she was safe, because he loved her. But anybody who said they'd been seen together was lying.

'Oh, come on,' said Hilary. 'Why should anyone want to lie about it?'

Head down, Darren said nothing. Then, suddenly, he looked up, his scowl clearing.

'It was that poxy old keeper, wasn't it? Wasn't it?' he demanded. 'Len Alger's always trying to get me into trouble. He's too old for his job, and he's afraid Mr Glaven will let me have it. You can't believe a lying old bastard like him!'

'We can't believe both of you, that's for sure,' said Hilary briskly. 'So what we're going to do, Darren – '

She was about to alarm him with the prospect of having his clothes taken away and examined for forensic evidence. But then she remembered something else.

'By the way – where's your shotgun?'

He looked blank.

'You had it with you on Saturday, didn't you?'

'No. No reason to have it. It's in its usual place at Len Alger's.'

'In his shed? It's not, you know.'

Darren shook his head impatiently. 'It isn't kept in his *shed*.

Mr Glaven would never allow that. It's always kept secure, same as the keeper's own guns, in a locked steel cabinet in his kitchen.'

Chief Inspector Quantrill spent the early part of the afternoon at Chalcot, checking the progress of the two investigations.

The interviews with Saturday's beaters and pickers-up – apart from Dorothy Wilson-Brown – had been completed. Frustratingly, in spite of the fact that they were all local men, not one of them had seen anything of any significance.

The beaters knew Laura Harbord by sight, but none of them had seen her at Belmont. By the time they had pushed their way through to the edge of the ride, flushing out the last of the pheasants, most of the shooting had already stopped.

Seeing the Guns in disarray, and saboteurs milling about at the far end of the ride, the beaters had kept their heads down. As soon as they realised that something was badly wrong, and that a girl had been hit, they'd hurried across the ride and tried to help. And that was all they knew about the shooting.

As Quantrill had expected, the elderly pickers-up had seen nothing of Laura either. He knew they always stood well back behind the Guns, waiting with their dogs for the shooting to finish. What he was sure was that they'd have noticed if any of the Guns had left their pegs during the drive; but if they had noticed, they weren't saying.

During the morning there had been four pickers-up, in addition to Mrs Wilson-Brown who always stood behind her brothers. By the afternoon, what with their age, the exertions of the morning and a hearty lunch, only two of them were still on their feet.

Understandably, those two had preferred not to walk all the way down the ride. As a result, the pickers-up were all positioned behind pegs one to four, where they saw nothing of the events leading to the shooting of Hope Meynell. And for whatever reason – whether it was true, or whether out of loyalty to Lewis Glaven on peg four – they had stoutly denied to their interviewers that any of the Guns had moved during the drive.

Still digesting this information the chief inspector took a walk

190

down the ride towards the scene of the shooting. There was a lot of activity in the bushes and among the trees, and he heard complaints of harassment from pheasants on all sides.

On the west of the ride, estate workers and villagers were continuing the search for Laura Harbord. On the east, the scenes-of-crime team were working in the woodland behind pegs five to seven, looking for further clues to the murder of Hope Meynell.

There had been so many people blundering about round the wounded girl after the shooting that the team had been unable to find any evidence to connect anyone with the crime. But they had found what they were specifically looking for: a single empty cartridge case, its orange-red colour making it difficult to spot against the russet of fallen leaves, lying in a position consistent with its ejection from the murder weapon.

The cartridge was an Eley number 6: six lead pellets to the ounce, the usual size for shooting pheasants. According to the forensic report, pellets of that size had been found embedded in Hope Meynell's face and shoulders.

Unfortunately, there was nothing distinctive about the make. Police enquiries had revealed that the nearest agent for Eley cartridges, a gun dealer in Breckham Market, had for many years supplied them in bulk to the Chalcot estate. He'd confirmed that he also supplied them to most other shooting estates in the district, including the Dodds' and the Treadgolds', and to the syndicate to which Reg Brunt belonged.

The scenes-of-crime officer, a greying detective constable, had found evidence further away, though.

'We know that a man stood shooting in a clearing in the wood about a hundred yards back,' he reported, when Quantrill visited the place where the shot was fired. 'We've found a heavily trodden patch of grass, a scattering of feathers, a shot-to-pieces hen pheasant and eleven empty cartridge cases.'

'Eley number 6?'

'Right. What's more there's a path, probably made by the keepers, that runs from the clearing to the edge of the trees about twenty yards away. Getting here would have been easy enough.'

Quantrill mulled over the information. He had to admit,

however unwillingly, that the case against Reg Brunt began to sound conclusive.

Certainly the man had a motive for killing Hope Meynell. He had parked his Fourtrak outside the estate wall on Saturday afternoon, so it was likely that he was the one who'd been in the clearing.

No doubt he'd fired the eleven shots so as to bring down a few pheasants and give himself a poaching alibi. His firing hadn't been heard by the shooting party, so presumably he'd done it when they themselves had started shooting. Then he'd gone along the path to the woodland edge and taken his twelfth shot, this time at Hope Meynell.

Yes – it all seemed to fit. And possibly, Quantrill conceded, it was nothing but a pig-headed determination to disagree with Martin Tait that kept him from admitting it without any reservation. But his instinct was still for Lewis Glaven and so he tramped off on his own, as he always liked to do, down the muddy ride towards peg number four.

The scenes-of-crime team had replaced the pegs the previous day, following Tait's directions. What Quantrill wanted now was to get the feel of standing on Lewis Glaven's peg. Specifically, he wanted to discover whether the landowner could have taken a concealed short cut from there to the place where the shot was fired. And to his satisfaction, he found that it would have been possible.

Lewis Glaven's peg was close to the seemingly impenetrable thicket that put a kink in the track, and hid the first four pegs from the last three. But a narrow path, its entrance half-concealed by an evergreen shrub, ran through the thicket and then up through the bushes to join another path on the edge of the trees. Standing on that slight elevation, Quantrill found himself looking down across the tops of the bushes towards the ride.

He could see the peg nearest this side of the thicket, number five where Martin Tait had stood. He could also see number six: Will Glaven's peg, behind which Hope Meynell had been standing, and from which she had made the run for what she imagined was safety.

Yes, it would certainly have been possible for Lewis Glaven

192

to have left his peg and shot the girl. But he couldn't have taken a shot at her *unless* she ran, for fear of hitting Will. That meant he would have had to hang about up here, waiting for her to move.

It was inconceivable that his absence wouldn't have been noticed. The two male pickers-up had denied he'd left his peg, but Quantrill was disinclined to believe them. If they'd lied out of loyalty, though, it might well be impossible to shake them.

True, there was still one other picker-up to be interviewed. But that was Mrs Dorothy Wilson-Brown. And according to Martin Tait, she and Lewis Glaven were old and affectionate friends.

Quantrill returned to Breckham Market to collect Sergeant Lloyd.

'Did you get anything out of the boy Jermyn?' he asked Hilary as soon as he reached his office. When it came to priorities, finding the girl who was missing concerned him rather more than finding the killer of the one who was dead.

Hilary explained that the evidence against Darren had collapsed. She'd sent a detective constable to interview Len Alger, who had reluctantly unlocked the steel cabinet in his kitchen and produced the boy's 20-bore shotgun. He'd forgotten, he said, that Darren kept it there. His memory wasn't as good as it had been . . .

The gamekeeper had also admitted that he could have been mistaken about seeing Darren and Laura Harbord together. Must have been a trick of the light, he said. It was nearly dusk at the time, and his eyesight wasn't as good as it had been either . . .

'Devious old bastard,' growled Quantrill. 'Well, we've no reason to continue the search at Belmont, so we'll call it off. That means we're no nearer to finding Laura – and she's been missing now for forty-eight hours.'

24

It didn't help that Martin Tait chose the next moment to ring from Saintsbury and enquire what news there was of Laura Harbord.

'Give us time, for heaven's sake,' exploded Quantrill. 'Hilary's just eliminated Darren Jermyn, so we'll have to widen the search.'

He glanced at the message pad that his sergeant put under his nose, and was pleased to see that his son had rung in with information.

'Peter's given us the names of a couple of anti-blood sport students,' he told Tait. 'Chances are they were among the protesters, so I'll switch the enquiry team from Chalcot village to Yarchester. Don't keep nagging me about it – I'm just as anxious as you are to find the girl. When there's any news I'll let you know. We're in the middle of a murder enquiry as well, don't forget.'

'Have you interviewed Reg Brunt yet?'

'No, we haven't!' Quantrill looked where Hilary was pointing, at the second message on the pad. 'We thought perhaps he'd done a runner – but his cleaning lady says he'd planned to go to Saintsbury today. We'll catch him at home this evening, after we've seen Mrs Wilson-Brown.'

'Oh, you're going to visit Doffy, are you?' Tait sounded intolerably familiar towards her, considering they'd met only once. 'She's a splendid old girl. Don't bother with her brothers, Tweedledum and Tweedledee,' he advised. 'They were drunk in charge of their shotguns on Saturday afternoon, so their evidence would be worthless. But you can rely on Doffy. She's very shrewd, very able – one of the pillars of the county.'

'So I've heard,' said Quantrill sharply. But he needed information, and so he moderated his annoyance. 'What I wonder is how she'll deal with a conflict of loyalties. Can we rely on her to tell the truth, if it means witnessing against her old friend Lewis Glaven?'

'It won't come to that,' said Tait with total conviction. 'Reg Brunt's your man, Doug. But in those hypothetical circumstances . . .'

He paused, thinking. 'Dorothy Wilson-Brown might avoid telling you the whole truth,' he concluded. 'But she wouldn't ever tell you a lie.'

By the time they reached Nether Wickford, the short November afternoon was drizzling towards darkness. There was just enough light in the sky for them to discern the prosperous size of the Treadgold family's Victorian farmhouse, just outside the village, and beyond its gardens the towering metal bulk of the farm barns and silos.

Most of the house was in darkness, but there was a light above the side door. Their ring was answered by Mrs Wilson-Brown, a big woman with an outdoor face and greying bird's nest hair. She sounded weary, and was obviously reluctant to bother with callers; but as soon as she knew who they were she said, 'Of course,' and invited them in.

The room she led them to was large and richly unpretentious, rather like Dorothy Wilson-Brown herself. It was softly lit by a couple of lamps and the flames from a log fire, and it contained a fortune in Victorian oil paintings and lovingly beeswaxed antique furniture. But Quantrill knew that his wife Molly would be ashamed to own such a shabby carpet, and such lumpy old chintz-covered sofas; and she certainly wouldn't approve of one of them being occupied by a snoring heap of dogs.

'Do sit down,' said Mrs Wilson-Brown, scooping newspapers and magazines about guns and dogs off the other sofa.

Her deep voice, deadened by sadness, was unmistakably out of the top drawer. Molly would have been impressed and even intimidated by it, thought Quantrill; but she'd have sent that baggy tweed skirt and vintage Aran cardigan to a jumble sale long ago.

'I've just made tea,' Mrs Wilson-Brown went on, 'but I doubt

195

my brothers will appear for it. They're deliberately keeping themselves busy with farm affairs – it's been a difficult time for all of us, as you know.'

Her eyes were dull with misery. Her gardener's hands – weighted with Victorian rings – shook a little as she poured tea from a brown earthenware pot into an assortment of china mugs.

'We do sympathise,' said Quantrill. 'Bad enough for you and your friends that Will Glaven's fiancée has died . . .'

'Yes.' Dorothy Wilson-Brown's voice tightened with suppressed emotion. 'Even worse to know that her death was intended, and that it was one of us who killed her.'

'Not necessarily,' said Quantrill, allowing kindness to overcome official caution.

'*Really?*' She looked at him with such astonishment and relief that he found himself hoping, after all, that Tait was right about Reg Brunt. 'But that's amazing!' she continued, her depression lifting. 'Who could possibly have – ? No, I know I mustn't ask. But – ?'

The chief inspector took refuge in police-speak. 'We always keep an open mind in cases like this. We do have several leads, and one of them points in a different direction. But I must tell you' – he put a warning note in his voice – 'that it's the shooting party that concerns us most. We'd like to ask some questions about it.'

'Of course.' Buoyed by hope, however insubstantial, Mrs Wilson-Brown sat forward almost eagerly and planted her hands on her parted knees. 'Fire away.'

Sergeant Lloyd took out her notebook. 'What we want to establish, Mrs Wilson-Brown, is the location of each Gun in your part of the line. I believe you were standing well back behind the Guns, so you were able to see all four of them quite clearly. Is that right?'

'Certainly. Barclay Dodd was on the first peg, then my brothers Jim and George, then Lewis Glaven on number four.'

'And there were two other pickers-up besides yourself, I believe. Are they men you know well?'

'Yes of course – Joe Gaskin and Harold Pike. Retired now,

196

but they used to work on the Chalcot estate. Known them for years.'

'That's useful,' said Quantrill. 'What we're wondering, you see, is whether their memories are reliable. They've both been interviewed already, and you've just confirmed what they told us about the Guns. But when they were asked whether anyone, themselves included, had moved during the drive, they said not. And I'm afraid I'm disinclined to believe them.'

Dorothy Wilson-Brown gave him a shrewd look, born of many years' experience in public life.

'What makes you say that, Mr Quantrill?'

'Well . . .' He put down his empty mug and hesitated for a moment, unable to shake off the outdated habit of choosing his words in female company. 'I understand that everybody had an excellent shoot lunch, with plenty to drink. It was a chilly day, and there was a lot of standing about before the afternoon drive began. So I'd be surprised if Joe and Harold, with a can or two of beer inside them, hadn't at some point felt the need to – er – disappear into the bushes.'

'Well of course!' She gave a robust upper-middle-class chuckle. 'I'm sure you're absolutely right. If they told you they hadn't moved, it wasn't because they were trying to mislead you. They probably thought that going for a pee didn't count.'

'Exactly.'

Quantrill paused, straight-faced: 'So what about the Guns, Mrs Wilson-Brown? Did any of them disappear into the bushes, too?'

Her amused expression froze. She knew now, despite his earlier kindness, where he was leading her.

'Quite probably,' she said, in a voice that was admirably even.

'All four of them, at one time or another?'

'Almost certainly. But I was there to watch where the pheasants fell, you see. I hadn't the time or the inclination to concern myself with anything else.'

'I think you would have noticed, though, if one of the Guns had left his peg for an unusually long time. Your host, for example?'

A flush of blood rose up Dorothy Wilson-Brown's neck, and turned her weathered cheeks a brighter shade of red. For a few moments she returned Quantrill's steady look. Then, with a social smile, she turned to Hilary.

'I don't know about you, Miss Lloyd, but I'm glad I live in a country where men don't pee in public. It's such a bore to find the Belgians at it as soon as one's crossed the North Sea.

'When we first motored abroad with our children,' she hurried on, almost as though the detectives were guests and she felt required to entertain them non-stop, 'I had to tell them not to stare at men who were standing by the roadside with their backs to the traffic. In England of course it's perfectly all right to look. When a man stands at the side of the road here, you know he's doing something interesting, like admiring the view or watching a bird.'

Her forehead glistened as she plunged on. There was a hint of controlled desperation in her voice, as if she didn't dare stop talking for fear of what would follow.

'My son, of course, thought the Continental practice was great fun. As soon as we came home, he took to spraying the garden. I soon put a stop to *that*. Ruins the plants. Though if I'd had my wits about me, I suppose I could have trained him to do some selective weed-killing – '

'Mrs Wilson-Brown,' said Hilary stopping her with quiet firmness. She admired the elderly woman's style and courage; she felt sympathy for her, and sadness for all the members of the tragic shooting party. But duty had to be done.

'I'm sorry, but we have to ask you this: did Lewis Glaven leave his peg on Saturday afternoon for any longer than a couple of minutes?'

'But that's what I've been trying to explain, Miss Lloyd! When a member of a shooting party disappears into the bushes, everyone knows why. One simply thinks, "Thank God for Englishmen," and takes no further notice. One doesn't watch to see which direction he goes in. And one most certainly doesn't make a note of how long he's been away.'

She rose to her feet, obliging both of them to do the same. 'Before you go – ' she said. 'Do please tell me: we're all

198

concerned about Mrs Harbord's daughter. Have you found Laura yet?'

The detectives arrived at Reg Brunt's bungalow in no mood to put up with any prevarication. If he was the man who had killed Hope Meynell – and they both hoped so; too many other lives would be devastated if it were Lewis Glaven – they intended to find out as quickly as possible.

The retired butcher had returned from his day out. His Daihatsu Fourtrak was parked in his driveway, next to the shop that he still owned, and the lights were on in the kitchen. The curtains were open and they could see him bustling about the tidy, cheerless room, putting a solitary plate of food on a formica-topped table.

Hearing their footsteps on the gravel, he turned anxiously to the window. With his bald head, his squat shape, his round eyes and wide slit of a mouth he looked, thought Hilary, remarkably like a toad.

Reg Brunt flung open the door. He looked anxiously apologetic.

'You must be the police,' he wheezed, before they could introduce themselves. 'Don't tell me – I know I'm in the wrong. Soon as I heard you were treating the girl's death as murder, I knew you'd find out that I'd parked my Fourtrak by the estate wall. Should have reported to you straight away – citizen's duty. Must apologise.'

They made the most of this minor admission of guilt and advanced into his kitchen. Reg Brunt retreated before them, bumping against the table and groping for a chair before sliding down on to it.

'So why *didn't* you report to us?' demanded Quantrill. 'What were you trying to hide?'

The man looked from one to the other and licked his thin lips. 'Poaching on Mr Glaven's estate . . .' he said reluctantly. 'Stupid thing – man in my position – great embarrassment. Never live it down in the village.'

It was the alibi they'd expected him to use. They sat down at the table, uninvited, and looked him over. He kept his eyes on his meal, a plateful of cold ham with oven-ready chips that looked as though they were made of polystyrene. A crusted bottle of tomato sauce and a can of lager stood on either side of the plate.

Hilary decided to add to his guilt by reproaching him.

'Poaching is just another name for stealing, Mr Brunt. We're surprised you should stoop to that. As you say, a man in your position . . . Why did you do it? We've heard that you're a member of a shooting syndicate at Horkey. If you wanted pheasants, you could have gone there and shot them legally, couldn't you?'

Slumped in wretchedness, the man nodded.

'So why *did* you take your shotgun to the Chalcot estate on Saturday afternoon?' said Quantrill.

Brunt picked up a chip in his fingers and chewed it dispiritedly. 'Another embarrassment,' he mumbled. 'Reluctant to reveal it . . .'

But embarrassment was evidently outweighed by indignation. He looked up, red in the face.

'Crack shot in my younger days – finest in the county,' he asserted. Like Mr Toad, he could soon regain his swagger. 'Always fancied going to a shoot on the Chalcot estate. And why not? Man of property – substantial business – mix with anybody. Heard they were short of Guns for Saturday's shoot, so offered my services. Prepared to pay, of course – expense no object.'

He began to swell with fury.

'But Mr Glaven turned me down, in front of his friends! They laughed at me – never been so humiliated in m'life. Decided then to shoot some of his birds at Belmont that afternoon, just to pay him back!'

Reg Brunt snatched up his knife and fork and began to fuel his anger with cold ham. Between mouthfuls, he confirmed that he had reached the wood early and waited in a clearing behind the line of pegs, so that he could pick off some of the birds the shooting party missed.

'Didn't want to be seen or heard, of course – wasn't going to risk being ordered off the estate. Didn't shoot until the others started. Then I heard a single shot, very much nearer. Afraid of being found, so I hurried out of the wood. Gang of saboteurs was just arriving, so I hid up till they'd passed – then came home.'

He sat back. Satisfied with his story, he poured himself a glass of lager and took a long drink.

Quantrill looked at him sceptically. 'What about the pheasants you said you went for? How many did you shoot, and where are they now?'

Reg Brunt looked uncomfortable.

'Poor visibility in that clearing,' he explained. 'Too far back – birds coming down through the trees, difficult to hit. Crack shot when I was younger, finest in the – '

'How many?'

'Only two worth picking up. They're hanging in the shed behind my shop.'

'And how many shots did you fire?'

'Just a few.' He moistened his wide mouth. 'It was the principle of the thing, you see – shooting at the same time as the shooting party. Only took a handful of cartridges with me.'

'Show us the rest of them, then.'

Reg Brunt bustled to one of the kitchen drawers. The detectives glanced at each other, appalled that anyone should fail to keep cartridges under lock and key; but this was not the moment to lecture him on gun safety.

'New supply for the start of the season,' Brunt explained, producing a shrink-wrapped pack of ten boxes of Eley number 6 cartridges. Only one box had been opened. Quantrill checked its remaining contents, and found that twelve cartridges were missing.

'You fired twelve shots, Mr Brunt?'

'Must have done.'

'Only eleven empty cartridge cases were found in the clearing. But one other was found not far away, at the spot where the gun was fired at Hope Meynell.'

Reg Brunt's eyes goggled. He stood with his back pressed against the kitchen unit, and his sagging throat gave a long visible gulp.

'You mean – the single shot I heard was the one that killed

201

her? But I've told you, I only *heard* it. I certainly didn't fire it! Why would I want to kill the young lady? I'd never even – '

Hilary interruped: 'What's your relationship with Ann Harbord?'

Confused by the ostensible change of subject, Reg Brunt turned his head towards the sergeant. 'Mrs Harbord? I – er . . .'

'She's a friend of yours, isn't she? A close friend, I believe. Someone you'd do anything for, isn't that right?'

He looked almost bashful. 'Fine woman – greatly admire her. Would be honoured if she'd agree to become Mrs Brunt.'

Hilary let that pass.

'Mrs Harbord wasn't happy about Will Glaven's future wife, was she? She was worried that she'd lose her job as house-keeper, and her home as well. I'm sure she discussed it with you. She didn't want the marriage to take place, did she? She wanted to get rid of Hope Meynell.'

Reg Brunt took a long deep breath.

'Certainly we discussed the situation,' he said with cautious dignity. 'As you say, Mrs Harbord was worried. She came to see me on Friday, and sought my advice.'

'And what advice did you give her?'

He held his head as high as it would go: 'I'm not a fool,' he said. 'Can't compare myself with Mr Glaven. Mrs Harbord will never marry me, because she wants to be near *him*. But that's no problem, I told her.'

His mouth widened to a smile. 'Big place, Chalcot House. Young Mrs Will Glaven – whoever she eventually is – won't want to run it single-handed. Only too glad of the services of an excellent cook – especially at weekends when Mr Glaven is at home.

'Ideal part-time situation for you, I told Mrs Harbord. And she and her daughter can live in one of my properties in the village, rent-free in return for a daily meal and a little company. What do you say to that? I asked her.'

He was beaming with satisfaction. Knowing that she had lost the initiative, Hilary asked patiently, 'And what did Mrs Harbord say?'

'She was pleased – most appreciative. Though ever since the shoot, of course, she's been very worried about her daughter.'

His smile was replaced by a look of concern: 'Fine girl, Laura – any progress in your search?'

Aggravated, Quantrill snatched back the initiative.

'What concerns us at the moment, Mr Brunt, is Hope Meynell's death. You took twelve cartridges with you to Belmont, but you can only account for eleven. Our view is that the twelfth of your cartridges is the one that killed her. What do you say to *that*?'

Reg Brunt said nothing. He frowned, and chewed his thumb in thought for several moments. Then his sagging face lifted.

He bustled to a tall kitchen cabinet, and reaching in behind an upright hoover he took out a side-by-side double-barrelled shotgun. Breaking it open, he said a shamefaced, 'Oh dear, oh dear . . .

'Only took one shot from my final reload,' he explained. 'That was when I heard the nearby single shot. Afraid of being discovered. Picked up my pheasants – hurried home – put the gun away without cleaning it. Broke all the safety rules, I'm afraid – should have known better – dangerous thing to do.'

He showed the detectives his gun, with the brass cap of the twelfth cartridge still sitting snugly in the breech of the second barrel.

Before returning home that night, Chief Inspector Quantrill made some arrangements for the following day.

First, he telephoned the Hertfordshire police, who were keeping in contact with the father of the murdered girl, and asked them to make an appointment for him with Mr Meynell.

Then he took the next step in the search for Laura Harbord.

If enquiries among the students at Yarchester had brought no results by ten the following morning, he wanted a televised press conference set up in time for the early evening news. The policewoman who was minding Mrs Harbord was to persuade her to attend, to make a personal appeal for any information whatever about her missing daughter.

25

The Meynell family lived in leafy suburban Hertfordshire. Their detached house was 1930s developers' Tudor, embellished with diamond-leaded window panes and black mock-timbering on white gables. It was set in a quarter-acre of garden, leaf-strewn on this soggy November morning but neatly landscaped with terraces and pergolas and lawns and flower beds. This was comfortable middle-class England: a place of double garages, living-flame gas fires, deep carpets and beautifully colour-coordinated soft furnishings; a world away from the draughty corridors and the doggy, shabby antiquity of upper-middle-class Suffolk.

The detectives were shown in by a fair-haired young woman whose attractive face was stiff with sorrow. She said that she was Hope's elder sister, Dawn, and that she and her children were there for a few days to keep her father company. Small voices raised in play, elsewhere in the house, lightened what would otherwise have been a sombre atmosphere.

Andrew Meynell, a dentist by profession, was standing with his back to the sitting-room fire. He was a dapper, balding man in his late fifties, in a dark suit and a plain navy blue tie. His face was drawn and his eyes were heavy with grief as he accepted the detectives' condolences, but he seemed fidgety.

He invited his visitors to sit down, but he himself remained on his feet. Bone china cups and saucers stood ready on a tray, and he waited impatiently for Dawn to bring coffee, in a matching pot, pour it and then go.

'I find this difficult to say,' he burst out. 'If I'm wrong, it's unforgivable even to think it. But I've been mulling it over, and I'm convinced that Lewis Glaven must have killed my daughter.'

He looked almost defiant, as though he expected the detectives to be either surprised or shocked. Quantrill sat back in his armchair and gave his coffee a methodical stir.

'What makes you say that, Mr Meynell?'

'I say it with great reluctance. I liked Will Glaven well enough – I didn't think he was the right man for Hope, but I couldn't fault the way he treated her. And she always said how kind his father was to her when she first visited Chalcot. In fairness to Lewis Glaven, I have to admit that he's shown me nothing but kindness and support, ever since the terrible event . . .'

Andrew Meynell shook his head in despair. 'It seems unthinkable that he should have wanted to kill my daughter. But I can see now what his motive must have been. Such callousness, though – such cold-blooded calculation . . .'

Hilary helped him get to the point. Prominent on a bookcase was a framed studio portrait of a beautiful, fair woman in early middle age. 'Has this any connection with your late wife?' she asked.

'Ah.' Meynell gave her a quick look. 'You've heard something about Carol, have you?'

'Only what Will Glaven told us. He already knew that your wife had died, but he didn't know the cause. On Friday, when they were on their way to Chalcot, Hope told him her mother had died in a psychiatric hospital.'

'I see . . .' It was Meynell's turn to stir his coffee. 'Hope should have told Will sooner, of course. But it's a very difficult thing for a girl to explain to the man she wants to marry. She was obviously trying to break the news bit by bit.'

'There's more?'

'Oh yes. And Lewis Glaven knew almost the whole of it, even if his son didn't. He came to call on me about three weeks ago.'

Andrew Meynell swallowed his cooling coffee in three long gulps, and parked his empty cup on the mantelpiece.

'Glaven telephoned me at the surgery. He said he happened to be driving through Hertfordshire, and asked if he could call late that afternoon to introduce himself. I knew that Will's family were landowners, and it did occur to me to wonder whether his father wanted to "look us over". That would have been intolerable. But he turned out to be perfectly civil, and appreciative of Hope.'

'Was she at home at the time?' asked Hilary.

'No, she wasn't back from work. She had a long journey from her City bank. He said she was a beautiful and charming girl – which of course we already knew,' added her father with a choke in his voice.

He walked quickly to a window overlooking a conservatory bright with floral cushions. For a few moments he stood rigid, trying to compose himself. The two detectives exchanged wry looks of sympathy for him, and Hilary got up to collect his empty cup.

Red-eyed, Andrew Meynell returned to the hearthrug and accepted Hilary's offer to pour more coffee.

'Lewis Glaven', he said, after taking a deep breath, 'told me that if Hope and Will decided to marry, he would do whatever he could to make her feel welcome at Chalcot. I took that at face value. But now, thinking about it,' – his fingers tightened angrily on his cup – 'I believe he was a thundering snob who considered that my daughter wasn't a suitable wife for his son.

'I think he came here to try to persuade me to warn her off. He said it worried him that Hope might not be happy at Chalcot, because life there was so different from the life she'd led here. He sounded apologetic about it – they were very old-fashioned and set in their ways, he said, and he was afraid their chief interests were dogs and guns and horses.'

'That's perfectly true, from what we've seen and heard,' said Quantrill. Oddly, considering that he'd come here to find the evidence he wanted against Lewis Glaven, he found himself inclined to defend the man. 'My own daughter Alison was there at the shoot lunch on Saturday – her first time too, and she felt completely out of place. She said you'd have to be born to that kind of life to fit in. Alison met your daughter and liked her very much, but she wasn't at all sure that Hope would be happy there. So perhaps Lewis Glaven was as much concerned for her as for his son.'

'Did you pass the warning on to Hope?' asked Hilary.

The dentist shrugged. 'I simply told her that Will's father had called to introduce himself. What was the point of telling her anything else?

'Hope was very much in love with Will and wanted to marry him. It's ungenerous to interfere, even if your daughter's set on marrying someone you don't consider right for her. Besides, it's a complete waste of time. If they want to marry they will, and there's no point in being difficult about it.'

Quantrill looked deep into his coffee cup, and said nothing.

'You were going to tell us about your late wife, Mr Meynell,' prompted Hilary.

'Yes. There's a lot to tell.' He parked his cup again and began to pace up and down the room.

'In fact,' he said, 'my wife Carol isn't dead.

'I say "in fact" advisedly. She's still physically alive, but' – he glanced sadly at her photograph – 'horrendously changed in appearance and personality. She was in a home for the mentally ill for some years, but she became too violent for them. She's now in a secure ward in a psychiatric hospital.

'We haven't forgotten Carol, or abandoned her. I visit the hospital every month, though I'm often advised against seeing her. Understandably, our children find visits too distressing.

'As you can imagine, knowing how to explain this to Will has been a great problem for Hope. I told her she must do it in her own way, and I can't blame her for telling him her mother was dead. If she'd told him the truth in the early days, before she brought him here, it would have destroyed their relationship.'

Hilary was looking shaken. 'I hate to ask you this, Mr Meynell,' she said, 'but if it makes it any easier for you to tell me, I once did some psychiatric nursing. Is your wife's illness hereditary?'

'Yes, it is.' He seemed relieved to be able to talk to a former professional: 'It's a genetic disorder of the nervous system, Huntington's disease.'

The name meant nothing at all to Quantrill, but he was watching Hilary and he saw her face turn sheet-white. For once she was speechless.

'You have our sympathy, Mr Meynell,' he said, conscious that whatever words he offered would be clumsily inadequate. 'This must be a terrible thing for you and your family . . .'

'It's something we've had to learn to live with,' said Andrew Meynell with dignity. 'My daughter's murder is a greater tragedy.'

'Yes, of course.' Quantrill returned to the enquiry. 'What

207

you're suggesting, then, is that Lewis Glaven killed Hope because he didn't want this disease passed on to his grand-children. But Will had no idea it was hereditary – so how could his father have known?'

Meynell took another deep breath.

'First,' he said, 'I want to make it clear that we as a family have strict rules of conduct. There's a history of the disease in Carol's family, so we knew that she and our children were at risk. We explained it to them when they grew up. We made them understand that it would be indefensible to marry without first telling their partners and discussing the implications.

'They also knew that *they* must do the telling. It would take a lot of courage, but it had to come from them, not from me. So I'm certain that Hope wouldn't have left Will in ignorance – she was taking her time, that was all. He'll have to hear the truth now, and I'd be glad if you'll tell him that.'

'Of course,' said Hilary. She was still white round the gills, but she was back at work. 'You still haven't told us, though: how did Will's father know that Hope was at risk?'

Andrew Meynell's shoulders drooped. 'It was my son, my oldest, who told Lewis Glaven. But I can't blame poor Roger for it. He's inherited the gene, and begun to show the symptoms.

'He and his family live about half an hour's drive away, and they arrived without warning just as Glaven was about to leave. Roger's an accountant, and he can still work from home. But his concentration is affected, he has alarming mood swings, and there's something – odd – about his appearance. His wife does all the driving now, because he sometimes loses control of his movements.

'The last thing I wanted was for Lewis Glaven to meet Roger, but there was nothing I could do about it. We all stood chatting in the hall for a few moments, then Glaven said he must go. Roger went to open the front door – but unfortunately he lost his balance and almost fell.

'Lewis Glaven was nearest, and made a helpful grab for him. But my son brushed him away. *Nothing to worry about*, said Roger bitterly, *I've got Huntington's, that's all.*'

Andrew Meynell's own voice was filled with bitterness. 'So

there you are: that's how Glaven found out, and that's why Hope is now dead.'

'But the name "Huntington's" wouldn't necessarily have meant anything to him,' objected Quantrill. 'It certainly didn't to me.'

'That doesn't affect my argument,' said Meynell. 'Lewis Glaven came here to try to stop Hope marrying his son. He met Roger, and was alarmed by his abnormalities. He then made enquiries about Huntington's, decided that the marriage had to be stopped at all costs, and invited Hope to a shooting party for the purpose of killing her. There's no doubt about it in my mind. I don't see how you can doubt it, either.'

Quantrill glanced at his sergeant. There was of course a gaping hole in Andrew Meynell's argument; but the man had grief enough, heaven knew, and this was not the time to debate with him.

'You've been most helpful, Mr Meynell,' said Hilary, as they both got to their feet. 'Thank you for telling us so much that's painful to you.'

'I admire your courage,' said Quantrill. 'We all have family problems, but most of them are *nothing* in comparison with yours. Tell me – if you don't mind my asking – how do you cope, with this terrible disease overshadowing your lives?'

Andrew Meynell gave a wry smile.

'In the first place,' he said, 'it's love. Carol told me her family history when I asked her to marry me, but it didn't put me off. With Huntington's, you see, there's a fifty per cent chance that any one child of a sufferer *won't* inherit the disease. And when you're young and in love you think you're bombproof, don't you?

'After the first flush of love, what keeps you going is optimism. You have to be positive. Carol was perfectly well until she was forty, so we had nearly twenty good years together. And we didn't hesitate to have children. We knew that even if Carol was carrying the gene, each of her children would have that fifty per cent chance of escaping it.'

He paused. 'As a family, we've always lived in hope. Hence my younger daughter's name.'

*

The detectives said little as they drove up the A10, through the late-autumnal countryside of Hertfordshire. Quantrill turned off at Puckeridge, and stopped at the old Fox and Hounds in Barley. They tottered into the pub, both of them shaken by what they'd heard.

Hilary's preferred drink was wine, but after she'd bought a modest half of bitter for the chief inspector, on the grounds that he was driving, she ordered a reviving gin and tonic for herself.

'Those poor Meynells,' she said. 'Huntington's is a terrible disease – it gradually shrinks the brain. I never had to deal with it when I was a nurse, but I remember seeing a horrifying case history.'

For once, Quantrill had lost his appetite. He'd asked for Stilton with granary bread, but he picked at it half-heartedly.

'Isn't there any cure for Huntington's?' he said.

'No. No prospect of it at the moment. It's a long downhill progress to insanity, poor souls . . . About fifteen years, from the onset of the disease to death.'

Hilary brooded over her drink. She hadn't felt like eating, but now she absently filched some celery from the chief inspector's plate and nibbled it as she talked.

'One of the problems with Huntington's is that the symptoms don't usually show before the age of thirty. The gene is passed on by both men and women. By the time they realise they've got it, they've probably married and had children of their own – like Roger Meynell. That means they could already have passed the gene to the next generation. And so it goes on.'

Quantrill had always looked to his sergeant for information on medical matters. But he'd recently taken an interest in genetics, on the strength of an article in one of the Sunday colour supplements, and now he had a point to make.

'There are blood tests for genetic diseases,' he said. 'Hope Meynell wouldn't have had to wait a decade to see whether the disease appeared, or to take risks with her own children. She could simply have asked to be screened. Then she'd have known for sure, before she married Will Glaven.'

'Oh for heaven's sake!' said Hilary crossly. There were times when she felt a great deal of sympathy for Douglas Quantrill's wife. 'Haven't you *any* imagination?'

'Yes, Hope could have found out whether or not she was carrying the Huntington's gene. And if the test had proved negative, she'd have been singing and dancing.

'But supposing it proved positive? How would she feel then, knwöing without doubt how hideous her future was going to be? I wouldn't want to know that, if I were in her shoes – and I bet you wouldn't either! Genetic testing's wonderful for curable or treatable diseases, but there can't be many people at risk from Huntington's who'd want to chance it. As Andrew Meynell said, what his family lives on is hope.'

Then she laughed: partly to unwind her own imaginative tension, partly because Douglas Quantrill looked so taken aback and she was really very fond of him.

'Go on,' she said, 'eat your Stilton, and tell me what we're going to do about Lewis Glaven.'

When they returned to the car, Segeant Lloyd made a call to Breckham Market for a progress report on the search for Laura Harbord.

There was no news of Laura from Yarchester. As Chief Inspector Quantrill had instructed, a televised press conference had been arranged for late that afternoon. Hilary confirmed that he would be there to front it, and was told that Mrs Harbord had agreed to appeal for information about her missing daughter.

Meanwhile, the detectives were on their way to Chalcot House. The time had come, Quantrill had decided, to confront Lewis Glaven.

They were still short of evidence against him. Everything they had was circumstantial. True, Andrew Meynell had provided a vital piece of information. But there was still a big credibility gap in their theory, and – irritatingly – it was the one that Martin Tait had pointed out.

No sane man, Tait had said, on hearing that his prospective daughter-in-law was at risk from a hereditary disease, would reach for his shotgun.

Certainly he'd oppose the marriage. But the natural thing would be to do everything he could to talk his son out of it. He wouldn't keep the information to himself, still less make an elaborate plan to kill the girl.

'It just doesn't make sense, does it?' said Quantrill. 'If I'd been in Lewis Glaven's shoes, I'd have told my son about it right away. And if that didn't put him off, I'd have wheeled out the family doctor and the family solicitor to have a go at him. I'd have made damn sure he knew the worst . . .'

'But if he still insisted on marrying her?'

'I wouldn't kill the poor girl, that's for sure. I'd feel more inclined to shoot my son for a fool.'

Hilary laughed. 'Now you're talking like Douglas Quantrill, not Lewis Glaven. Why would *he* want to kill Hope Meynell – that's the point, isn't it? Why would he want to kill her without even giving Will a chance to call off the engagement?'

They had entered Suffolk at Six Mile Bottom, over the railway crossing that gives the impression of being a frontier post against would-be despoilers of the county. Now they were driving through Newmarket, the capital of the English racing world. Traffic along the old Bury road had been halted to let a string of racehorses, stable lads up, cross from the gallops to their yard.

Distracted from her argument, Hilary was watching the elegant, high-stepping horses with admiration.

'Aren't those thoroughbreds *beautiful*?' she said. 'I can't bear to watch jumping races on television – I'm so afraid they'll fall and have to be destroyed.'

'Oh for heaven's sake,' complained Quantrill, mocking her affectionately: 'I've never known such a sentimental woman over animals!' And then, as the last of the horses disappeared behind high brick walls and he put the car into gear, he had a thought.

'Lewis Glaven's a breeder, of course. Not of horses, but of pedigree cattle. And I reckon that breeders must see life and death – and bloodlines – differently from the rest of us.'

212

26

The police officer on scenes-of-crime duty at the gates to Chalcot House was also keeping a discreet eye on Lewis Glaven's movements. When Chief Inspector Quantrill and Sergeant Lloyd drove up, he directed them to the estate farm.

The main entrance to Home Farm was about half a mile further on along the road. The farmhouse, late Victorian with ornamental barge-boards, and looking pretty as a dolls' house in the watery November sunshine, was backed by a great metal shed and a couple of silos. Beside the concrete entrance road, high on a post, was a painted sign: THE CHALCOT HERD OF MURRAY GREYS – LEWIS GLAVEN, CHALCOT HOUSE.

The detectives found his mud-splattered Range Rover, with the dogs in charge, parked next to a tractor in the yard behind the house. Glaven himself could be seen in the cavernous interior of the open-sided shed.

Half the shed was occupied by baled straw, and the remainder was railed off to form cattle pens. All the pens were empty except one, and in it stood a solitary cow, hock deep in loose straw. Lewis Glaven, in cap, dirty old wellies and Barbour, was leaning over the rail scratching the animal's poll.

'That's useful,' said Quantrill to Hilary as they approached the shed. 'You can go in first and talk to him about cattle.'

'Why me? I don't know anything about cattle.'

'That's why. You'll be able to lead him along without making him suspicious.'

While the chief inspector loitered, Hilary approached Lewis Glaven and wished him a disarming Good Afternoon.

Surprised, he turned towards her. He was, she thought, such an upright and distinguished-looking man, with his high-boned pink cheeks, his silvery wings of hair and neat moustache; it was difficult to think of him as the probable killer of Hope Meynell.

'Good afternoon to you!' he said, tipping his cap. His eyes

were wary, but his voice was courteous: 'What brings you to the farm?'

'We're on our way to talk to Mrs Harbord,' Hilary told him. 'I expect you know that she's agreed to make a television appeal for news of Laura. She'll be collected from your house at four thirty, and we'd like a word with her before then. You've no objection, I hope?'

'On the contrary. Relieved you're stepping up the search for the child – she's been missing too long.'

'Yes. But we're living in hope,' said Hilary. 'We all have to do that, don't we?'

She leaned on the rail beside him, smelling the comfortable warmth of the cow. She had expected a Murray Grey to be grey, but instead it was a rich cream colour, darkening softly to mushroom on its ears and poll. It looked back at her ruminatively, through the thick pale lashes that fringed its large brown eyes.

'I'm no countrywoman, I'm afraid,' she said, 'and I've never been this close to a cow before. She really is a beauty. Does she have a name?'

He introduced the animal with affectionate pride.

'This is Chalcot Alicia. Champion breed heifer at the County Show last summer. I call her Alice. She was coughing a bit last week, which is why I brought her under cover. Vet says she'll be well enough to return to the herd tomorrow. She misses their company.'

Hilary gave the cow's placid face an experimental stroke, and found her short stiff hairs surprisingly silky. 'Has she had any calves?'

Glaven laughed kindly at her ignorance. 'As I said, she's a heifer. A maiden. She'll have her first calf next year.'

'Then I'm sure it'll be a beauty too. But supposing . . .'

Hilary abandoned the cow and turned to look directly at its owner.

'I know this doesn't bear thinking about: but supposing the vet found that Alice had some invisible, incurable defect? Something genetic that she would probably transmit to any calves she had. What would you do then, Mr Glaven? You'd

214

have to protect your pedigree herd, wouldn't you? So what would you do – slaughter her?'

He had been leaning casually on the rail. Now he stood up, slowly, his profile stern. Turning to Hilary, he gave her a strained smile.

'No, no! We farmers are sadly misunderstood by you towns-people. You think we've no concern for our animals' welfare, or sentiment for them. Quite untrue. I'd never slaughter Alice in those circumstances. Wouldn't breed from her, of course, but wouldn't dream of killing her. No, Miss Lloyd.' His tone remained courteous but his eyes hardened. 'You're mistaken.'

'Quite probably, if it's cattle you're talking about,' said the chief inspector's voice from behind them. 'You're the expert there, Mr Glaven – but that's because you're in complete control of your herd. They can't breed without your say-so. It's different with people, though. The girl your son wanted to marry, for instance . . .?'

Lewis Glaven's moustache twitched uneasily. His eyes moved from one to the other, but he said nothing.

'We had a long talk with Andrew Meynell this morning,' Quantrill continued. 'We know, as you do, that his daughter was a possible carrier of Huntington's disease. You wouldn't have wanted a terrible thing like that in your family, would you? But you couldn't prevent *her* from having children – so the only way to save your family from Huntington's was to kill her.'

Glaven stood his ground, an upright country gentleman beside his champion heifer. 'Have you any evidence for what you're suggesting?'

'Enough,' asserted Quantrill. That wasn't true; what's more, the credibility gap was still there; but the only way forward was to try to get a confession out of the man.

'We know how you set up the shooting party, so as to make her death look like an accident. And we know about the hidden path through the bushes, from your peg to the place where the shot was fired.'

'Circumstantial evidence, that's all,' said Glaven brusquely. 'Wouldn't do for a court of law.'

'You mean you'll plead Not Guilty? That's a shabby way to treat your old friends. You arranged things at the shoot so that they wouldn't be involved, didn't you? Surely you don't want them to be put in the witness box and cross-examined by some hostile prosecuting counsel?'

For the first time, Lewis Glaven looked shaken. Hilary took advantage of it.

'Mrs Wilson-Brown, for example,' she said. 'Such a delightful woman, and so loyal to you when we questioned her. It was obvious that she knew you'd left your peg for long enough to shoot Hope, but she refused to say so. We didn't press her – but the prosecution will. Do you really want to make her stand up in Yarchester Crown Court and endure that?'

There was a tense silence. Then Lewis Glaven gave his cow a final pat, and turned to the detectives.

'You're right,' he said. 'Dishonourable to plead Not Guilty. Before you charge me, though,' he added quickly, anticipating Quantrill's next move, 'I have to tell you that it wasn't selfishness that persuaded me to shoot the girl. "The only way to save my family", you suggested. Not true.

'Didn't want Will marrying her when I knew about Huntington's, of course. Asked a London psychiatrist, and was horrified. But if I'd been solely concerned with my own family, I'd never have shot the poor girl. What would have been the point, once I'd made damn sure that Will wasn't going to marry her?'

'That's what we've been wondering,' admitted Quantrill. 'Why didn't you discuss it with your son, and pressure him to call the engagement off?'

Lewis Glaven shrugged. 'Because I'm a breeder of pedigree cattle, I suppose. If Alice here had a genetic defect – as you hypothesised, Miss Lloyd – I would *never* pass her on to an unsuspecting farmer for breeding. Wouldn't be right, would it?

'Well, then: in the same way, how could I reject Hope Meynell for my own family, but leave her to carry the Huntington's gene to another? The girl was a walking time-bomb. Deeply regret the necessity of killing her, but it had to be done.'

His face had darkened and his voice became vehement. 'D'you know what the pyschiatrist told me? He said the disease could be stamped out in a decade, if only the affected families

216

would stop having children. And yet Hope's brother and sister are already breeding, and Hope herself said how much she wanted a family! Totally irresponsible. Wickedly so.'

'Inadvisable, yes,' said Hilary, 'but not wicked. Far less wicked than murder. We're not talking about cattle here, Mr Glaven, we're talking about the death of an innocent girl.'

He gave her a small stiff smile. 'You think me callous, don't you, Miss Lloyd? That's not so. I'm a very experienced shot, and I hate to see pheasants wounded and suffering. Intended to give Hope Meynell a quick, clean death, such as I give my birds.

'But compassion got in the way, d'you see? Not callous enough. My hand shook, I botched my shot, and as a result she suffered. Never forgive myself for that . . . Never forgive myself.'

Having charged Lewis Glaven with the murder, Quantrill agreed that he could change out of his farm clothes before being taken to Breckham Market police station.

The sun was setting among low pink clouds as they drove in procession along the back road to Chalcot House. Glaven led the way in his Range Rover, slowing to look as he passed the field where his pedigree herd was pastured.

When they reached the yard behind Chalcot House they found a car already parked there, a clapped-out Ford Escort with its bonnet up. Lewis Glaven took no notice of it. He let his dogs out of his vehicle and walked quickly with them to the back door, his head held high.

Hilary was about to follow him. Her mind was now on the search for Laura Harbord, and what she was going to say to the girl's mother about the forthcoming press conference. But Quantrill was already out of the car.

'Hold hard,' he said, 'what's Peter doing here?'

His son emerged from under the Escort's bonnet, and grinned with relief when he saw who had arrived. He hurried over to them, putting on his mock-Australian accent: 'Good on yer, Dad! My starter motor seems to be jammed – can you give me a push?'

217

'I daresay I can, when I know what you're up to.' And then, seeing the grin on his son's face widen, Quantrill added quickly, 'Have you found Laura Harbord?'

Peter paused, relishing his achievement. He was, thought Hilary, a very good-looking lad, with his thick dark hair and his green eyes; Douglas's son, and no mistake.

'I've just brought Laura home from Yarchester,' he said casually.

'Thank God for that! Is she all right?'

'Fine. She'd run out of money, and she hadn't any spare clothes, and she hated being in a squat with students who lived on beefburgers. Otherwise, no problems.'

'Excellent!' Hilary dived into the car, and radioed Breckham Market to call off the search and cancel the press conference.

Quantrill looked at his son with approval. 'Good man,' he said, deciding there and then to buy a reconditioned engine for the Escort without even being asked. 'How did you find Laura?'

'Just asked around,' said Peter. 'A bit of persistence – you know how it is.

'She told me she'd got involved with some of the protesters at the shoot. When things turned nasty, they ran for their van and took her with them. She forgot that she'd left her bike and her sports bag by the side of the road. When I found her she was wandering round the university car-park, trying to hitch a lift home. Seems she's got some pheasants to look after . . .'

'How did her mother react when you brought her back?' asked Hilary.

Peter snorted. 'Gave her an earful, from what I could hear. Sounds as though Laura's having a go as well, though.'

The back door of Chalcot House had been flung open. A defiant figure, just inside, was rounding off a shouting match.

'Thanks for the welcome! I'm going to look for Fred and Francis – at least *they'll* be glad to see me!'

'Oh dear,' sighed Hilary as they watched the girl rush out, her long fair hair furiously flying, her black sweatshirt bannered with SHOOTING PHEASANTS IS WRONG. Seeing the three of them, Laura checked, scowled, and ran in the other direction.

'It's not that Ann Harbord doesn't love her, I'm sure of that,'

Hilary went on. 'It's just that she's no idea how to express it. What that girl needs is a big hug.'

'I rather think she's about to get one,' observed Quantrill.

Will Glaven had just come round the corner of the house, hands deep in the pockets of his Barbour, head held sadly down, dog sloping at his heels. But then he saw Laura. He did a double-take, shouted her name with relief, and held his arms wide in a brotherly gesture of affection.

'Well, then,' said Douglas Quantrill.

'Well, then,' replied Martin Tait.

The two men were standing on either side of the Quantrill family hearth, filled glasses in hand; abandoned by their womenfolk, they were wondering what to say to each other.

Molly and Alison were clearly having a much nicer time in the kitchen, laughing and chatting happily as they prepared a special engagement supper. And fortunately, thought Quantrill, with Alison – her sprained ankle well on the mend – in charge of the cooking, it was a meal to look forward to. It might well be full of garlic and other foreign stuff, but he couldn't deny that it smelled delicious.

'I suppose,' said Martin with guarded jocularity, 'that this is the moment when I say, "Is it all right with you if I marry your daughter?" And then you say, "No, it isn't – and considering you've been living with her for over a year, you've left it a bit late to ask."'

'Something like that,' agreed Quantrill. 'But you can delete the objection,' he added, bearing in mind what Hope Meynell's father had said. 'If Alison wants to marry you, I'm not going to be difficult about it. Just take care of her, that's all.'

'Of course. And – er – thank you.'

Martin hadn't been looking forward to this evening of compulsory togetherness. He'd fully expected to be on the receiving end of a lot of aggravation from his prospective father-in-law. But now, with the irritant removed, he felt relaxed and happy.

'You won't be going to any more shooting parties, I imagine?' said Quantrill.

'Never again, after what happened at Chalcot. Anyway, I agree with Alison: killing birds is an objectionable sport. I'll shoot clays at the gun club in future.'

'You're not giving up shooting, then?'

'Certainly not. Shooting clays is excellent sport – it's skilful and exciting, and it does no harm to man, beast or bird. Or to woman either,' he added sadly, remembering Hope Meynell.

'Where are you keeping your shotgun now? At the gun club, I suppose?'

'No, at home. In a locked steel cabinet, of course.'

'That's not the point.'

Lulled by the withdrawal of Alison's father's objection to their marriage, Martin had thought they were having an ordinary conversation. Now he realised that Doug Quantrill had been interviewing him, and was seriously displeased with his answers.

'Good God, you should know better than to keep a shotgun in your own house! You've no reason to do it – you're not a farmer, and you're certainly not a country gentleman. I'm not having my daughter marrying a man who keeps a lethal weapon at home just to bolster his own ego. If you must shoot, you're to keep your gun in the proper place, locked away at the club. *Right?'*

Coldly angry, Martin Tait clamped his mouth shut while he selected his reply. Damn it all, he was Doug Quantrill's future boss! Yes, all right, the man was his host and his prospective father-in-law; but he wasn't going to let him get away with this.

They were supposed to be celebrating, though, and Alison wouldn't easily forgive him if he spoiled her parents' evening. Besides, with youth and future rank on his side, he had a better way of scoring a point.

Instead of coming out with a crushing retort, Martin looked kindly on the older man. He gave him an indulgent smile.

'Right, Dad,' he said.